are u 4 real?

are u 4 real?

Sara Kadefors

TRANSLATED BY TARA CHACE

Dial Books

First published in the United States 2009
by DIAL BOOKS
A member of Penguin Group (USA) Inc.
Published by The Penguin Group
Penguin Group (USA) Inc., 375 Hudson Street, New York, NY 10014, U.S.A.
Penguin Group (Canada), 90 Eglinton Avenue East, Suite 700, Toronto, Ontario, Canada M4P 2Y3
(a division of Pearson Penguin Canada Inc.)
Penguin Books Ltd, 80 Strand, London WC2R 0RL, England
Penguin Ireland, 25 St. Stephen's Green, Dublin 2, Ireland (a division of Penguin Books Ltd)
Penguin Group (Australia), 250 Camberwell Road, Camberwell, Victoria 3124, Australia
(a division of Pearson Australia Group Pty Ltd)
Penguin Books India Pvt Ltd, 11 Community Centre, Panchsheel Park, New Delhi - 110 017, India
Penguin Group (NZ), 67 Apollo Drive, Rosedale, North Shore 0632,
New Zealand (a division of Pearson New Zealand Ltd)
Penguin Books (South Africa) (Pty) Ltd, 24 Sturdee Avenue, Rosebank,
Johannesburg 2196, South Africa
Penguin Books Ltd, Registered Offices: 80 Strand, London WC2R 0RL, England

Originally published in Sweden 2001
by Bonnier Carlsen under the title *Sandor Slash Ida*
Published in the English language by arrangement with Bonnier Group Agency

Jacket design by Jeanine Henderson
Book design by Jasmin Rubero
Text set in Columbus MT

Printed in the U.S.A.

1 3 5 7 9 10 8 6 4 2

Library of Congress Cataloging-in-Publication Data
Kadefors, Sara.
[Sandor slash Ida. English]
Are u 4 real? / by Sara Kadefors ; translated by Tara Chace.
p.   cm.
Summary: After meeting "online" in an Internet chat room and helping each other deal with
family problems, Kyla and Alex, two very different sixteen year olds, decide to meet in person.
ISBN 978-0-8037-3276-6
[1. Interpersonal relations—Fiction. 2. Friendship—Fiction. 3. Family problems—Fiction.
4. Online chat groups—Fiction.] I. Chace, Tara. II. Title. III. Title: Are you for real?
PZ7.K116466Ar 2009
[Fic]—dc22
2008046257

Acknowledgments

I'd like to acknowledge the invaluable help of
Kristen Pettit and Evelyn Berger. Thank you both!

In addition, grateful appreciation to
The Swedish Arts Council for sponsoring translation costs.

$It's$ the same as always. He reaches the bus stop with a gnawing sense of apprehension.

An old woman with two overfilled bags of groceries limps out of the mini-mart—otherwise, nothing. Not even cars at the gas station or anyone outside the library. Good.

He walks quickly across the rutted, cracked asphalt. The bus sits there vibrating, spewing exhaust into the already gray November air.

He speeds up. Sometimes it leaves early. He's run after it too many times, trying to catch it, the words *crap, crap, crap* throbbing over and over again in his head. He's never shouted or flipped the driver off. That wouldn't be like Aleksandr Borodin. He's not the kind of guy to kick the bus or pound on the window; he's just the kind who *imagines* it. The kind who trudges back home because the next bus won't be coming for forty minutes and it would be lame to just stand there, waiting.

So he sits at the kitchen table instead, staring into space for fifteen minutes, until it's time to go back to the bus stop. Today he gets there several minutes before any driver would dare leave. When he shows his bus pass, he's met by the driver's surly, almost disapproving look. As if he'd done something wrong by getting to the bus in time.

"Problem?" he wants to ask, casually, sarcastically. But instead he just pockets his pass and sits down in his seat.

His seat. It's true; it's always the same one, fifth row back on the right. As if he were an old man going to the same job every day for forty years.

Sometimes it feels that way to him, this slog to the studio. Like a tired old man, Alex sits there because he must. Because this is what is expected of him. Because he can't imagine doing anything else.

There are only three other people on the bus, no one he recognizes, no one under fifty, mostly old women. Relief washes over him, and he prepares for a pleasant thirty-minute ride. Alex leans back, closes his eyes, recedes into himself. He hears the doors close, feels how the driver shifts the bus into gear and how it gradually pulls away from the stop. Alex sighs, but then his sense of safety is upset by someone screeching outside the bus.

"Heeeeeeeeeeeeeey!"

He opens his eyes. Oh no. They're running behind the bus. Kevin screams, "Dude, hold up!" at the driver. Val follows, "Yeah, pull over!"

Both boys pound on the bus with their fists. Alex is instantly on the driver's side—hopes he'll floor it just to be spiteful. Alex tries to send encouraging thoughts to the driver, but instead of accelerating and lurching away from the stop, the old man eases off the gas and slowly presses down on the brakes.

The doors open. Kevin and Val tumble in, panting, their faces bright red. The driver starts driving again and mumbles bitterly, "Next time, be on time."

Kevin attempts a retort: "Yeah, well, you shouldn't . . . you . . ."

Val fills in, "You can't leave the stop three minutes early!"

The old man has his eyes on the road. "My watch said half past."

The two boys snicker at the driver, though there's really nothing funny. "Half-dead jerk," Kevin mutters just loud enough as he rummages around in his pocket for his pass. Val sneers.

Alex winces. His peaceful trip has turned into a hostage situation. He wraps his fingers around his messenger bag, hoping a tight grip and sheer will can safeguard the gear inside: white tee, black tights, and, of course, his dance shoes. It's going to be thirty-five minutes until the bus pulls to a stop and the doors open. That's an eternity, a whole chunk of freeway, all the way across the bay and into San Francisco.

"God, I wish I had your body!"

Kyla pretends she didn't hear, just continues putting on her makeup. She takes a sip from her tall glass of vodka and then, with a newly-manicured pinkie, dials up the volume on her iPod dock. She hums along with the song. It's Madonna—"Borderline." Old-school, but without a doubt Kyla's favorite.

The sound temporarily drowns out the voices of her friends, and Kyla sighs. Sweet relief! She sings a few bars, then worries. What if her mom wakes up? Susanna and Therese can *not* see her right now. That would be a disaster. She waits for the end of the chorus, then nonchalantly turns the sound down again.

Susanna is sitting on the bed, studying her every move. "I mean, I just can't wear pants like those. They don't work on me." She sighs dramatically, pauses for effect. "I'm too fat. I admit it. I'm totally, disgustingly fat."

Kyla glances to the left. As usual, Therese appears to be ignoring this conversation. She looks like a crazy woman, frenziedly sucking in her cheeks, swiping at her face with a monstrous brush full of bronzer. Her eyelids glow a sickly lavender. Kyla squints. The shade is familiar. Is that Kyla's eye shadow, or did Therese buy the same kind Kyla uses?

Susanna continues to stare at Kyla, her big, wet eyes filled with admiration. "I've got to go on a diet," she says. "Or I'll never be able to compete."

Therese purses her lips, finally irritated by Susanna's fawning. Now Therese grabs Kyla's lipstick too, casually spreading it on in a thick layer. Therese's complexion is completely different from hers; the color looks a bit ridiculous. But it's not worth trying to help Therese. She'll just laugh and flip you off.

Kyla tosses her eyelash curler into her cosmetics bag. "C'mon, Suse! Enough already!" She doesn't want to say "I'm not pretty," even though she knows it's what's expected. That it's as unavoidable as "you're not fat." But isn't it true what they say, that you should never do anything you don't want to?

She refuses to play the game, and keeps applying makeup even though she's actually done. Ten seconds go by, twenty, maybe even forty. No one says anything. Susanna's words hang in the air. Kyla feels cornered, surrounded, like a hostage in her own bedroom.

What would happen if she said: *"Know what? You're right. You'll never be as gorgeous as me, and you're just going to have to learn to live with it."*

Kyla sighs. Armageddon, that's what would happen. Nuclear explosions. Fire and brimstone. The entire world as they knew it exploding in a nightmarish, catastrophic end.

The thought of it cheers her, gives her just enough strength to go on. She tilts her head forward so that her gold-white hair cascades over her eyes. Then she tosses it back as the other two watch. It lands on her shoulders, thick, full of body, and enviable—like a shampoo commercial, live and in person.

"Susanna," she coos sweetly. "You are not fat, and I'm not that pretty. And anyway you're every bit as pretty as I am!"

That should end it, but Susanna does exactly what she always does—pretends she's shocked, opens her eyes wide, fishlike, as if she hadn't heard Kyla tell her this ten thousand times before. "Yeah, right. Very funny, Kyla. I'm just as pretty as you. What a joke."

Kyla takes another swig of her vodka and rinses it down with a beer. It tastes awful. No wonder, considering how cheap it was. But she enjoys its amazing warmth in her body; so much so that it feels almost nice when she puts her arm around Susanna and says, "Listen to what I'm saying, you crazy bone pile. You are *not* fat!"

Susanna smiles sheepishly. "You think?"

Kyla takes another sip.

There. Now she'll feel much better.

He hunches over in his seat, willing himself to be more invisible. Leans his head against the cold window and pretends he's asleep. He's not particularly believable. Who could sleep in such an uncomfortable position with all that drama going on? But it's the best he can come up with.

He sits completely still and waits for them to walk past him. Even prays, *"Oh God, if you exist, please don't let . . ."* A faint whiff of tobacco wafts past along with the rustling of a couple of varsity jackets, and then they keep going toward the back of the bus. He sits motionless for a good minute before he dares to relax. When the bus gets on the on-ramp, he smiles to himself, thinking, Well, sometimes you're lucky.

He focuses on the lesson ahead, and his favorite part of it: Christina. He has almost managed to bring the image of her delicate face into focus in his mind, when he feels a faint puff of air on the back of his neck. He pretends it's not there, but then it happens again. It blows right in his ear. The scent of cigarettes is overwhelming. He turns around reluctantly.

They're sitting there grinning. Kevin cocks his head to the side. "Sorry. Did we wake you up?"

"What? Nah," Alex replies, even though he knows the question was rhetorical.

"Maybe you were having a little daydream?" Val adds with a snort.

"Maybe." Alex turns his head back around to mark that the conversation is over. He stares straight ahead, hoping they'll give up for lack of opposition.

"So what are you dreaming about then?" Val asks.

Alex doesn't respond. An intense sense of discomfort permeates his entire body. Fear, probably, but at the same time he feels sorry for them. He tries to remember that they're pathetic, insecure people and not dangerous at all. Isn't that what they say about bullies?

They pile into the seat in front of him now, hang over the back, and scrutinize him intently.

"Maybe you're dreaming about a *boy*friend?" Kevin pesters.

Val bursts out laughing. But his laughter sounds hollow as usual, almost nervous. Suddenly Alex feels tired. Tired of the whole situation, which is just like yesterday and the day before. He wonders what would happen if he didn't look away and mumble something inaudible. What if he actually *answered?*

It must be unexpected help from a God who doesn't exist that makes Alex dare to look Kevin in the eye. He sighs dramatically and responds, "No. Are *you*?"

Silence. They're just as surprised as he is. Kevin's mouth is hanging open. His face is strangely vacant. "Huh?" he mumbles.

"Nothing."

Kevin leans into his face. "Is there something you want to say to me?"

Val isn't snickering anymore; the only noise is from the bus engine. Everything else has faded into the background. Alex focuses on Kevin's eyes. The seconds go by. Suddenly he can't remember what this is all about. Why are they sitting here? Who said or did what and why?

"I said, was there something you wanted to say?" Kevin repeats.

Alex snaps out of his trance. There it is: two against one on a bus, like some scene from a bad after-school special. And now it's time for the moral of the episode: *Listen up, kids. If you're being bullied, don't take matters into your own hands. Tell a parent or trusted adult. Take a stand. Lend a hand. Let's stop bullying now!*

But in real life there's no voiceover. And, really, what would Alex gain by taking a stand anyway? Respect? Hardly. The thought's almost laughable.

Alex looks away. "Nah, sorry. It was nothing."

Kevin scoffs. "That's what I figured."

When you link arms, close your eyes, and sing at the top of your lungs, that's when life is best. Like now. There's no stopping them.

They're sitting in, or rather *on,* the backseat of Richie Turnbull's convertible, singing as loud as they possibly can. They're stuck for the moment on the 405, and Kyla feels the other commuters' eyes on her. Truth be told, she enjoys it—thinks they're probably envious. Look how *free* they are!

It wasn't hard getting Richie to play chauffeur. All it took was one call from Kyla. She hopes for Richie's sake that someone from school will see them. It'd probably raise his status for the rest of the year.

Traffic comes to a standstill and Richie hits the brakes. Kyla loses her balance. She pulls the other two down with her as she falls, so they all wind up in a big heap on the trunk. They shriek with laughter—Richie too—making quite a scene. It's a bit ridiculous.

They pick themselves up with enormous effort, holding on to each other, helping and supporting each other into their seats while the car inches along. How could she have had such negative thoughts about Therese and Susanna back in her room? They've been her friends forever; they call her every day and make her feel important and needed. They would do, and *have done,* almost anything for her: lie to the teachers at school, protect her reputation, stick up for her when somebody tries to mess with her.

Really, they've been friends since elementary school. That's just the way it is, and that's the way it always will be.

They keep singing as Richie turns off the highway, but soon Kyla has to remind the others to get it together so they can get in. There's already a crowd. Crap! No choice but to go stand at the end of the line. Kyla senses the other chic club-goers looking at them skeptically, wondering, What are those little girls doing here, they're hardly old enough to have boobs, but she's not sure.

Well, it's worked before. Kyla knows that she can pull off eighteen if she wants to, and Therese has her sister's ID. Susanna usually gets in because she's with them. But it all depends on the bouncers.

She focuses on the two musclemen up by the entrance. They look extremely unapproachable, with tired icy eyes. They move as if each motion and response were rehearsed. Kyla can imagine doing the same thing every night: Open the door or close it, say "Hello, welcome to Area," "Goodbye, have a nice night," "Do you have ID," "You should start heading home now," "Everyone back up a few feet, otherwise no one is getting in." On and on and on. Poor guys.

A party of four approaches. The bouncers light up and the door opens wide. Kyla scowls. In L.A., there's always someone eager to get ahead of you. Someone with a brand-new hit movie or hot single, someone more special, someone, Kyla thinks, like her dad. Suddenly, she feels like an idiot for feeling sorry for the bouncers.

Kyla bats her eyelashes at Muscleman No. 1. He can't help it: He checks her out quickly but obviously. Therese and Susanna know their roles; they close ranks behind Kyla and try to look indifferent. Kyla tosses her hair, smiles provocatively at Muscleman No. 2, and then back at No. 1.

Kyla raises her eyebrows questioningly. "Problem?"

A little smile from the bouncer. "Nope, everything looks fine from here."

Yes! He opens the door to let them in. But then he stops, eyeing Therese and Susanna critically. Instantly Susanna gets babyish and hesitant. "Um," she pleads, "we're with her?" She points at Kyla. The bouncer isn't convinced and demands, "Can I see some ID?"

Therese quickly pulls her sister's license out of her purse and the bouncer checks it carefully, skeptically. Susanna is standing there, shaking. Therese's lips are pursed in panic. Dead giveaways, the both of them.

Kyla intervenes. She lowers her eyelashes, lays her hand on the bouncer's forearm, and composes her features into The Look That Always Works.

"I'll take care of them tonight. I promise," she reassures him. She smiles.

He doesn't want to let himself be taken in, but finally he grins back.

The bouncer nods at Kyla. She's won.

He's been standing by the exit doors for several minutes before the bus pulls up to the stop. He doesn't want to be there a second longer than necessary. The doors finally open. The reassuring noises of downtown San Francisco envelop him, and he quickly hops down the stairs. Kevin and Val are behind him in a flash, almost on top of him.

"Don't overexert yourself!" Val chides.

"Yeah, make sure to save something for your boyfriend," Kevin adds.

They disappear off down the street, laughing and throwing punches at each other.

Finally Alex is just a person in the crowd, a nobody. No one gives him a second look. It's paradise. When he gets to the studio, he flings the doors open and is greeted by the familiar scent, a mixture of sweat and something indefinable, something invigorating and peaceful at the same time.

It seems empty, just as he'd hoped. He walks into the locker room and changes quickly, hurrying so he can practice by himself for as long as possible. Changed and ready, he slips into one of the rooms and heads straight to the stereo. He flips through the CDs and picks one, shoves it in, and presses play. Music fills the room. Alex fixes his posture and lifts his chin.

She doesn't care that the dance floor is almost empty. She doesn't want to dance with anyone anyway, doesn't want to feel trapped in front of some guy who thinks he's entitled and might try to pull her against him to start making out.

So she dances by herself. She lets her arms, legs, and hips find a rhythm. Kyla's hair swirls around her head, it whips her in the face and sticks in her makeup, but it doesn't matter. Her body is alive, *she* is alive. At last!

He's alone in the studio. It's been two days since his last practice, an eternity: How has he managed? How did he live for so many hours without dancing, the only thing that makes him feel alive?

He dances Kevin and Val away, dances away the stiffness that had taken over his body on the bus. Softly, slowly, carefully, he moves, timing his steps to the melancholy strings, then to thundering drums. He leaps, he lurches, intensely, savagely: *You can't get to me because I couldn't care less about you!*

The other boys evaporate along with the anger. There's only Alex, his body, and whatever's inside. For a moment he wonders, Is this happiness?

The door jerks open. Scott Henning steps in to watch, upsetting a private moment with his critical eye. Alex becomes self-conscious. He keeps dancing for a while under Henning's gaze, trying to ignore his audience. Then the music stops. Henning's serious expression bursts into a smile.

"Looking good!" Henning applauds. And then comes the sigh, the fretting. "Your *grand jeté* is still better than mine. I'm going to have to practice."

As the dance reaches a thundering pulse, she realizes that nausea is taking over. She tries to suppress the feeling, pretending it doesn't exist, like when you're half-awake in the middle of the night and have to pee but refuse to give in.

13

But the retch becomes more and more intense. Until it's inescapable. She races off the dance floor and flings the bathroom door open in desperation.

It's full of girls, a line in front of each stall door. She looks around, is forced to draw attention to herself. "Excuse me, but I'm feeling a little . . ." she mumbles, then stops, pressing her hand over her mouth, but she can't hold it in any longer.

The other girls squeal and jump back.

The contents of her stomach just explode, right onto the floor.

No one can see him from here. The trees cast big, dark shadows over the street, obscuring the light from the streetlamps. He steals along the sidewalk edge, getting closer and closer to home, passing by the other shoebox dwellings in the line of time-worn townhouses. The light is on next door, in Toby's room. What is he up to? Building a gigantic space station out of LEGOs? Mixing hydrochloric acid with lemonade? Uncovering another "fascinating" fact about the Vikings?

Alex smiles. In his best friend's parlance, the answer is likely D, all of the above.

Alex slowly approaches the front gate, where the mailbox is marked clearly—even the script looks different from everyone else's in this neighborhood, as Russian as his parents—"Borodin."

He doesn't go in that way; instead he steps over the small, thorny bushes, the ones that were supposed to get big and full in one summer and clearly delineate the tiny yard from the street and the neighbors' yards. The bushes were a disappointment. They had grown just as slowly as Alex's social life over the last three years. He can't help but feel a kind of kinship with them.

He carefully slips through the yard, crouching as he passes the kitchen window. He slinks up the front steps and takes three deep breaths. Then he cautiously presses down the handle and opens the door without making a sound. *Yes. He's going to get past her. It's going to work this time!*

He freezes in the doorway. She's standing there, parked right in front of him, the corners of her mouth curling up in an expectant smile. No way! It's as if she hadn't moved during all the hours he's been out. How does she do it? Is it telepathy? X-ray vision? Mental illness? Alex sighs. The answer is likely *D, all of the above.*

"Hello, my love! How did it go? Wonderful? You were able to get the S shape into your *cabriolés?*" she asks, her eyes twinkling.

"I'm working on them," he says.

His mother is not satisfied. Eagerly, she continues, "Let me see . . . a *sissone ouverte* at the barre and then *au milieu* into *arabesque* or *grand pas devant?* Then a *temp levé* on the supportive leg? Then up to the working leg and bring your calves together . . ." She illustrates with the palms of her hands: Smack! And continues, " . . . and drop to *demi plié . . .*"

He shuts the side door and starts untying his shoes.

His mother is still talking. " . . . and then raise the work-

15

ing leg and complete the exercise with *assemblé* or *pas de bourrée*. This is right?"

"Yup," he mutters.

She peers at him inquisitively and proceeds, "So you are getting the help you need? It is one of the most difficult . . ."

"I'm *getting* help—" he begins.

"Paulina must understand that you must be challenged too, though you are the best—"

"I'm not the best."

"Shall I speak with her, Sasha? She must look at your individual needs . . ."

He bristles at the nickname—a holdover from Russia, just like everything else in his mother's head.

Maybe there, half a world away, Sasha is acceptable. But here? Here it sounds childish and soft. Why doesn't she understand? "Don't worry about it, Mom, okay?"

He takes his jacket off and brushes past his mother on his way into the kitchen. She follows him close on his heels.

"I tell my students always how important it is not to become lazy. 'You must do your best every time,' I say when they think they know a step. And I remember my teacher at the Vaganova Academy . . ."

Ah yes, the world-renowned Vaganova Academy. School of Balanchine, Baryshnikov . . . and Olga Borodin. This monologue is one of his mother's greatest hits. He could practically deliver it for her.

He opens the refrigerator door and takes out the milk,

casting a stealthy glance her way. She's standing in the doorway, still yammering. And, yup, her forehead is creased in concern.

". . . if you want to be the best, you must want this one hundred percent."

The front door opens and Alex thinks, *Thank God!* His mother reacts right away—vanishing in half a second. He quickly pours some milk into a glass and sneaks past her while she angrily greets Nina.

"You were to be home at ten thirty," she scolds.

"It's ten thirty-five," Nina says.

"Yes. *Thirty-five,* not thirty."

"Mom, stop nagging!"

"I must nag, this is what a mother . . ."

On his way to the stairs, Alex peeks through the half-open door into his dad's office. The glow from the computer screen lights up his father's face. He's fully absorbed in work—glasses on his nose, fingers moving at full speed.

It's so quiet in here, so different from the rest of the house, which is his mother's domain. Alex has an urge to open the door, go in, and sit down next to his father. Maybe to read what he's writing, maybe to learn something. Or maybe, to be close to him?

He opens the door a crack further. "Dad?"

There's no response. Not even a movement, save the tapping of the keyboard.

Alex doesn't press his luck. He pads away from the door and walks quietly up the stairs to his room.

It's the middle of downtown L.A., but right now, the streets are deserted.

On the way home she sees only a few solitary people out walking their dogs. It's creepy, no doubt, but she has to get back one way or another. So she pretends she's the heroine in a Lifetime Movie of the Week: a strong, scrappy, uncommonly-attractive-yet-approachable young receptionist who refuses to let her life be ruled by fear.

There is a man on the other side of the street, walking his dog. She imagines that the dog is just a cover for the story's villain—an abusive ex-husband, or a kidnapper.

She glances at her watch and thinks of her father in New York, probably just going out for his morning run. He once told her that the reason New York was so safe was because the people who think about committing crimes are never sure if the people they're targeting are crazier than they are. Of course there *could* be men who are crazy enough to attack a crackhead, she reasons, but there can't be that many. So she contorts her face so it's unrecognizable and starts walking funny well before the man passes her. Just to be on the safe side.

A few blocks later, and she's too tired to even feel afraid. When she gets to her building she takes the elevator up to the fifteenth floor and tries to unlock the door to the apartment. There's no need—the door's already unlocked. Kyla sighs and steps into the dark hallway.

Through the window on the other side of the apartment, the lights of the city are twinkling through the night. Inside, though, it's completely black, not a single lamp is on, waiting to welcome her home. She takes her boots off, hangs her jacket on the hook. Her mom's door is half-open; there she lies, snoring away as usual, completely zonked and unaware of everything that could've happened in an unlocked apartment.

"Mom?"

No reaction.

"I'm home now."

Her mom grunts and turns over in bed, quickly becoming motionless again. Kyla watches her for a while and wonders what it would be like to have another kind of mom. The kind who waits up for you, who worries when you're not in the door exactly when you said you'd be, who cares where you're going in the first place.

Kyla frowns. *Yeah, probably a huge pain.* She sighs again and goes to her own room.

It still smells like smoke from the cigarettes they were smoking earlier. She still feels a tinge of nausea, a reminder of what happened in the bathroom, so she opens the window to let some fresh air in and sinks down onto the bed. Thankfully, the nausea eventually fades. *What a night! What a waste.*

Therese and Susanna stayed at the bar, nursing the beers she bought for them. They were totally confused when she said she had to leave. "What do you mean you threw up? You?" Susanna seemed concerned. But Therese gave a little smirk. Did she enjoy Kyla's misery? Or was she just happy there'd be less competition?

Dutifully they asked if they should take her home, but she could see how excited they were because a couple of guys were standing near them. They were not at all cute, and nowhere near sober, but still they were older, which was always worth something. So she said she'd go by herself. Just as well. It'd be nice to just sit here in the quiet, alone. But now, it's almost *too* quiet.

She thinks of her father again, turns on the radio and the computer and types quickly.

> dad! it's been so long since we talked. how are things going? how are the girls? has cecilia started walking? is madison still causing trouble? and you? how's business in the big apple? or are you on location somewhere, shooting your latest blockbuster? it's so hard to keep track. it'd be great to know exactly when you're coming next and how long you'll stay. i know you're totally busy, but it would mean a lot to hear your voice. hugs and kisses, kyla

She hits SEND and sits there idly in the desk chair. She can't go to bed yet. And she has no desire to call any of her friends. So what now?

She stares vacantly at her AOL home page. Then she shrugs and logs into a chat room.

He sneaks downstairs in just a T-shirt and boxers. His mom and dad are in bed. Nina and Andrei are in their rooms playing music—no one notices Alex. He cracks open the door to his dad's office. It's quiet and dark. He walks in, turns on the computer, logs into the chat room he likes to loiter in now and then. He quickly scans the comments. *cuz she's a *beeatch* w no life!* And a big debate about a basketball player. That's pretty much it. A bunch of nothing. He sighs and puts his fingers on the keys.

The chat room window is open. Kyla doesn't plan to write anything herself, but she's fascinated at how worked up people get about pointless crap. Wait—what's going on now? A discussion about the hottest girl on a new reality show and some stuff about basketball. She shifts on the bed and adjusts her laptop. At least she's not the only person who's up and alone at two a.m.

Kyla yawns. Maybe she should catch a couple of Zs. She's about to log off, when something grabs her eye.

> **Alex592:** I cnt sleep. Tried, but no go. I just want to talk, but w who? No one 2 call. :(So I'm here. Alone is nice sometmz, but not usually. Does any1 else understand?

Kyla stops and reads the message again. Alex. Just as lonely as she is.

She watches the answers to Alex's plea pop up, one after another: *quit w ur moanin and *lightbulb*: git urself a friend! and ltz tlk grls in miniskirts. i wanna know why ur such dumbasses. y wear minis if u don`t want to b calld sluts?*

Kyla sighs and shuts down the computer.

lightbulb: git urself a friend!* He groans and turns the computer off.

They say families are supposed to eat breakfast around the table, to spend quality time together. Obviously she's seen what that looks like, both on TV and over at Susanna's house: Mom stands while everyone else sits, she moves in the official kitchen triangle between the refrigerator, stove, and table; Dad mutters absentmindedly as he reads the paper; and the children bicker loudly about who finished all the Frosted Flakes and took the toy. Frankly, it doesn't sound that great.

Kyla has MTV on. She's dancing in front of her closet with a mouth full of buttered toast while she picks out what she's going to wear to school. She hooks herself into her black gel bra—the one that makes her boobs look huge. Then she flips through her hangers. She doesn't choose anything earth-shattering, just a concert T-shirt and a short skirt that goes with her tall brown boots.

The girls in the video are prancing around in gold bikinis in a desert somewhere. Kyla is about to turn it off, but flips through the channels first, winding up on a nature documentary. She lingers there. A bunch of horses galloping wildly across the screen, their long manes waving in the wind, their bodies pounding rhythmically. Kyla stares, hypnotized. They're so . . . free. But then the music fades and it cuts to a commercial.

She checks to see if she's gotten an e-mail response from her father. A sting of disappointment: nothing. On the way out she passes her mother's door. She stops and looks at the pool of brown hair and notices the stuffy, stale smell wafting from the room. She's about to move on, but stops suddenly, struck by a horrible thought. Someday, any old day, as Kyla walks by on her way out the door to school to meet her friends and doze through homeroom, her mother could actually be dead. While she sits in the cafeteria complaining about rubbery fries, her mother could be lying in bed, stiff and cold and abandoned. What if she lay there for several days before Kyla noticed? But no, Kyla knows that no matter how dead her mother looks, she never is—Mom is just *depressed.*

Since her parents' divorce her mom refers to depression as if it were her period, something that everyone just has to accept and deal with, whether they want to or not.

Oh, it's just a little something I take for my depression. No, I don't think I can go to the beach today, honey—my depression.

But still, what if . . .

Kyla pushes the door open a smidge and creeps into the semi-darkness.

"Mom?"

Her chest doesn't seem to be moving up or down. Kyla moves closer. Her mother's face is turned toward the wall. Kyla takes a deep breath before she quickly leans over the body to try and see how she looks on the other side: alive and asleep, or dead? Impossible to tell. Greasy ribbons of hair hide her mom's face.

She just can't make herself touch the body—what if it's totally cold? She gathers her courage and pats her mother hard on the cheek, shakes her a bit, and whispers, "Mom?"

Nothing happens. She's not particularly cold. Is she? Kyla quickly raises one of her mother's eyelids like she's seen them do on TV. She doesn't have any idea how to interpret what she sees in there, the white of an eye. It's white, does that mean that . . . ? Her heart almost stops.

Her mother shudders and snaps awake. She gapes at Kyla with wide, startled eyes. Her face is creased from the pillows, and her eyes are puffy, but Kyla can still see traces of the beauty that her mother was not so long ago—the glamorous model her father fell in love with while he was still filming fashion events.

They stare at each other. Kyla relaxes first. She smiles gratefully at her mom, squeezes her shoulder, and says, "It's just me. Sorry."

Her mother starts to get her bearings, begins to recognize her daughter. "Why—what are you doing in here?"

"I didn't know . . . I just wanted to make sure you . . ." Kyla stammers.

Her mother sinks back down into the bed, puts her hands on her head and moans, "Oh God, my head is killing me." She glances at Kyla, smiles with a questioning expression and asks, "Honey, have you eaten? You have to eat. Aren't you going to . . . Isn't it a weekday today? Don't you have school?"

Kyla gets a lump in her throat. She's so touched by the unsuccessful attempt to act like a parent that she strokes her mother's cheek tenderly, as if she were the responsible and caring adult.

"Yeah," Kyla answers. She hugs her mom, takes a deep breath, and breathes in all her smells without her stomach turning. "I just wanted to say bye first."

Her mom hugs her back, confused. "Oh. How nice. Bye, sweetheart."

Kyla watches as her mother turns over in bed again. Face to the wall. "Um, do you think you could find something to do today?" Kyla asks. "Even if it's just going outside for a little fresh L.A. air?"

It's a joke they used to share, but she hears how forced it sounds, feels the pools of water in the corners of her eyes. Her mother hardly reacts, mumbles something inaudible in response, something that doesn't sound anything like "Absolutely. I'll definitely do that," but more or less the opposite. Kyla swallows and blinks away her tears.

"So I found out that it *is* possible to sleep standing up. Check this out!"

Toby's pointing to a photo in a book. Alex is leaning against Toby's bedroom doorway with his backpack over his shoulder. He glances at his watch: They're going to be late. "Not now, man. We're not going to make it," he prompts.

Toby holds the book in front of Alex's nose and says, "Look. They sleep tethered in, standing up. Just look at that!"

He's breathing hard, almost agitated. And he smells like sweat, just like he always does. Should Alex say something? A little by-the-way or a there's-this-thing-I've-been-meaning-to-tell-you? Neither seems feasible when it comes to Toby. He can just hear Toby's response. "So?"

Toby, continuing to demand his attention, continues, "There's no up or down in space. That's why."

Alex snorts in irritation. He regrets it a second later. This is how Toby reaches out. He ought to show him a little sympathy. *He* of all people ought to understand how it feels not to be taken seriously. So he looks down at the book and says, "Wow."

Toby lights up. He gazes intently at Alex and explains, "This is how they sleep on Skylab. Isn't that cool?"

"Mmm."

"And on Mir before that."

"Yeah?"

"Imagine how that would feel! Sleeping standing up!"

Alex can't take any more. He looks at the time, exaggerating the motion and making a face that says "Uh-oh." Then he says it out loud: "Uh-oh! Shouldn't we get going?"

"I promise you, I'm going to go some—"

"Yes. That's great, but right now it's time to go to school."

Toby continues as if he didn't hear Alex. "—and live on a space station like that. They get water and food and books and everything they need from an unmanned spaceship."

"How convenient," Alex says, his voice dripping with sarcasm.

"Imagine!" Toby continues. "Just doing scientific experiments all day long, every day. That's my dream."

"Yeah, and I'm going to dance with the American Ballet Theater, at Lincoln Center in New York. That's *my* dream." Alex waits for a reaction, but Toby's expression doesn't change; he just keeps staring at the book.

"You can sort of get a sense for what it's like if you—"

"Toby? I'm leaving now."

"Sorry, sorry. I'm coming," Toby says.

Finally. They walk past Toby's parents' bedroom. His dad is sitting on the edge of the bed, his back bent, in just his underwear. He glances up and raises a hand in greeting. "Hello boys!" he says.

"Hi," Alex replies quietly, continuing quickly into the entry hall.

"Bye, Dad!" Toby calls cheerfully.

She's waiting for the elevator, exasperated. It's ten to. A door opens, the neighbor's door.

Kyla prays: *Oh, God. Seriously, not today.* But of course it's Elizabeth, running late too. She comes swooping into the stairwell with her black backpack slung over her shoulder and her long, smooth bangs covering half her face. Kyla slips on her giant sunglasses so she can glare unnoticed. She glances sideways, jealous of those perfect bangs that always look freshly washed and wholesome. Since their friendship broke off in the fifth grade, Kyla can never escape the truly petty urge to want to take a pair of scissors and snip them off.

Elizabeth locks the door to her apartment. *Please let the elevator come before she notices me,* Kyla pleads. *Please, God?* But no. Elizabeth turns around. They don't acknowledge each other.

In silence they wait at a safe distance. Elizabeth gives Kyla a once-over. Kyla tries to look as though she couldn't care less, hopes it's working.

Finally! The elevator takes an eternity to stop. The doors open. Elizabeth quickly slips in before Kyla's able to push her way past.

Elizabeth's eyes are focused on Kyla's tall, expensive boots, judging her. Kyla despises her right back, with her perfect life and Goody Two-shoes reputation. The contrast hurts so much that she can't stop herself.

"Are you sure you brushed a hundred strokes today?"

Elizabeth doesn't get it.

"I mean," Kyla continues, "you might have cheated. And just brushed those bangs ninety-eight times."

Elizabeth rolls her eyes, disgusted, and flips her bangs back. "Oh, whatever."

Just then the elevator stops. Kyla readies herself to serve up a frosty smile. As the doors part, Elizabeth walks out with her head held high. "Have a nice day now," Kyla calls in a singsong voice.

"You too," Elizabeth responds in the same sickly sweet tone.

Only one class left to go. Today really felt like The Day That Would Not End. Alex wondered if he'd be at school forever, trapped in a world of graffiti-covered lockers and old wads of chewing gum. If he would die here without ever getting to become anything at all.

He remembered a movie Andrei rented one time, the one where the same day kept repeating over and over. Andrei had laughed like crazy, but it just made Alex nervous. Because that's pretty much how his life already felt: All the days were the same, equally meaningless. What he wouldn't give for something new or exciting to turn everything upside down.

The wall of sound surrounding Alex as he makes his way through the hall is massive. He hears everyone else, and yet he doesn't. People are standing in groups, chatting loudly and gesturing. Only he and a few other students take their seats early, waiting for class to start. Beside him, Amanda gives him an unenthusiastic smile, lets him know she's over today too. Amanda's kind of cute with her red-brown hair and the swipe of freckles across her nose. She and her best friend Shauna are nice. They have no problem with Alex and he has no problem with them.

He'd consider pursuing her, asking her to study, or go with him to the Starbucks for a Frapawhatever, but whenever he thinks of another girl *she* always slips into his mind. Christina—so graceful, so beautiful. If he's lucky, he'll see her at practice tonight.

The bell rings and Mrs. Wallgren enters the classroom, her back stiff. Someone walks in behind her, a tall blond man most likely in his twenties. He looks around the room, seems honest and forthright. A few people look up.

Mrs. Wallgren clears her throat and shushes the class. "Everyone take your seats," she instructs.

The students do what she says, although most do it somewhat unwillingly. "We have our annual guest here from the Gay-Straight Alliance today," she explains.

Alex's heart reacts immediately, beating harder. Every year since seventh grade this visit goes down the same way, and some of his hard-acquired self-confidence with it.

As usual, the word *gay* is like the crack of a whip. Suddenly it's dead quiet in the room.

This year's visitor is Kent and he's twenty-eight. He explains that he's the GSA social coordinator for the East Bay, and that he loves to give outreach talks to junior high and high school students. The class has practically stopped breathing. Alex can hear what they're thinking: *Here it comes!* Kent smiles at them calmly.

"I'm going to talk about my experience as a gay man," he says.

Everyone stares; only Toby peers distractedly out the window, indifferent.

A bit of embarrassed chair adjusting and whispering can be heard. Alex looks down, but it's hardly an effective shield for his classmates' snickering. The worst of it comes from Kevin, Val, and three others. He knows exactly which ones—Kevin's lackeys from the soccer team. As he stares intently at his desk, he feels his body temperature rise to an abnormal level inside his sweater. The redness creeps slowly, crawling up over his neck. It moves toward his face and spreads out onto his cheeks. He can't stop it. *Please, please, just let this be over soon.*

Kent doesn't seem to register the murmuring, or he doesn't care. He talks as if nothing is happening, explaining what it means to be gay, and adding that lots of people have questions about their sexuality when they're juniors.

When *he* was sixteen, he says, he was terrified to think he might be gay, but it's actually just as natural to be gay as straight. The love is the same, regardless of gender. That's why gay and straight teens need to work together to support each other, and teach the facts to people who don't know them. Alex catches only fragments.

"There are still so many prejudices against gay people. I mean, do I look gay?" He holds his arms out. "Well? Do I *look* particularly queer?"

A few isolated *no*s can be heard.

"Exactly. But you still have a particular idea of what a gay person looks like, don't you?" Kent asks. "So what does one look like then?"

Alex hears the voices now, they're just loud enough to make out clearly: *Alex . . . Alex . . . Alex . . .*

Mrs. Wallgren shushes them, but Kent carries on, unconcerned.

"You think a gay man has to be effeminate, right? Want to do so-called girl stuff?"

The voices are louder now, they've become a drone: *Alex . . . Alex . . . Alex . . .* Mrs. Wallgren shushes them again; the heckling is even worse than last year. Amanda turns to Kevin in irritation and says, "Shut up, would you!"

"Well, that's not true," Kent continues. "You don't have to *be* any particular way to be gay. We're all extremely different, just as different as all of you in here and . . ."

The drone isn't a drone anymore. What those two, maybe three, people are saying is quite audible now: *Alex . . . Alex . . . Alex . . .* and it has clearly made it to Kent at last. He stops talking and looks around pointedly. The voices keep murmuring, escaping from behind the hands people have over their mouths. Kent's eyes finally meet Alex's, and Kent understands. His eyes are filled with compassion. Is he going back in time now, picturing himself as an insecure sixteen-year-old?

Alex screams silently. He doesn't care if someone else is, but he *isn't* gay. Which means he and Kent are *not* on the same team; they have nothing to do with each other.

The whispering continues. Kent's eyes are on Alex. Alex feels like he's going to pass out. But then Kent moves his gaze and glances around the class seriously. His eyes move from one student to the next and then stop again. On Kevin, who is still making noise. Is Kent going to beat him up? It looks like it. The look Kent gives Kevin is as focused as a laser beam. Kevin squirms, finally stops mumbling. Only then does Kent ease up. Then he smiles at the class as if nothing had happened.

"Hi, my name is Kent. I play hockey and chew tobacco. And I'm queer."

They're at the café again. No one feels like going to math today. Susanna found a new kind of bubble tea she *just loves!* She's sitting there slurping up her tapioca balls, on her third sickly pink drink, still full of excessive enthusiasm. Every so often she glances furtively at Kyla, whom she finally convinced to try it.

"Yummy, isn't it?"

It isn't. It tastes like plastic.

"Pretty good," Kyla lies.

Therese has a glass of warm water in front of her. She calls it "silver tea" and says she doesn't want anything else, but Kyla knows that's not true. Therese has water because it's free. Why can't she admit it? They would understand—she's short on cash. Her dad hasn't had steady work in years, and the well dries up pretty fast when your cult-hit

TV series is canceled, doomed to spend the rest of its life airing only in syndication.

Why are they here anyway? Kyla can't stop thinking that she should have gone to class. If she doesn't pass math, she won't get into the AP courses her father seems insistent on. If she even *wants* to get in. But what else is she going to do? Lie around like all the other kids with industry big-shot parents, unconcerned about the future because, well, there's really not much to be concerned about?

"What AP classes are you applying for?" Kyla asks. "Chem or Spanish or what?"

The others don't hear the question. Their noses are buried in a magazine full of women with long legs.

"Miss Arizona, *obviously*. She's the prettiest." Susanna places her cup down resolutely.

Therese flips through the portraits. "Her face, maybe. But her legs look freaky, kind of knock-kneed." She puts her finger over one of the girl's kneecaps. "There! Now she looks better, doesn't she?"

"What AP courses are you guys going to apply for?" Kyla asks again.

They look up from the article in their magazine. "Do we have to talk about that stuff now?" Susanna pleads.

"Well, we've got to talk about it *sometime*."

"I don't care about any of it," Therese adds.

"Very mature," Kyla fires back.

Susanna glances down again and asks, "How in the world can you tell? You can't possibly tell she's knock-kneed from a picture."

Kyla stares out the window. Time creeps slowly along, and one day she'll be thirty-seven, tanning-bed shriveled, with no education and no job—but lounging poolside and still pretending to care. Surely depressed too, seeing as how it appears to run in the family.

"My life is going nowhere," Kyla sighs.

The others look up from the magazine.

"What are you talking about?" Susanna asks.

"I'd just, you know, like to find a niche. Something I'm good at. Besides guys—and getting into bars."

Susanna stares at her a moment, then smiles. "You're crazy! But it's good to dream big."

Therese looks at her skeptically. "I figured out when my dad lost his job that you can forget about dreams. The only thing that matters is what we're doing right now."

"No. I don't know . . ." Kyla fumbles, trying to find the right words. "I just think if, maybe, if we tried a little more—"

"Look. Just drop it, okay?" Therese sighs. "Some people are just brainiacs who take AP courses and get into Ivy League schools and go on to cure cancer. Others aren't. I hate to break it to you, but we fall into the 'aren't' category."

Kyla shakes her head. "It doesn't have to be like—"

Therese slams her cup down on the table. "What is *wrong* with you? Your dad is like the biggest director in the *world*. Most people . . . *tons of people* would die to be in your shoes. I don't understand why *you* can't be satisfied with it."

The discussion is over. Kyla stares at her friend, remembering all those elementary school afternoons when Therese used to beg Kyla's mom for advice on how to be a model, when she was so serious about becoming one herself. It was a goal that might not have been out of reach, if Therese still cared about anything.

"Sorry, Suse," Therese continues, "but Miss Michigan has it all."

"But she's kind of *too* thin, though. Kyla, what do you think?" Susanna wonders.

"Kyla?" Therese prompts.

Kyla stirs her fake-strawberry tea, then looks Therese right in the eye. "I think you could have made it."

He's walking behind a girl whose rear is encased in shiny, tight-fitting fabric. You can't not stare. It's so ridiculous. Again and again he tries to look somewhere else; his eyes keep wandering back to her butt. Katy's butt. He glances over at Toby, who's walking next to him. Toby's eyes do not settle on the obvious. Toby is looking at everything but. It's as if Katy doesn't exist.

Katy's shoes are the kind that Alex's mom forbade Nina to buy, insisting she'd sprain her ankles. Katy's long hair swings softly across her back. It's blond, but almost black up at the part. She needs to do her roots. Is there something wrong with him? Is he being a perv? Is she as hot as people say? He surely has a mind of his own. But in this case, it appears that Toby's the only one who's different.

Or is he just pretending? Did he maybe he sneak a peek when Alex wasn't looking?

"Hey. Do you think she's cute?" Alex whispers.

Toby is startled and looks confused. "What? Who?"

"Katy."

"Katy? What about her?"

Alex shushes his friend and points ahead of them. Toby peers at Katy as if he's only just noticed her—as if she's some rare species in need of a genus and phylum.

"You want to know if I think she's *cute?*"

"Yeah. Do you?"

Toby looks tormented. He's on thin ice when the topic has nothing to do with archeological findings, space, or eleventh-century expeditions.

"Cute . . ." he tries hesitantly. "I . . . don't know."

Alex considers just dropping it. But he doesn't. "All you have to do is say yes or no."

"Yeah, I get it, but . . . cute? Well, where?"

"What do you mean, *where?* Just cute! The whole package! Everywhere!" Alex doesn't recognize his own voice.

Toby looks at Katy again and sighs, really concentrating. "All I can see is her back."

"Exactly!" Alex's eyes bore into Toby's.

And suddenly, Alex makes up his own mind. He's a marvel of decisiveness. "*I* don't think she's cute. She's kind of cheap somehow. Not my type."

Alex looks past Katy. A little farther ahead Kevin and Val are hanging out by the mini-mart. He deflates, the resoluteness he'd had five seconds ago lost in a flash. They haven't noticed him yet. They've only seen Katy. Kevin whistles. Val whistles.

"Ooooooh, baby, come over here a minute!" Kevin taunts, but Katy just keeps walking. "Katy?" Kevin continues, suddenly sounding uncertain. She just raises her hand and flips him off.

"What the hell's your problem?" Kevin yells angrily.

"Yeah, what!" Val yells lamely.

Katy stops and slowly turns around. "Poor little Kevin," she coos, "things are tough for you, aren't they?"

Kevin loses his triumphant smile. He seems to attempt a retort, but just mutters something under his breath. He lost. The next second he catches sight of Alex and Toby. "Well hello, ladies! How's your relationship working out? Is it *good*? As a new member of GSA, I want you to know that I'm concerned about how are you two lovebirds are getting along."

They keep walking. Katy turns around and looks right at him. She rolls her eyes. Alex blinks; she's thinking the same thing he is about Kevin and Val. That they're total losers.

Strange—that's never happened before. Not with a girl like Katy.

Alex rolls his eyes back. And smiles.

Kyla walked Susanna home, and now she's standing next to her in the dining room, feeling awkward. The whole family is gathered around the table. Susanna's little brother,

Michael, is impersonating his fourth-grade teacher. He sticks out his upper lip, imitating a severe overbite, and lisps, " . . . sho you musht all shtrive to do your besht . . ." Her mother, father, and Susanna all giggle.

There are candles on the table. Steam wafts up from the dishes of baked chicken and sweet potatoes. It smells delicious—it smells like a home. Her father grins as he turns to the girls. "Susanna, there you are! Kyla, hello! I hope you two have been out studying?"

Susanna sighs and tells him that everything is *super-hard* right now, but she'll finish her homework later. He offers to help however he can while her mother fusses over Michael, insisting he take more carrots. Then she looks up and asks, "Kyla, won't you stay for dinner?" Susanna looks like she'd be okay with it, and Kyla's stomach cries out in hunger. But she can't. She's got to get home, back to her mom, and make sure there's some food on that table.

"Thanks, Mrs. Swanson, but I can't."

Fag. That's not so bad, is it? Being called that over and over?

Some people travel back and forth between a house and an apartment and have two sets of toothbrushes and gym clothes. Others have parents who drink or get beaten up by sleazy uncles. What does he have to complain about? Kevin and Val don't even touch him. They've never shoved his head in the toilet or forced him to smoke cigarettes until he puked, nothing like that. And he actually has a friend. Sure, Toby isn't much for conversation and the guy borders on the truly weird, but so what? Some people don't have anyone. And then he has his family. All he has to do is open his mouth and just try: "People think I'm gay. What should I do?" If he could get the words out, he's sure they'd listen.

He leans over the porcelain sink, slowly washes his face and studies it in the mirror. Is that a new Alex he sees? A bold, take-charge guy who speaks with heartfelt honesty about life and its hardships? Yes, he's sure it is. And today is the day the new Alex starts a *real* relationship with his parents.

His mother's in the kitchen. She's listening to the television and making dinner. He watches her back moving under the fabric of her blouse; her flab seems to have a life of its own. At one time she'd been thin and in peak condition, but that was so long ago, before Alex was even born, back when she was a prima ballerina in St. Petersburg.

"Mom?" Alex asks.

"What is it, Sasha?" she asks without turning around.

"What are you doing?"

"Shhh!" she shushes him, as if she were listening to something important. But the TV program is about insects. Dung beetles. Since when does she care about beetles? The host of the program informs viewers that beetles are in the scarab family.

He sits down at the kitchen table, unsure of how he should begin. "Uhh," is all that comes out.

His mom whips around in a flash and demands, "Did it not go well today at rehearsal? But you said that—"

"Oh, yeah, it was fine but . . ." he starts.

"You have to promise me you will not give up," she insists, shaking a wooden spoon in his direction. "Even when it feels hard, Sasha. It will be worth it, you know."

He grits his teeth. "Yeah, I know."

She smiles quickly and turns back to the stove. Dung beetles burrow in piles of manure.

"It isn't that," Alex tries again.

This time she doesn't turn around. Dung beetles build branching tunnels underneath manure piles.

Louder now, to drown out the television: "It isn't that."

"Hmm?"

Dung beetles lay their eggs in the tunnels and haul the dung down to feed to their larvae.

He's yelling now: *"It isn't that, I said!"*

His mother whirls around, a crease in her brow.

"Why do you shout, Sasha? I'm listening to a program. What is it?"

There are ninety species of dung beetles in the United States.

"Never mind."

Alex leaves the kitchen.

Kyla hears the sound from the TV before she even closes the door behind her. Good, so her mother is up. Her mom mostly watches reality shows. Sometimes, when Mom is kind of alert, they watch together, making comments like,

"I *cannot* believe he said that!" and laughing when shiny, fake tears flow and the characters squeal and cry about their botched love affairs.

She takes her coat off in the hallway and braces herself for the disheveled head on one arm of the sofa and the legs stretched over the other. Covered by that shabby old blanket from back when her father was around. And she's right. Her mother glances up with one eye.

"Hi, you," she says.

"Hi."

Kyla goes into the kitchen. There are almost no dirty dishes in the sink, just her stuff from breakfast this morning. In the fridge there's only some peanut butter, a moldy onion, and an almost-empty bottle of ketchup. She ate the last of the bread this morning. Suddenly she wants to cry, she's so tired and hungry. Thinking of Susanna's family dinner, she's just angry. Couldn't her mom have at least gone to the store? What the hell did she do all day?

Kyla storms back out to the living room. "It's ten o'clock. The fridge is empty and the grocery store is closed. What are we going to eat?!"

Her mom drags her eyes away from the TV and wonders, "Didn't you eat at whoever's house you went to?"

"Why would I have done that?"

"I don't know. I just thought that—"

"Oh, you did? You thought about it? Otherwise, you're saying, you would have made dinner." Her voice sounds hard and sarcastic.

Her mom looks at her nervously and mumbles, "I—I'm sorry, I didn't know . . ."

Kyla feels the anger run out of her like gushing water when a drain is opened. Anger takes just too much energy. She flops down next to her mom on the sofa and leans her head on her shoulder. "It's okay," Kyla says. "I'll call down to Mr. Chow. Jeff will send up something." They offer each other small smiles.

"Do you want kung pao, Mom?"

"No, thanks . . . I had a sandwich or two earlier on."

Kyla feels her stomach knot up. "I doubt it. We don't have any bread."

Her mother sits up straighter and demands, "What, you're checking up on my diet now?"

"I just don't think that, on top of everything, you should starve yourself too."

"I'm not starving myself," her mother hisses, lying back down. The knot in Kyla's stomach gets even tighter.

"You know, Mom, if you don't eat you'll be able to do even less. You have to eat something!"

"I don't *have* to do anything!" Her mom climbs clumsily off the sofa and stomps her way to her bedroom. *Bang.* The door slams shut. Kyla's whole body starts trembling. *God, this is so screwed up!*

Kyla goes to her room and locks the door. She turns on her stereo, trying not to cry. Madonna's voice fills the air. Madonna, who's several years older than her mother, even though she seems so young. Why couldn't her mom be more like that? Madonna's had her share of crises, but then she started doing yoga and got all cheery. And when she had kids she even seemed *happy*. Her mom had her a thousand years ago—well, sixteen years ago anyway, but she's nowhere *near* happy. Maybe yoga is all that's missing. Can you trick someone into doing yoga?

Kyla checks her e-mail, sees that she has a new message. *Please, let it be from Dad!*

> Hi, Sweetie!
> Great to hear from you. Cecilia took her first steps. She looks so happy as she totters around the house. And Madison is livening things up here at home as usual. It's not easy having little kids, especially when I have to work so much. It's a good thing it's fun too.
>   Don't be too disappointed, but I had to cancel my trip to L.A. Such a shame, I know, but a few things have come up on the set (actors!) and unfortunately I just can't leave. Maybe I can get away later or you can come here on your next vacation? It must be a good six months since you've been here by now, right? I was at your favorite restaurant the other night and Mario said he missed you. (So you know that I do too!) E-mail me back so that I know you're not too bummed. I put money in the account as usual.
> I love you,
> Dad

She just sits there for several minutes, staring at the screen. Slowly she realizes something is dripping on the keyboard. Small pools have formed between D and F and N and M. Frustrated, she clenches her hands into fists.

Damn it, Dad! Don't you understand what's happening here? We're drowning—and you have no idea.

Worse, she realizes, she has no way to tell him. Not without him trying to fix things—and then he might try to seek custody, and take her away.

That can never happen. Ever.

She unlocks her door and steps out, flings her mother's door open. Of course, Mom is asleep, her face to the wall. No, that can never happen. Because without Kyla around, what would happen to *this* family?

Alex gives up on his dad the second he sees him. The idea of the two of them being able to talk to each other is almost ludicrous. How would that conversation go?

Hey, Pop, what's happening?

Well, son, today I installed a new server that will host the company's super-awesome software I created that you don't understand or know absolutely anything about. How about you?

Well, I performed some wicked grand jetés today. I mean, I really set it off! But earlier, around noon, Toby and I ate lunch right next to the most gorgeous girl in school. Seriously! I mean, she didn't know we were there, but man, if she had turned around she would have been looking right at us!

That's fantastic, son, I'm so proud. Come over here and give your old man a hug!

Yeah, right.

Instead his father grunts as he rises from the dinner table, clearly done for the evening. He sits down in front of the television as Alex slips up the stairs.

He goes to Nina's room. He can feel the hip-hop beat from the hallway. The door is ajar. Nina is practicing air guitar in the cramped space in the middle of her floor; she's totally sweaty and completely absorbed. He knows how she feels. He can feel the energy just watching her. They're actually not that different, he and Nina. She's only a year younger. They really ought to be able to get more out of each other, but she's so wrapped up in her own stuff all the time. Like now. She obviously doesn't want to be disturbed.

Nina gave up ballet years ago, and Alex wasn't sure his mother would survive the blow. The yelling and the tears never seemed to end in those days. Yet somehow, they were all still here, all alive, and Nina first got to explore other forms just for the fun of it—like hip-hop, jazz, and modern—and then quit all together. Their mother had even accepted it when little Nina joined an honest-to-God rock band—as the lead singer.

They've played a few gigs for friends and at the all-ages venues. Someday, maybe he'll get to see her perform.

Alex is simultaneously in awe of Nina's freedom and jealously aware that he doesn't have the strength to face his mother the way she did.

The next room down the hall is his brother Andrei's.

Andrei calls him "bro" in a way that's almost affectionate. Andrei's nineteen and is going to have to move out soon, according to their father. Does he have time for a heart-to-heart before he goes? Alex puts his ear to the door, but doesn't hear anything. He tries to peek through the keyhole. No luck. He knocks lightly, then carefully opens the door. At first he thinks the room is empty, but then— he shuts the door again. Andrei was on his bed with a girl. Just kissing, but still. Alex blushes.

He goes into his own room and sinks down on the bed. Then he gets up and slips back down the stairs and into his father's office. There's got to be someone, *anyone* who will listen.

⌖

She tries to think positive for a minute. After all, plenty of people have it worse off: people who are starving, orphans. She has a mother, even if she is depressed, and she has a father who loves her, even if he's far away. She has friends, even if they're superficial and boring. And Therese is right, there is plenty of money. So why, *why* does she feel like there's something tremendous missing in her life? Like there is a giant hole in her, aching to be filled by ... what? She wishes she knew.

She goes over to the computer, turns it on, and logs back into the chat room. If she can't figure it out, maybe someone else can.

She reads. Just a bunch of empty words and meaning-

47

less opinions. What was that guy's name, that guy from the other day? The one who felt lonely and just wanted to talk?

> **kyla16:** hey, alex from yesterday, are u 4 real? u said u were lonely and wondered if any1 else felt the same way. *i* sure as hell do. u there?

He just stares. Kyla16 can only mean him. Suddenly he's nervous. Someone noticed him. Remembered him.

> **Alex592:** Kyla! Yeah! I'm here. But I don't really get why. Everyone just seems to be typing a bunch of crap.

He waits anxiously. Is she still there? Or maybe he wasn't fast enough? Maybe she logged off and went to bed? But then it appears:

> **kyla16:** hi there. ;) i know. sometimes i wonder if there's something wrong with me, cuz i just can't deal with the bullshit. what if the whole world just gave all that up, got real 4 even a day?

He has to know more about her. He clicks on her name to pull up her user profile.

Blank. Darn it. He'll just have to keep chatting.

Alex592: That'd be crazy. ;) Sometimes it's like no one wants to know who I really am, like no one cares. How do you get people to listen?

kyla16: im not sure. hw old r u?

Alex592: 16, u?

kyla16: same

They create a private chat room.

kyla16: people think they know me, that's the worst part

Alex592: Sometimes I think OK, now I'm going to be myself, u know, and then things always go wrong. Does that mean that I'm wrong?

kyla16: i don't think so. i just think people suck. i don't even try now. besides, how can i expect people to know me for who i am? i don't even know who i am!!! lol

Alex592: I think I know. But then maybe I don't . . . imagine if i die b4 i figure it out! Will anyone have gotten to know the real me? Does that even exist?

kyla16: someone's got 2 know the real us . . . god?

Alex592: Never heard of him. ;) Anyway, he doesn't seem to drop by my life much.

kyla16: well if there's no god what about satan? i'm pretty sure he xists. cuz there are times it feels like he's right there messing around w me

Alex592: So you're not alone!!

kyla16: lol! no i guess . . . my little demon is always right there, sitting on my shoulder

Alex592: I could use some company 2 . . . I'm not even picky enough to refuse the underworld.

kyla16: u don't want my guy . . . he smells. *scent of gym socks in hellfire 4 u*

Alex592: \<runs away in terror> Bleck! But really, why does everyone exist in their own self-centered universe?

kyla16: maybe we're just as bad, we just don't realize it? we r sitting here talking about ourselves, btw ;)

Alex592: True, but who can blame us when we finally get the chance?

kyla16: listen, i have 2 go, but I don't want 2 stop chatting. i'll send u an email l8r, k?

Alex592: ☺

She isn't human. She moves like a bird—no, not a bird, like an angel. Or maybe a fairy, hovering over the floor.

Skinny body and translucent skin. She looks like someone born premature, fragile and frail. You can see the veins at her temples. Her skin is so fair, her legs are covered in patterns from the blood vessels near the surface. You want to take care of her. *He* wants to take care of her. Wrap his arms around her, or at least hold her hand.

Sometimes he gets to touch her when they dance. Her body is hard, but her skin is soft. She weighs nothing. When he lifts her way up in the air she rarely looks him in the eye; she's off in her own world. Maybe she's just concentrating on the dancing?

They see each other four times a week, he and Christina. They have for over a year, but they've hardly said a word to each other. She doesn't talk to anybody. Sometimes she flashes a small, shy smile when someone makes a mistake. Otherwise, she's unapproachable.

She always wears her hair up. Alex fantasizes that when she unwinds it, it reaches down to the back of her knees, flowing like a blond river. Her nose is so thin, it's almost just a line, with a little swoop on each side. Her mouth is small, her eyes light blue, almost gray. What's weird is that she has black eyelashes even though she's so fair. And narrow, black eyebrows.

Christina dances better than anyone else in the group. She's going to be a prima ballerina one day, says Paulina, who has her favorites even though she's not supposed to. In the case of Christina, that's all right, Alex thinks. Because she truly is phenomenal. And someday, someday she'll notice him.

"This is phenom," Adam says. "It's totally amazingly awesome. Right, Kyla?"

She doesn't know what he's talking about. Adam is leaning against the wall with his skateboard under his arm, as if he were posing for a picture. Nonchalant. Jake is sitting on his board a few feet away. He hocks a loogie the way he knows a cool skateboarder should. Everything seems posed, calculated. Therese and Susanna are smoking. Therese is blowing smoke rings because she just learned how. Susanna is the only one who responds. She peers admiringly at Adam.

"Totally!" she squeals, way too upbeat. "Hella cool."

But Adam is waiting for a response from Kyla. He doesn't take his eyes off her. "Kyla?" he prods.

She smiles quickly. "Um, cool, yeah," she agrees, without a clue as to what they're talking about.

Adam looks satisfied. Walks over and strokes his index finger across her forehead. She jumps.

"What are you doing?"

"You had something there," he explains.

"What? Where?" She waves him away with her hand. "Cut that out."

Adam's shoulders slump. "Chill. It was just a piece of hair."

She can't look at him. Can't stop wondering why she slept with him. Well, she knows *why*. It's because they were partying, and she was *very* drunk, and at the time his arms felt warm around her. Kissing him made everything tingle and every little voice telling her not to, to just *shut up*. The next day it was never quite so Zen. Especially after she realized that Adam could barely string a sentence together without needing to go Ollie or whatever skateboard guys do. She's avoided him since.

So why are they here? Therese and Susanna. They begged Kyla to come hang out. They think Adam and Jake are cute, despite the fact that Kyla's been with both of them.

Yeah, yeah. She slept with Jake too, but it was two years

ago, so he's easier to look at. Jake doesn't say much and wears his pants so far down on his hips that they once fell down to his knees. It took him down a notch when it happened. It's still a little funny to remember.

Therese apparently liked Jake then too, way back freshman year. Kyla hadn't known it then, and Susanna hadn't told her until it was too late. Therese never said anything about it herself, just started acting weirder and weirder— like everything that'd changed about Therese, it was another rift they'd probably never address. At this point, Kyla just throws her hands up in frustration. How could she have figured out a secret Therese kept even from her best friends? Was she supposed to be a mind reader?

Kyla sighs. Susanna giggles like a little girl at one of Jake's skateboard tricks.

Is this how it's supposed to be? Kyla wonders. *I mean, life, is this really it? Because if it is, well, just shoot me.*

"You children are making me crazy!"

There's something wild in their mother's eyes. Her arms are full of stuff that she begins to fling onto the floor in front of Alex, Andrei, and Nina.

"Look at these things *now*!" she orders. Then she disappears back into the closet again. Rummaging around and pulling stuff out. Her backside swaying back and forth. When she comes out again, she's holding a dusty old baseball glove.

"As I said, what is this? Who is using this?"

Andrei grabs it away from her. "That's mine."

"Yes, but when do you use this?!"

"When do I use it?"

"Yes, when. Let me hear!" Their mother stands there with her hands on her hips, her eyes wide and expectant, strands of hair flying every which way. "Yes?" she urges.

"Chill out, Mom," Andrei says, thinking. "I . . . I might start playing again."

That's not good enough. Their mother smiles triumphantly.

"Ha! But you have not touched this in two years, my *dorogoi*. So I am not planning to 'chill out.' It's going!"

And she's back in the closet again, her rear still vibrating as she sorts madly. She comes out with a bunch of sports equipment of various types and dumps it in front of Andrei. "We cannot keep these hockey sticks. They make this closet full. You must keep them in the shed or in your own room."

Andrei sighs and mumbles something to himself before grabbing his stuff and leaving.

There's a pile of old games and clothes in front of Alex, a tangle of Barbie dolls in front of Nina.

"Now I see organization," a jubilant voice calls from inside the closet.

But suddenly her backside is completely still. Their mother slowly emerges from the closet. She has something in her hand.

"Oh," she whispers. Her eyes are full of reverence for Nina's old toe shoes with their long, pink ribbons. She's

holding them as if they were something delicate and fragile. Immediately Nina's lips purse, looking grim.

"Oh . . ." Their mother holds the shoes out toward Nina.
"Look!"

"Yeah, we can toss 'em," Nina says stonily.

Their mother looks at Nina, the corners of her eyes gleaming. "Are you sure?"

"Yup."

"But you cannot be very sure, can you?"

Nina sighs. She puts a hand on her mother's back. "Listen to me," Nina begins. She emphasizes each word: *"I. Am.
Never. Going. To. Dance. Again."*

Their mother turns away, but Nina is ruthless: This time
her words will finally get through. She walks to her mother's
other side and presses her nose up into her face. "Do you
hear what I'm saying, Mom? *Never again!*" She picks up the
toe shoes and deposits them in a nearby wastebasket. Then
she turns around and goes to her room.

Alex is still standing there. His mom is shaking and
trembling, but it's just pretend crying. Maybe *she* actually
thinks she's crying for real. But she's not. Everyone in the
family knows it.

"Oh, Sasha. My little Sasha, how lucky there is you."

Yes, Alex thinks. *Lucky, lucky me.*

Dear Kyla,
I hate myself. I didn't protest or scream that
I'm not the momma's boy they think. I just
stood there . . . I must be the biggest wuss in

55

the world. My head's so full of how I should react. How everything should be, but none of it ever happens, ever.

Do you realize, Kyla, what an idiot you're e-mailing with?!!

Grrrr!
—Alex

Kyla hurries, walking the path along the beach way ahead of Susanna and Therese. She wants to go home and write to Alex.

They've exchanged several e-mails already. She's not really into all the online stuff, other than occasionally updating her Facebook page, and she certainly wasn't looking for an online *pen pal*. In fact, she suspected online relationships were mostly for the extremely weird or socially inept. But why should that be true? Alex is not a loser. He's got real thoughts and feelings. He listens, thinks, asks questions. She feels warm when she thinks about him. And they don't even know details about each other.

That's all right; she doesn't need to know. They chatted again last night for two hours, and it was the best conversation of her life.

"Kyla, quit walking so fast!" She is wrenched away from her thoughts by Susanna's whiny voice from behind her.

"I wanna talk about Adam," Susanna coos. "He's so hot. Don't you think?"

"No."

"You don't?" Therese jabs. "It sure seemed like you did last month."

"Strange. Because I don't."

Therese giggles and asks, "Why are you so flustered then?"

"I'm not flustered! You two should go for it."

The other two get quiet, look at each other and make faces. Fine, just let them—she's trying to help. "Go hang out with your skateboard lovers," she teases. "See ya."

She turns toward her apartment building, leaving the two of them behind.

Only one more block and—*oh no*. Elizabeth. And her friend Jenny. No one says hi. Elizabeth and Jenny are walking just in front, but they've noticed her. At first it's quiet, except for footsteps and a couple cars that speed by. Suddenly Kyla hears a giggle. She tries to ignore it, to think instead about the e-mail she's going to write. But they giggle again, louder this time, and she senses it throughout her whole body: That laughter is meant for her.

Elizabeth and Jenny think she's worthless in every way: shallow, dumb, and cheap. The two of them with all their books and brains and honor societies, they think they're so superior.

She picks up her pace and interrupts. "What the hell do you want?"

Elizabeth stops abruptly and says, "Sorry?"

"Obviously something is really funny."

"What, now we can't even laugh?" Elizabeth looks at Jenny with a smile. "Well, I beg your pardon. I'll never laugh again."

She turns around to leave. But the anger wells up in Kyla. She wants to strangle Elizabeth for making her feel so worth-less. "You'd better watch it!" she growls, low and menacing.

But Elizabeth doesn't intimidate easily. "What is that? Some kind of threat?"

"Take it however you want."

Elizabeth's cheeks redden. "I'm not afraid of you."

"Well, you should be," Kyla hears herself say.

They've never been this close to getting into a fight. Elizabeth casts an anxious glance at Jenny, who's trying to pull her along.

"Screw her. C'mon!" Jenny says. But Elizabeth is pissed.

"You're really not that perfect and popular, you know. We *used* to hang out. I know what your deal *really* is, you—" Elizabeth hesitates. Kyla knows what's coming, but Elizabeth isn't actually the type to stoop so low, is she?

" . . . you slut!" Spit sprays out of Elizabeth's mouth.

Kyla slaps her with the palm of her hand.

oh, alex . . . i just wanna scream. i'm not what they think! not inside. but obviously no one would believe me. i do stupid things that i don't mean to do, always the same stuff. it

58

just happens. why? y???!!? the world is spinning. i don't get myself. it's like i've turned
into somebody else. am i crazy? all i do is mess
shit up for everyone and myself worst of all. oh
god. what if i end up like my mom? i'm clearly
almost there and i don't know what to do, how
to change how everything is and where it all
seems to be heading. help, please . . . kyla

P.E. sucks, but today it's not as awful as it usually is. Because
now there's Kyla, which there never was before. She's more
than a friend; she's like a sister, or what do people call it—a
soul mate? She's so different from anyone else he knows.
He hardly dares to talk to Christina, even though he loves
her from afar. But he can tell Kyla anything.

He was sad and, at the same time, strangely honored
to see her e-mail last night. She was obviously going through
something terrible and she chose to share her feelings
with him—she reached out to *him* for help.

He hoped his response helped. He told her that it didn't
matter what anyone else thought; she knew who she was
inside and as long as she stayed true to that person, well, then
screw everyone else. When he thought about it now, it made
him smile. Maybe he should try following his own advice.

Everyone has their gym clothes on and is sitting on the
benches. Coach Platt and his whistle are full of their usual
energy.

"Today, my friends, I'm going to teach you something completely different. You're going to learn how to waltz."

Groans echo throughout the gym. They don't stop until Coach Platt smiles. "Okay, okay, some of you can play soccer then. If you'd like to learn a useful social dance, go join Mrs. Kirby in the annex."

The guys whoop and cheer "Yes!" Kevin stands up, demanding attention. "Hey, Teach!" he calls.

"Yeah?"

"What's Alex gonna do? I mean, maybe he'd rather *dance.*" He flutters his fingers in the air on the last word.

Coach Platt shoots him an irritated glare. "Cut it out, Briggs."

Kevin turns toward him. Alex doesn't look away. Thinking about Kyla, out there somewhere, facing her own problems, helps him to be strong.

"Why don't you come with us, Alex?" Kevin taunts. "We know how much you like to play with boys."

Alex knows he's being baited, and normally he'd ignore the challenge, but he's feeling sort of exhilarated today. "Sure, I'll play."

Kevin sneers. "Oh goody." He turns to Val. "He can be on *your* team."

Kevin's never seen Alex play soccer before. Kevin started going to the school when they were all in the fifth grade. Before that, Alex used to play all the time. Andrei always told him he had a good sense for the ball. Alex hopes he's still got it.

He plays midfield. Ballet hasn't left him much time for anything else recently, but this still feels good, and the moves come naturally.

He receives passes, sends them on, and doesn't hear a single negative comment. Everyone's playing fair. Alex dribbles a little, drives the ball forward, and feels his energy start to flow. He's fast, like a lynx on the field. He dribbles between defenders, weaving quickly around their attacks. Everyone else eyes him appreciatively, nodding in approval. He feints left and manages to get past a player from the other team and then quickly passes to Javier, who attacks the goal.

"Nice one, Alex!" Anton yells.

A couple of people even clap. Kevin, on the opposing team, flashes him a nasty snarl. Alex realizes that Kevin isn't going to just accept this. He's going to put a stop to it, and Alex doesn't have to wait long. The next time he dribbles along the outside edge, Kevin comes thundering over and hurls himself down in front of Alex. Alex stumbles and goes flying. He really jams his knee.

"Man, that tackle was messed up!" someone shouts angrily.

Platt blows his whistle. "Yellow card!"

Alex tries to walk it off, but Coach leans down to examine his leg. "Better not push it, kid. Nice work out there. Hit the lockers."

He limps off toward the locker room thinking it all worked out great. At least now he's shown that he's a force to be reckoned with. He hears rapid footsteps behind him and turns around. It's Val; he looks sincerely concerned. "Hey. Are you okay?"

How's Alex supposed to take this? Is it just a joke? Is he being set up, as usual?

"Is it your knee?" Val asks.

Best not to answer.

"I can help you to the locker room," Val offers.

This definitely smells like a trick. Val holds out his arm for Alex to support himself on.

"Nah," Alex mumbles, "I'm fine."

"Oh . . . okay. I was just wondering."

Kevin is standing off in the distance, watching them. "Hey!" he yells. "We've got a game here. You playing or what?" Val grins and jogs back over to Kevin, who punches him in the arm.

Alex winces, but feels a swell of pride on his way back to the locker room. His knee isn't that bad; he'll just have to be careful at the studio later—maybe let Henning have the upper hand for once.

It was totally worth it—he can't wait to tell Kyla about today.

> Hi Kyla!
> I hope things are a little better than yesterday.
> I wanted to write you to let you know I had a pretty good day, because of you.
> I was thinking about our conversation, and then this guy in gym was giving me a hard time. I decided to do exactly what we said—be com-

fortable with myself, not let his words matter so much. And you know? It basically worked. Miracle!

So anyway, just wanted to tell you. I'm so glad you decided to contact me in that stupid chat room. And, well, thanks.

—Alex

Susanna must've told Kyla how awesome she was at least twenty times in the past hour. Even Therese thinks Kyla is the coolest person in the world for having the guts to slap Elizabeth. Kyla doesn't say anything. Her so-called guts are in a knot and she's deathly afraid every time the café door opens. What if it's Elizabeth?

"So anyway, this party is going to be hot. *Everyone's* going," Susanna squeals.

What if it's true what Alex said, that she *can* change?

". . . and Christopher's family's like, totally loaded, so the party's going to be in his pool house and backyard. They're in Malibu and have a sick view. Plus, I heard his older brother totally knows about it, and is helping him throw it. There might even be *actual bartenders!*"

But what if Elizabeth reports her? What if her mom finds out? As if Mom doesn't have enough to deal with right now. . . .

"By the way, Jake is coming, and Richie and Adam too. Doesn't Adam have a great smile?"

What if the police come to her house to talk to her, and

see her mom, and institutionalize her with a bunch of other psychos?

"... nah, you can't get drunk on beer. Can't someone score some hard stuff?" Therese complains. "I have *got* to hook up this weekend . . ."

Or what if they forced Kyla to move to New York?

"... we'd better go hang out by the liquor store again . . ."

Her mom wouldn't be able to handle it if they were separated. Oh, God. She might try to . . . What if she tried to . . .

Therese slaps her hand down on the table. "Kyla!"

She jumps. "What?"

"It's your turn!" Therese gives her a stern look between jet-black streaks of eyeliner.

Kyla tries to figure out what they're talking about. Christopher's party on Friday? "But—"

"Don't even try! How many times have I gotten the booze?"

"Yeah, but—"

"*Yeah, but* what!?" Therese fumes. "*Someone* has to do it! Why does it always—"

"*Yeah, but I can't even go to the party!*" She hears the echo of her own voice in the café, startling herself. Therese and Susanna are stunned.

"Can't go? What are you talking about? Why not?" The bead in Therese's tongue gleams behind her parted lips as her mouth hangs open. Susanna stares so hard that her eyes look like they might pop out of her head. But Kyla isn't planning to take it back. She thinks about Alex's e-mail, how he managed to stand up for himself. She's going to be true to herself.

"Uh, it's my mom," she says quietly. "She's not doing that well."

"So you're just going to sit around the house for your mom's sake?" Therese asks.

Kyla is quiet for a moment, and Therese quickly tries to recover.

"Sorry. It's just—" She leans in over the table, cocks her head, and speaking softly says, "So what does she have? It can't be that serious, can it? I mean, she's not in the hospital. And your sitting at home being miserable isn't going to help *her*. Seriously."

Kyla can feel them looking at her, looks that sting, claw, pressure her. But she won't give in. She may be using her mother as an excuse, but this is what she really *wants*. "I know, but I mean, I should stay home *occasionally*," she argues. "You guys can go on your own, can't you?"

Therese and Susanna look at each other nervously. It's dawning on them that Kyla might be serious. Susanna swallows. She looks like a begging dog. "I guess, but you were the one who was invited. *You're* the one he asked."

"So?"

Therese smiles, reaches forward to touch Kyla's hand. "*You're* the one they want to see. *You*. Have. To. Go."

Kyla wants to put her hands over her ears, to melt into the floor and disappear. She can't go. She can't. She knows how the evening will end, and she doesn't want to spend another early morning piecing together where she's been and who she's been with.

She's about to just get up and go, when the door opens and Elizabeth walks in.

Jenny and Kim come slinking in behind her. All three of them stop when they see Kyla. Their eyes scream that she's something dirty. Does it last for seconds or minutes? Everyone in the café can feel the tension. Can't they? Kyla's legs are shaking under the table.

"We're not staying here," Jenny announces loudly. She turns up her nose.

"This isn't our kind of clientele," Kim chimes in, her eyes resting on Kyla. "Right, Liz?"

Elizabeth doesn't respond. She stares coldly at Kyla. Kyla just clenches her teeth and stares back. They regard each other for a long time. After a while Kyla forgets what the whole thing is about and starts thinking about Elizabeth's eyes, how they're an unusual color, kind of blue and brown at the same time.

Elizabeth looks away first, sighs as if she were actually tired, and then deliberately stares at Kyla, Therese, and Susanna one at a time. "None of these girls are worth the trouble."

Everyone watches Elizabeth walk out of the café in surprise. Therese is fuming, and Susanna looks like she inhaled too much hairspray. It would almost be funny if Kyla didn't want to shrink into oblivion.

They're not worth the trouble.

Kyla wonders, *really* wonders, if Elizabeth might be right.

i'm so pathetic! 1 second i think i've gotten somewhere, and then everything blows up in my face. i can't live this way, in a stupid shadow of a life, but i don't know how 2 b any other way. so many times, i feel like no one cares, if i vanished no one would notice. so how the hell am i supposed to be strong? how did *u* do it? and is there any point? maybe this is really just the way i am. maybe if i ended up somewhere on the other side of the world where no one knew me, maybe i would still be exactly the same. maybe u would 2. kyla

Dear Kyla,
I'm sorry you're so frustrated. I get that way too—I don't have to remind you of that after all we've talked about it! So you know I'm hardly the one to offer advice, after one small success in a lifetime of failures. But you should never feel like no one cares. Because it's not true. You should never feel like you could just disappear because . . . well, I'd come looking.
—Alex

~~~

Alex must be the only sixteen-year-old in the whole world who's never even held a girl's hand. He never really even flirts—doesn't want to put himself on the line like that. Is that dumb? What if there's actually someone who would want to make out? It kind of doesn't matter who it is, it would be good to get the first time over with. That way when he kisses Christina, he'll be like a pro.

Alex studies her as she stands there by the barre: her feet in first position, her abdomen and butt tucked in, her shoulders lowered, her arms rounded, fingers extended, arching toward her thumbs. God, she's so beautiful.

She is just as preoccupied as always. He's gotten used to letting his eyes rest on her. He glances quickly at everyone else, suddenly catches Henning's glare. Did he notice Alex checking her out?

He tunes Christina out and does his part on the floor. Everything works today. All of a sudden he feels a rush of exaggerated self-confidence. He feels deep in the marrow of his bones that he's almost magnetic, like her—maybe even sexy?

Paulina scrutinizes his dancing with stern attention. She gives a hoot of joy and gushes, "Alex! Wonderful! Perfect!"

He beams at her as the sweat pours off his forehead and his T-shirt clings to his chest. This is really thanks mostly to her. She's the one who's helped him discover the strong dancer inside. Christina is watching him through her luminous eyes, behind those dark, thick lashes. She's smiling. Is she in love too? Maybe. He grins back. It lasts a few glorious seconds, then Paulina announces, "That's it for today."

Christina unties her shoes and disappears toward the changing room while Alex dwells on her shy smile. Maybe today is the day their lips will meet for the first time?

No, geez, that sounds like a cheesy movie. But maybe he should ask her to go out afterward. Like for coffee? Or just to the mini-mart to grab a soda?

He showers and gets dressed quickly, but spends an extra-long time in front of the mirror combing his hair. He's looking pretty good, actually. Henning is watching. Why? "I'm going to start taking extra lessons on the weekends," Henning says.

"For the jumps?"

Henning nods. No one is as focused as Henning, or as driven. Henning occasionally asks him if he wants to do something after practice, but Alex always says no. All Scott Henning ever talks about is ballet.

Alex waves good-bye. Once outside, he leans against the front of the building to wait for Christina and watches the cars driving by in the street. A silver Mercedes is parked right in front of the entrance.

The door opens. Christina steps out onto the stairs with her wet hair in a knot, not wearing any makeup, just like always. Alex doesn't hesitate. He walks up to her and says, "Hi, I was thinking—"

The door opens and Henning appears on the stairs. Alex pauses, not knowing how to proceed with an audience. Christina raises her eyebrows questioningly, but only for a few seconds. Then she heads down to the sidewalk, turning quickly toward Alex and raising her hand before stepping over to the silver car. Or is she waving at Henning? They both wave back.

The woman in the car leans over the passenger seat and opens the door from the inside. Her neck is so long she looks like a swan, and her hair is pulled tight at her temples. Then the car drives away. Henning and Alex stand next to each other and watch it go. Their eyes meet. There's something comical about the whole thing; Alex can't help but smile.

"See you tomorrow," he says.

Henning smiles back, and nods. "Tomorrow."

What do people think when they look at me? That I'm a total loser, a stud, a freak? Or D, all of the above? What do they say about me when I'm not listening? Should I even care? Maybe I should only care about what certain people say. Like you, for example. To be honest, I'm a little afraid of what you'll think if you know everything about me. Do you feel the same way? Is that why we're tiptoeing around and avoiding a bunch of stuff? Is it like we think everything is going to fall apart if we tell the truth?

We're totally being chickens. I haven't asked before, but now I just have to. Where do you live? What is your life like? Basically, who are you really?

—Alex.

They're standing outside the liquor store. It ended up being her and Susanna. Therese got out of it at the last minute. Kyla and Susanna both know it's so she can avoid chipping in, but neither of them will ever call her on it. Kyla wants to go home and write to Alex. Usually she answers him right away, but this time he started asking questions. Suddenly he wanted *details*. What happens if they're totally different? What if he can't stand party girls who hang out in front of liquor stores trying to get alcoholics to buy booze for them? She has to consider how much she should reveal— not her last name; she can't make herself Google-able, or give him the chance to find her Facebook page. She's not ready for that. She's been loving privacy for a change.

Susanna is going on and on about Therese: "She's always so sulky these days! We haven't done anything to *her*. It's just like . . ."

Kyla keeps scanning for someone who can buy for them, but the people she sees seem kind of freaky, walking around and mumbling to themselves. She considers for a second why people go crazy. Hopefully the world they live in is nicer than this one, where you hide shit from your friends, where she even wants to hide from Alex. "You know, Suse, we should just cut her some slack."

"You can't really mean it. I mean . . ." Susanna giggles nervously. "Okay, promise you won't tell. You have to promise!"

"What?"

"I said *promise* first!"

Kyla sighs. "Okay, okay. I promise."

Susanna takes a deep breath. "Therese talks shit about you."

It's not a surprise, but still it feels like someone punched her in the stomach.

"We're all best friends, but she says you're a stuck-up bitch and that you sleep around. Just because she's jealous. I promise you that's why, just because your dad's so famous and you're prettier and—"

"Enough."

"She just can't deal with everything and just blathers on and on about how you always have to make all the guys fall in love with you and . . ."

Kyla wants to be anywhere but here. She sees a man walking toward them with a jerky gait. She drags Susanna along, just wants to get it over with.

"Hey, excuse me! If you buy us a bottle of vodka, we'll give you ten bucks." The man is confused. His eyes are clear and lucid. This guy's no boozer. He furrows his brow in concern and looks almost sad. "Are you girls really going to drink?"

Kyla feels ashamed. Both because she thought this guy

was an alcoholic and because she revealed their plans. "Yeah, we were planning to," she mumbles.

He slowly shakes his head. "No, I'm sorry. I mean, I don't think that's a good idea." His eyes linger on her. She looks away. He walks on in his jerky motion, maybe from cerebral palsy or something else far more tragic than her life.

"God, how embarrassing!" Susanna whines. "I'm gonna *die*!"

The pointlessness of this whole situation weighs on Kyla with such force that she feels weak. She leans against the wall of the building. She can't believe she's demeaning herself like this when she didn't even want to go to the party, just because Therese nagged her. Therese, who disses her behind her back.

Susanna picks up where she left off: "Guys just don't fall for her, because she can't relax . . . and you know what? Want to know what she actually said? Promise you won't tell her I told you, but it was *soooo* awful . . ."

Kyla can't bring herself to say anything; she just nods.

"She said that it's true what Elizabeth said. That ever since your dad went to New York you're a total slut. That really sucks, doesn't it?"

Someone calls out to them, "Kyla! Susanna!" Oh, God. It's Therese. Susanna puts on such a big, forced smile she's unrecognizable. *"Hiii!"* she shrieks, flinging herself around Therese's neck and kissing her on both cheeks.

"How's it going? Have you gotten anything yet?" Therese leans over and gives Kyla a light peck on the cheek.

Very light. Their skin doesn't actually touch, but she's still smiling through bright red lips—that same wrong color, Kyla's color. Somehow that sparks resolve. Kyla spies a twenty-ish guy parking his car and heads straight for him.

"We haven't gotten anything," she reports. "But we're about to."

> so ur curious about my life. there isn't much
> to tell really. we live in the southern california
> hills by joshua tree. it's gorgeous out here and
> super far to the nearest town—i take the bus to
> school. mostly i spend time outdoors and hike
> around the desert, and then i ride. we have a
> few horses of our own and i love them more
> than anything, even chocolate. lol! one's white,
> one's bay, and one's appaloosa, and then there
> are the four fillies. tell me about where u live.
> what do u like 2 do?

He has time to think about Kyla on his way home from school. He pictures her on horseback, with long hair blowing in the wind, just as free as the wild landscape around her. The truth about Kyla's life came as a little bit of a shock. He'd been picturing something totally different. He definitely had her pegged as a city girl. But obviously this is cooler: Kyla from the desert, who goes

74

on nature walks from her back door. His life is way less exciting. It seems too lame to even tell her about: living in a long line of townhouses in downtown Oakland, and then dance class in the city? It's pathetic. Guys must be so rugged in the desert that they'd die laughing at the *thought* of dancing. And being *almost* bullied probably isn't earth-shattering either. For the first time since he met Kyla, he feels glum.

He hears someone running up behind him. Swivels around quickly, prepared for anything. It's Val coming toward him, panting. *Just* Val? Where's his sidekick?

"Hi!" Val calls out.

Alex says hi briefly, almost soundlessly, and keeps walking.

Val walks along next to him for a while without saying anything. When and where is Kevin planning to show up?

"You left so fast. Are you off to practice, for dancing, or what?"

Alex tenses, nods.

"Do you practice every day?"

"Four days a week."

"That's intense. We practice three days a week. For soccer, you know."

Alex doesn't respond. What's he getting at?

"Well, I was thinking . . ." Val begins. Then he stops and then starts again. "There was just something . . ."

Yes? Alex thinks.

"I mean, have you ever thought about quitting? The dancing, I mean."

Alex is quiet. What answer does Val want?

"I mean, maybe if you're tired of it . . . ?"

"No," Alex says quickly. "I've never wanted to quit."

"Oh, okay. I just wondered if, maybe—you could be on our soccer team, instead."

Alex stops dead in the middle of the sidewalk. Is he kidding? Just a few weeks ago Val was calling him a fag left and right. "Me?"

Val blushes, genuinely embarrassed. "Yeah, you're so good! I'd forgotten. You always used to play, back before Kevin—"

Alex starts walking again, hurriedly. "Yeah."

Val hurries to catch up. "I mean, I understand if you don't want to. But the season is starting soon. Would you think about it? The practices are fun. Really."

It seems like he means what he's saying. But why would Val want to hang out with him? He dismisses the thought. Obviously the whole thing is some kind of a trap.

Yeah, Alex scoffs to himself, he wouldn't be surprised if Kevin taunted him about it tomorrow, teasing about how he almost fell for the Fake Soccer Invite.

He breaks into a run. "Sorry, I've got to hurry," he mumbles. "Bye!"

Kyla—

Your life is so different from mine. I live right in downtown San Francisco, in a North Beach apartment with my mom and dad. I'm always out, going clubbing and hanging with my

friends. And at practice. My parents think I should spend a little more time at home, but obviously I don't want to. In my free time I mostly play soccer and hang out with my girl–friend, Christina. We've been together for two years. She's totally incredible ... I sometimes think she could leap tall buildings in a single bound. ;) Have you ever felt like that? That there's this one person, who's *the* one?
—Alex

She's succeeded in getting delightfully drunk and has almost blocked out the fact that Therese thinks she's a total ditzwhore. Anyway, *whatever*. Worse things have happened. Now they're hanging off each other like they're the best of friends, so it's all okay.

There are tons of cute guys at the party, most of them a little older. They must be Christopher's brother's friends. Kyla knows some of them, but nowhere near all. Who knows, maybe one of them is the guy who's going to bring her back to life again.

Kyla hasn't really had a chance to come down to earth after reading Alex's e-mail. A *romantic jock*, it kind of doesn't go together. Or maybe she just has a thing against soccer players. But she likes that about Alex. He's surprising.

Madonna is on and Kyla feels happy. She dances with her eyes closed. For a second she *becomes* Madonna, they're one and the same, proud and self-confident and not the slightest bit stupid. The kind of person Kyla wants to be, the way she *is*. Right now.

Susanna goes out to get another drink while Kyla takes a breather next to the dance floor. She still can't get the thoughts of Alex out of her head. On the one hand it's nice that he has a girlfriend and that he doesn't want anything more, but on the other hand . . . On some level she feels disappointed. Was she hoping that Alex was her *one*? That he would sweep her off her feet and into a new life? Maybe she *is* one incredible ditz.

"Hey, there!"

It's a guy she doesn't know. Older, maybe nineteen or twenty. Very preppie-cute, trendy, well groomed. Kyla doesn't usually go for that type, but she can't deny that he's got a kind of movie star quality to him.

She gives him a quick nod, then glances out at the dance floor. She's going back to her Madonna moment.

He makes a new attempt. "So who do you know here?"

"That's not exactly an original line."

He laughs. "True. What should I say then?"

"That depends on what you want," Kyla fires back. Totally smooth.

It's quiet. She waits for his next move. She's not planning on doing anything—she knows perfectly well how to get him interested. *This is fun.*

"What if I really wanted to know?" he wonders.

"To know what?"

"Exactly what I asked."

"Well, then you could ask."

"Okay."

They're silent again. What's he waiting for? Suddenly he laughs. "Aren't you going to answer?"

"Aren't you going to ask first?" She can't help smiling.

"Didn't I already?" He chuckles.

She bats her eyelashes flirtatiously. "I'm sorry, why don't you try again."

"What's your name?"

"Kyla."

"Lucas."

"That's not original either."

She looks into his eyes. They're saying that he wants her. They make her feel like a woman, not some little brat who isn't good for anything besides starting a catfight.

When Susanna gets back, Kyla is gone. She sees Susanna spot her from a distance, dancing with Lucas. Kyla can hear what she's thinking: *Not again!* But Kyla doesn't give a damn. Because, in this moment, Lucas is all about her, and that feeling is totally incredible.

That night he feels guilty. Why did he tell Kyla a pile of lies that will just make things complicated? Now he's going to have to make sure everything is consistent every time he wants to talk to her, and if they ever decide to meet in person—God, he doesn't want to think about it. Maybe he should tell her the truth now, right away, tell her that he lied. Before it's too late.

What an idiot she'll think he is. Maybe he can call her and explain? But how? He doesn't even know Kyla's last name, so he'd never find her number. In the darkness his thoughts get weirder and weirder. When he considers trying to find a bus to Joshua Tree in the middle of the night, he realizes it's time to do *something*.

He goes down to the kitchen and gets a glass of water. Types a new message. Short and sweet. "Where are you tonight?" Only then does he feel a little better.

She only *almost* throws up. The fact is, all that comes out is mucus and stomach acid. Looking in the mirror she realizes that it's time to go home, she's obviously trashed. Lucas is standing outside, waiting. He can tell too. He holds up her jacket courteously and helps her to the entryway, where there's a guy passed out on the floor. Lucas steps over the guy and holds out his hand to Kyla. As if she were a princess and not some drunken slut.

"I want to go home," she whimpers.

"I know," he reassures her. "We're going now."

"No, *I* want to go on my own."

He looks at her quizzically. "But we can keep each other company."

"Do you live in my direction?"

"Nah, but I don't want you to go alone. I mean, you've been drinking and . . ." He looks her up and down. ". . . yeah."

She can't help but like it. Does he actually want to make sure she gets home okay? To impress her with his car? Or does he just want to sleep with her? She giggles, remembering a line Alex wrote: *D, all of the above.*

Therese comes wobbling out into the entryway with a hazy look in her eyes.

"Kyla, darling . . . !" she drawls.

Darling?

"You're leaving *already?*" she continues as she checks Lucas out.

"Yeah," Kyla answers curtly. "Bye. Come on, Lucas."

He smiles gratefully and follows her like an obedient dog.

"So this one is Lucas?" Therese yells after him. "What up, Lucas!"

He turns around and nods. Kyla leans her head against his shoulder. He puts his arm around her. The envy on Therese's face is so apparent she's practically green.

Kyla holds Lucas tighter. It's nice to have someone to hold on to.

She doesn't say much on the way home. Lucas does the talking. About France, where he should've been born, and something about cheese. He nervously tries one topic of conversation after another. But Kyla just mumbles and nods in response. She can't wait to get home and into the bathroom, where she can stick her fingers down her throat. But then she feels sorry for him and takes his hand.

"Sorry, I'm just so tired," she says.

He smiles at her, relieved.

Outside Kyla's building he asks for her number. When she doesn't respond, he takes a business card out of his pocket and says, "Or you call me."

She wonders what kind of a guy makes a business card when he's just a student, but doesn't say anything. He leans in and kisses her. She kisses him back. Then she pulls herself free and hurries inside. She has to run up to the apartment and puke.

They have a half day; they get to leave after lunch. Toby suggests that they go to his house and watch *Star Wars: Episode IV,* the *uncut* version. Alex declines. He isn't a big fan of science fiction, and the idea of sitting and listening to Toby's nerdy factoids about the movie for the millionth time is not a big draw. He takes the bus into the city instead, can't come up with anything else.

He drinks two cups of coffee at a Starbucks, feeling lame he couldn't find someplace cooler. But he's too distracted . . . Kyla still hasn't responded. He waited for an e-mail all day yesterday, but nothing. Was there something in his story that didn't hold up? He tries to remember every detail he wrote, but can't detect any holes. After a while he decides to go to the dance studio. Maybe there's a practice room free.

There are more people there than he was expecting. The children's lessons are in full swing. He glances at the schedule and sees that all the rooms are taken, and he's just about to leave, when he spots her through the pane of glass. Her posture is impeccable. She's guiding a group of uncoordinated preschoolers with deadly seriousness. They wander around the room like little pink birds, each off in her own world. It's the first time he's ever seen her teach. With a no-nonsense look on her face, she demonstrates a few easy steps. Two or three of the children make serious attempts to imitate her, the rest do whatever they feel like doing. She shakes her head, obviously disappointed, and demonstrates the same thing again.

He turns away. He doesn't want to see any more of his mother.

Kyla suffers at her desk the whole morning. She overslept and put her makeup on in three seconds. When she walked by, her mom was lying in bed like a dead seal. She hesitated at the doorway, but decided: No, she really didn't have time. The thoughts came later: What if today is the day she . . . ? The classes plod along.

When there's a knock on the door during social studies—she knows exactly what's happened. The assistant principal pops his head in and says sorry to interrupt. Then he slowly turns toward her. A serious look on his face.

"Kyla, can you come with me?" he asks.

Everything stops. She gets up, her legs shaking. Terrified, she meets him outside the door. He puts a hand on her shoulder, as if to comfort her.

"There's a phone call for you in the office," he says. "We don't usually take calls for students, but this one . . . well . . ." He smiles suddenly. "I'm sure it's nothing serious."

"Who is it?" Her voice is too high.

He shakes his head. "You'd best hurry."

Kyla rushes through the corridors. *No, no, no. You'd better not have taken all those pills. Please, you can't leave me alone. You wouldn't, would you?*

The receiver is lying on the desk in the office waiting for her. She stands there in the doorway, thinks she sees it glowing with danger. She takes a few slow steps. The tears erupt behind her eyelids. She slowly lifts the receiver and raises it to her ear, holds it a bit away from herself, as if to defend herself against whatever might follow.

"Hello?" she ventures.

A proper man's voice bellows, "Is this Kyla Billings?"

Weakly she says, "Yes."

She's about to burst, crack, fall apart. *She doesn't want to live with her father. Yes, she loves him, but he has his new wife and the kids. He's never told her he wants her there with him, never asked if she would want to move. No, they can't handle another one, there isn't room even in their huge brownstone. Where will she go then?*

Keep living in the apartment alone? With Mom's smell. Visit her grave on Sundays . . .

The man on the phone laughs loudly and says, "I'm obviously good at this. They seemed to think that someone died or something."

She doesn't understand. Slowly, slowly it dawns on her that this man doesn't have anything to do with her mother.

"I'm sorry, who is this?" Kyla asks, still in a state of shock. Her mom isn't the least bit dead; she's probably just lying there at home sleeping, or staring blankly at *The Price Is Right.*

"Who do you think?"

"I don't know. Would I have asked if I knew?"

"It's Lucas!"

Lucas? Lucas who? Suddenly she makes the connection: Lucas from the party. Jesus! Anger wells up inside of her. "What do you want?"

"I—I . . ." Lucas stammers.

The words just pour out. Her whole body is trembling. Her voice too.

"I am so . . . *so* pissed off. Who do you think you are? How could you . . . ? This is so totally . . . disrespectful!"

Silence.

"I . . . crap. I'm sorry." His voice sounds small and ashamed. But it doesn't help.

"I have class now!"

"Wait! Don't hang up! You never called, Kyla. I just wanted to talk to you . . ."

"Screw. You." Kyla slams down the phone.

Alex is walking around outside of his father's office. Won't he ever quit working? Alex pulls some leftover borscht from the fridge and eats it directly from the Tupperware. He takes his time and scans the paper although he doesn't really notice what it says. When he's done, he tries again, but the chair in front of the computer is still occupied. Doesn't he ever run out of code to write? Or is he e-mailing his coworkers, after office hours, when normal people are vegging out in front of the TV, or spending time with their kids?

Alex scowls and sits down on the stairs to wait. Then he walks over to the door again and peeks through the crack. He's about to go sit down again, when the clicking noise from the keyboard suddenly stops.

"Aleksandr!"

Surprised, Alex pops his head in. "Huh?"

"What are you doing in the hallway?" His father sounds irritated.

"What do you mean?"

"You are hovering. Do you want to use the computer?"

"Um, yeah."

His father takes off his glasses. He sighs, rubs his eyes, and says, "Do you have the time for that? Don't you have homework?"

"No."

His father regards him with concern. As if he were lying.

Alex shrugs. "I did it already."

In his father's eyes the only *really* important thing is for

Alex to graduate with good grades, to make something of himself in this country. To his father, that means Alex should focus on his schoolwork—nothing should get in the way of his studies. If Olga had had any say, Alex would go to the performing arts school in the city and wouldn't even have to take academic classes in the evenings.

"Who are you writing to? Do I know this person?"

Alex chuckles. "Who would that be? Who do you know?"

His father looks surprised. "I . . ."

Alex folds his arms. In a moment his father will realize the truth, that he doesn't know the first thing about Alex's life, and go back to work. But that's not what happens.

"You sit here almost every night. Who do you get e-mails from?"

Grudgingly, Alex tells his father about Kyla.

"So you're saying you have never met this girl?"

"Nope."

"So she could be *anyone!*"

"Sure, but she isn't."

"There's no way you can know. All that she writes may be made up."

"It could be," Alex acknowledges.

"This *she* could actually be a *he* for example. Isn't that right?"

Alex shakes his head, nearly laughs. "No. I trust her."

"Alex, I don't want you to be hurt." His father looks *very* concerned.

Alex just sighs, having long since tired of this version

of a heart-to-heart father-son talk. "Aleksandr, there is so much for you to do in this life, activities that are enriching, so many books to read . . ."

Books to read! He feels his irritation rising. All he ever does is study or dance. Things his *parents* want him to do. How dare his father try to control the way he spends the tiny crumbs of time that are left?

He speaks the words slowly but firmly. "She's my *friend.*"

His father looks for a second like he's trying to understand, then he gives up and turns back to the computer. "Yes, okay. I just believe . . . I believe it is more sensible to have real friends."

He wants to punch his father in the jaw—the man obviously hasn't considered the fact that Alex doesn't have any friends. No, he's obsessed with his work—*that's* the only thing that matters. Who knows, maybe someday he'll regret it. Maybe someday he'll realize everything about his children he's missed.

The doorbell rings. His dad looks pointedly at Alex and then at the time.

"It's not for me," Alex insists.

It rings again. His father gets up with a great deal of effort and bumbles off to open the door. Behind his father's shoulder, out on the stairs, Alex catches a glimpse of Katy.

Jesus! Katy from his class, Katy of the fine backside. What does she want? To talk to Alex? About what? Teaming up to get revenge on Kevin? That might be fun. Or maybe the math test on Tuesday? Or maybe she has a secret crush on him. He pricks up his ears.

"Hi. Is Andrei home?"

He feels indignant even though it's stupid. Andrei and *Katy*?

"Andrei?" his father calls, annoyed. *"Andrei!"*

No response. His father shuffles past the kitchen on his way to his other son's room. "That boy knows a lot of strange girls," he mumbles, shaking his head.

Alex dashes into the office and opens his e-mail.

She reads her own words on the screen. A lot of what she wrote is true, but not everything. Her hand is on the mouse, the cursor over SEND. Just one little click. But can she really send it? It feels so wrong to keep lying, but what's the alternative? She's already made her choice. She can't tell him now how drunk she got at Christopher's party the other day. That wouldn't jive with the cowgirl-in-the-desert image. If she confesses, she risks losing him entirely. It seems opposite of what little she's surmised about real friendship, but to hold on to him, she can't reveal herself now.

She can't deny that it's exciting to be someone else. Isn't that what she's always longed for? And without all the work she'd have to do to truly change. Just a little typing and, *presto,* there's the new Kyla. A sweet, innocent girl on a horse.

i'm glad u have christina. it must feel so amazing to love someone! i don't know how people fall in love. can u make it happen yourself, just by deciding? sometimes i pretend i'm interested in a guy but it's not really about love, u know? it's more about, i dunno, feeling like at least someone is interested. i've never really believed in the soul mate idea. i don't get how ur supposed to meet that person if there's only 1 in the whole world. what if he lives in australia and u live here and even if he did live here, how would u recognize him, even if he was right next to u? am i making any sense? i've actually never had a real boyfriend ☹ *shrug* so, was christina the 1st for u? what was it like???

His thoughts are churning a mile a minute. How can he write about sex he's never had? Apart from what he's seen in sex ed, he has absolutely no idea what happens.

They brake suddenly and he's jolted from his thoughts. The car in front of them is turning. His mom isn't the most with-it driver.

She just mutters a small *"Bohze moi!"* after missing the bumper by a fraction of an inch.

He studies her. She's wearing big, heavy earrings and

vivid makeup. She looks so happy. Alex likes seeing her like this, as mother and son are on their way to the ballet in San Francisco. It costs a ton, but she always manages to get discounted tickets through her job at the dance studio. She loves the War Memorial Opera House; the building is pristine and beautiful and reminds her of the lavish Mariinsky Theatre in St. Petersburg.

And he goes along for her sake. He actually isn't particularly fond of *watching* ballet. When he dances, it's a totally different story—he loves it.

Or . . . does he? Sometimes it's like he can't separate his own feelings from his mother's. If she were a soccer nut instead and had started making him practice penalty kicks in the yard at home from the time he was three—would *that* be what he loved? It's an unsettling thought.

"Mom, when you were younger—"

She presses down on the gas and zooms past an old Volvo at about seventy-five miles an hour. She swerves quickly back into the right lane again. The Volvo is forced to brake and then honks.

"Yes?"

"Did you ever, you know . . . ?"

"What?"

"Well, did you ever wonder . . ."

They're stuck behind a truck. His mom sighs impatiently. "Did I *what*?"

"Did you wonder what you actually wanted, well, what you wanted to do with—"

"Sasha, please tell me. What do you want to say?" Her

brow is furrowed into deep troughs. She decides to pass the truck.

"—what you wanted to do with your life? What you wanted to *be*?"

She's going almost ninety.

"Did you ever have any doubts, I mean, about dancing?"

His mother's eyes leave the road in a flash. She stares at him as if he'd just said he'd grown another toe. *"Doubts?"* she repeats, incredulous.

The car shudders. He lets out a little yelp. She swoops back over into the right lane again without a word, driving along in silence.

"There wasn't *ever* a time when you thought about doing something other than dancing, not even when you were a kid?"

She slams on the brakes. It frightens him even though he's used to it. The brakes squeal as she swerves off onto the shoulder just before the bridge. The cars behind them honk. She turns to look at Alex.

All right! he thinks. *Here it comes.* Finally, she's going to tell him about her doubts and the pressure from her strict parents, about how she understands everything, *everything* he's going through.

She enunciates each word carefully. *"I have never thought to throw away the unique gift I have from God. I have never questioned what was and is still my true dream."* Her face melts into a loving smile and she puts her hand on his cheek. "Dancing is my life. Exactly as it is for you."

She puts the car in gear and pulls onto the road again.

Alex slouches farther down in his seat. How can she be so *sure*?

"Oh, yes," she adds, as if nothing in particular had happened. "We are going to a party in Los Angeles in a month, your papa and I. We will stay with Vladik and Eva. You must remember them? Papa's childhood friend and his wife?" She doesn't wait for a response. "We thought maybe you would come with us. There are so many beautiful performances to see. That would be great, yes?"

She tiptoes into the apartment even though she knows it isn't necessary. But then she notices that her mom's door is wide-open. The overhead light is on and the bed is empty. Kyla looks around in astonishment—no one in front of the TV either. There are noises coming from the kitchen.

Her mom is sitting at the table, dressed, with her hair up in a ponytail. Kyla is dumbfounded. The radio is on. A gigantic bouquet of flowers is sitting in the middle of the table. Kyla's whole body feels warm. Mom must have met someone! Did she sneak out sometime when Kyla didn't know about it?

Her mom lights up at the sight of her. "Hi! I was wondering when you'd get home!"

"Hi, Mom." Kyla sniffs the flowers and asks, "So who sent you these? Some new admirer?"

"Those aren't for me. They're for you."

"For me?" The bouquet is *enormous*. What kind of teenage boy sends flowers?

"A delivery guy brought them. There's a card too." Her mom picks up the card and reads melodramatically, *"I'm sorry."*

Kyla laughs. "And?"

"Nothing else. Don't you know who they're from?"

"Yeah, probably." Kyla sinks down at the table. Lucas must really be crazy. Or just Bel-Air rich?

"Ah, if only I had such an admirer . . ." Her mother almost giggles in pretend envy.

"This one's just a pain."

But Kyla's annoyance doesn't last long. Her mother is *dressed* and upright. What could the occasion be?

"So," her mom announces excitedly, "I almost got a job today!"

Kyla rejoices silently. "You didn't!"

"Well, not a *real* job, you know, but the employment office actually managed to set up a great . . . um, what was it called? Some kind of workplace traineeship or something? I don't know . . . but it sounded good. At an insurance company. I'll be at the reception desk to start with and then maybe start doing office work."

"Mom, I can't believe it!" Kyla flings her arms around her mother's neck. "Congratulations!" She doesn't think any ugly thoughts about how it will only last until her mom gets tired or sick again. Kyla just wants to feel happy for now. Her mom pushes her away, as if she could read her mind.

"And it's *not* going to get screwed up this time, I promise you that, Kyla."

Kyla wants so badly to believe her that she decides to.

"And tomorrow," her mom continues, "I want us to do something together. I've been lying around this apartment for way too long."

There's an intermission. People are mingling with glasses in their hands. Alex is sipping some sickly sweet fruit punch. His mom is holding a glass of champagne to mark this ever-so-special occasion. She scans the room, mumbling something he doesn't hear. There's something roosterlike about her. Then she begins to wave her hand wildly and calls through the sea of people, "Greg! Fanny!" Alex wants to sink into the ground. You just can't do that—stand there hollering like a diva. But his mom takes him by the arm and forces her way through the crowd. They end up in front of a middle-aged man and a woman. Their smiles are uncomfortable. Does his mother embarrass them?

Alex studies her, tottering on her ridiculous heels, her red and green print dress clinging to her round form. Her hair is piled high atop her head in a riot of swoops and twirls. The woman before him, on the other hand, wears a crisp gray suit, and her makeup, if there is any of it, is natural and subdued.

Alex knows what these people see when they look at his mother. He can't help but see it too. It makes him feel angry at their shallowness—and then ashamed.

"Olga, how nice," the man mutters while the woman agrees, "Really."

"This is Aleksandr!" His mother beams.

At the same time his mother explains that the Hansons are the parents of little Phillip, who dances in his school's children's group. The woman smiles—very stiffly. Then Alex recognizes her, the woman in the Mercedes, the woman with the swan neck. Even before his mother is able to say it, he knows.

"You have an older girl who dances with my Sasha."

Alex blushes at the thought of Christina. He doesn't have a chance to snap out of it before she's standing there in front of him, a glass of the same terrible punch in her hand. She waves shyly.

"Ah, yes, here's our Christina," the father says, putting his hands on her shoulders. "But you two already know each other, don't you?"

Alex shifts. Christina doesn't say anything. It seems as if she's struggling not to collapse under her father's heavy hands.

Her mother talks in a low, languorous voice. "Christina has made enormous progress lately, we have great hopes."

Alex's mom nods encouragingly. "How nice!"

"But we can't have her neglecting her schoolwork. We've told her that, that it's important to get a good education."

"Yes," Alex's mother agrees, putting her hand on his shoulder. "His papa is also very stern about this. Isn't he, Sasha?"

Alex fidgets. He wants to take Christina's hand and fly out the window, disappear into the atmosphere. But her father's hands are holding her in place and her eyes are distant, just like always.

"Christina does well at whatever she chooses to put her mind to, so we don't really worry," her mother says with affected nonchalance.

"Yes, I have heard that Christina is talented." His mom laughs and adds, "But so then is Sasha, if we must brag."

Christina's parents' tight smiles don't waver; they might as well be carved out of bronze.

"I suppose you've heard that the San Francisco ballet is looking for a young couple for the next performance," Christina's mom continues dutifully.

Alex's mom gasps. "Oh?"

"Yes, there are auditions in a couple of weeks. Christina is going to try out of course."

Alex's mother looks at him, her eyes full of accusation. "That's marvelous. Why have I not heard about this?"

Alex has heard about it, for sure. Everyone in the group was told. But he doesn't want to try out. Dancing at the Opera House, drawing that kind of attention to himself, would just lead to more crap at school.

His mom's eyes twinkle at Christina. "Then maybe you and Sasha will be together on the stage here soon. That would be wonderful, yes?"

Only then does Christina look up. She looks right at him, her eyes unwavering. And smiles.

The first time with Christina took my breath
away. We were out in the woods that day.

97

The wind was warm and the sun caressed our bodies. We got to this field full of flowers and we stopped there because Christina wanted to pick a bouquet. Suddenly she put down the flowers and turned to me. "What is it?" I asked, but she didn't answer. She started unbuttoning her top, button after button, and slowly it slid down off her shoulders. She wasn't wearing anything underneath it. Her naked breasts were exposed and I had seen them before of course, but they had never been as perfect and pert as they were now. Then she took off her jeans and her underwear. Then she was standing there in front of me, completely naked, surrounded by wildflowers. I just stood there and watched. She came over and took off my clothes. Then we lay down in the grass and she took my penis in her hand and guided it toward her vagina. I stroked her breasts. Then I penetrated her. Everything around us disappeared. Afterward we lay there and held each other in the sun. We'd never experienced anything so beautiful and we promised that from then on we would be together forever.

Kyla can't help but crack up. Is there any way this could be true? It sounds like a mix between a bad romance novel and a sex manual. Or else she and Alex are so different from each other that even *sex* is different for them. Can being in love with the other person *make* it "so beautiful"? She doesn't want to believe that Alex is lying, but this is just too much. Besides, a field of wildflowers? In downtown *San Francisco*?

Or, she thinks, *what if Christina doesn't even exist?* After all, if Alex had such a wonderful girlfriend at his side, why was he feeling so lonely to begin with? Why would he need someone to talk to, to confide in?

But then, why would he lie to her? Sure, *she* lied too, but she actually has something to hide—the fact that she's a spoiled Hollywood bimbo with stupid friends and a psycho mom.

What if there's something wrong with *him*? Maybe he's hideously ugly or tragically handicapped or both? Or maybe he has ADHD and can't recall what he's said from one moment to the next?

"Kyla, let's go!" her mom calls.

Kyla shuts off the computer and runs out to meet her mom, who's ready and waiting in the hallway. She's is wearing a scarf in her hair today, just like Kyla sometimes does. It looks silly, sort of girly, but that doesn't matter. Her mom looks *happy.*

They take the bus. Neither of them knows where they should get off—they've never gone this far east before, but then they ask someone where they can find a trail to go for a walk and hop off somewhere beyond the suburban sprawl.

Everything goes wrong. They can't find the trail, and they wind up on the shoulder of a freeway in the middle of nowhere with a ton of cars driving on it. So they have to walk in single file along the edge of the road while the cars zoom by.

"God, this is the worst nature hike I've ever been on!" her mom cries over the drone of the engines. Kyla giggles.

Eventually they find something that looks sort of like countryside. There are some scrubby fields with cows in them and they climb over the fence and walk several hundred yards to reach the sheltered area they can see in the distance. Kyla's mom doesn't say much. She just keeps taking deep breaths and plows straight ahead through the manure with her impractical shoes.

Kyla almost feels shy around her mother—there are so many things she wants to ask. Why everything turned out the way it did with her father and why they had Kyla in the first place. How did they think *that* was a good idea? And after she was born, was that the first time her mom started feeling bad? Was that what made her give up modeling? And why couldn't she pull it back together after dad left? Could she not handle being alone? Or was Kyla too much for her?

She wants to let the questions spill out, but she doesn't. Everything feels so fragile right now. She doesn't want to ruin it.

It's been a long time since she's been so far away from school and Susanna and Therese and, well, *everything*. It feels good. She wonders what Therese would say if she knew what she was up to. Because Kyla didn't tell her the truth; she came up with some story about having a headache and how shopping was just out of the question. She scowled at her own weakness, but at least she avoided any unwanted questions.

They approach a paddock with horses in it, big horses that Kyla wants to see closer up. She watches the horses move, is completely engrossed—this is better than any nature special, or that *National Velvet* movie that was her father's favorite, the one they always used to watch when she was little.

"To think that I used to ride when I was little," her mom says. "It feels like such a long time ago."

"What? You used to *ride?*"

"Yeah, I was a summer kid," her mom continues, eyes on the horses. "Like a summer cat, one that you adopt while you're on vacation and then abandon when the vacation's over just sort of hoping it will still be there next year." She laughs and turns to look at Kyla.

"Wait, but what does that have to do with horses?"

"Well, I got put in touch with this family that lived on a farm in the Central Valley. I don't really know why. Maybe so my mom and dad could take a break from me. Or maybe they just thought I should be able to get out of the city for a while."

"And you learned to ride a horse?"

Her mom smiles proudly. "I did."

"Was it hard?"

"Yeah, it was hard."

"How hard?"

"Well, I think anyone could do it, but someone has to teach you. The mother of the family taught me. They had their own horses."

Kyla considers. If her mother could learn, surely she could too. "But weren't you scared?"

"In the beginning I was, but then I wasn't. Do you want to learn how to ride, Kyla? I didn't know that."

"I . . . I don't know. I don't know anyone else who does it."

Her mom puts her arm around Kyla. "Well, that doesn't matter. Of course you'll learn to ride. You just have to ask your dad for the money."

"Yeah . . . maybe."

"Promise me you'll do it."

They keep walking. They reach a more wooded area and pick their way through one of the paths for a while. Soon their shoes are soaked and they start missing home. It gets dark before they find their way back to the road. They haven't eaten anything in hours and hours—obviously no one thought to pack a lunch. Still, things feel right. Kyla takes her mom's hand. Her mom is surprised, but she smiles as she gives Kyla's hand a squeeze back.

mom and i got out of the city today, it had been such a long time since we'd done anything together! i feel relaxed for the first time in so long, and strong, like i'm not worthless after all, like everything *could* be different. but who am i kidding? everything will probably be the same as ever when i get together with my friends. topic change: there's something i've been thinking that i have to say. i just . . . i hope that we can be honest with each other, u and me, and not waste each other's time with a bunch of bullshit. lying sucks. otherwise what's the point in keeping on doing whatever we're doing here? so, you know, you first. if there's anything you need to come clean about, just tell me. i'll understand. if not, then we're all good. k? i'm not saying that i think you lied, but i've heard of people making things up when they meet someone online and i just want to make sure that's not us.

Alex sits there as if paralyzed. Does Kyla suspect something? How could he have been so stupid? Writing about sex even though he's never had it! Should he take back all the lies? *Now?*

He reads her e-mail again. Then he notices something: *mom and i got out of the city today.* What city? Doesn't she live in the desert? He reads the e-mail again. *everything will probably be the same as ever when I get together with my friends.*

The same as what?

Maybe Kyla isn't who she claimed to be either?

Kyla!

I hate it when people lie. But if you lied, I'd forgive you. You have to think of what's more important: our friendship, or some stupid pride issue? I kind of don't know what to write now . . . Crap, I totally hate myself. But you can't turn back the clock. So, I admit it. Your suspicions are true. I lied. I can't explain it any other way than to say I was afraid. I know, that's stupider than stupid . . . aaaarg, i'm so sorry!!! I'm a total idiot.

—Alex

A week goes by. Every night, Alex slips into his father's office to check his e-mail, but there's nothing there. He's going crazy. Why won't she answer? If she did the same thing herself, surely she ought to be able to forgive him. Or had she not lied after all? Maybe he got confused and misinterpreted things and then it came as a complete shock to her when he turned out to be a fake. Maybe horse-riding desert women only want safe, earthy friends who never make mistakes.

The insecurity and the waiting are taking their toll on him. He isn't eating much, can't concentrate during dance practice. He's snapping at his mother, not picking Toby up in the mornings, and consistently avoiding Val, who keeps watching him. He doesn't even shower Christina with the usual amount of attention; he can only concentrate on the void of Kyla's absence.

Sometimes she feels angry. Angry that it's like she thought. Angry that she's forced to picture a new Alex. Maybe some lame-ass wuss, a fat slob with zits and bad fashion sense, someone who has to make friends on the Internet just to have any. When she thinks like that, she gets scared. What if he's obsessed with her and gloms on to her? What if he suddenly shows up at her door and throws his arms around her neck like in the movies? Is it worth the risk of having everyone laugh at her and her freaky stalker from San Francisco? Does he even live in San Francisco?

Even more, which is hard to admit, she's afraid of what he'll say when he finds out she lied too.

Well, maybe she never has to tell him. Her mom is better now—she has a job and gets up in the morning—so maybe Mom can take Alex's place in Kyla's life. Or Lucas, if she gives him a chance.

Right, she doesn't have to tell Alex anything. She just wishes she didn't miss writing him so much.

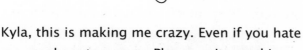

Kyla, this is making me crazy. Even if you hate
me, you have to answer. Please, write anything—
that you never want to have anything to do

with me again if that's what you want. Just
something. Anything!
—Alex

They're wandering around the open-air mall, trying on
clothes and testing makeup. The others keep asking: "Is this
one cool, Kyla? Does it look good on me?"

"What do *you* think?" Kyla always fires back, which
makes them feel nervous and insecure, even Therese, who
stands there rummaging around in the sale bin—everything for $4.99. "So how's it going with Jake?"

Kyla rolls her eyes. "*Jake?* You know there's nothing
going on with him, T., there never really was." Kyla's quiet,
trying to look at her friend pointedly, to offer some kind of
apology if that's what her friend wants.

"Oh, right." Therese sighs. "Except that you *slept* with
him." She pulls out a sheer top with a snakeskin pattern on
it. "What about this?"

"Butt ugly," Kyla answers, even though that's not what
she thinks. She's pissed, even if she doesn't really have a
right to be.

Therese drops it back into the bin and Susanna snatches
it up. "Is it really?"

Kyla pretends to inspect it more closely and then says,
"Nah . . . actually it *is* cool, isn't it?"

Susanna smiles, satisfied. Therese lowers her chin, deflated.
Kyla ignores it.

"Well, what about that loser from the other night?" Therese demands. "Lucas or whatever his name was?"

This startles Susanna. "Hey, hello? Who are you calling a loser? He was totally hot! You said so yourself at the party."

"But I was drunk then, wasn't I?"

Kyla takes a deep breath and says nothing.

Therese keeps rummaging around in the bin. "So are you going to see him again then?"

"Yeah, I am." Kyla tries to make it sound as exciting as possible.

Therese stops, her eyes wide. "Really? When? Where?"

"Tonight. That's why I wanted to buy something new."

Susanna's eyes gleam with curiosity. "God, how . . . Oh, crap!"

Something's startled her. Kyla turns, and spots Elizabeth in another part of the store, Elizabeth—with a guy. She knows who it is. His name is Erik. He graduated last year, and he's generally known as an unfaithful jerk. What's a girl like Elizabeth doing with a guy like that? They have their arms around each other and are smiling like they're all in love. Kyla has to get out of there. There's time; Elizabeth hasn't seen her yet. "Come on, we're leaving."

Susanna sputters, "But, I haven't had a chance to try the top on yet and . . ."

"Well, *I'm* going." Kyla makes her way toward the exit. The other two follow reluctantly. When they're almost out, Therese finally spots the couple. She points at Elizabeth and Erik, who are standing in line at the cash register. "Look!"

Kyla feels herself break out in a sweat. Therese's eyes are wide. "Is she with Erik Donahue?"

Kyla keeps walking. "Like that would matter. I don't care."

"But she called us *worthless*!" Therese howls. "And she called you a slut."

"I'm leaving."

Once they get outside, Kyla can almost breathe again. She walks away quickly, weaving around the potted palm trees and shoppers dripping with bags, the other two fast on her heels.

Please, God, don't let anyone see me. I promise I'll believe in you from now on. Alex is out with Toby in his go-kart. Yes, that's right, *go-kart*.

Toby built it himself, of course, and doesn't care that sixteen-year-olds just don't do that kind of thing. There's a part of Alex that respects Toby for that—admires the fact that he doesn't give a damn about what you're *supposed* to do. It's why no one really irritates him. He goes through life without noticing he's being picked on, or made fun of. Because he just does not care.

He sits behind the wheel like the cart is a sweet sports car. He looks just as proud as if it were.

"The design turned out. I didn't think it would!"

"You're a real genius when it comes to mechanics," Alex agrees, and means it.

They take turns pushing the car down the straight stretches. It speeds up on the downhill. Then they both ride. There's a front seat and a backseat. Toby's enthusiasm is contagious; on a particularly steep block, Alex feels his stomach drop, feels the wind whistling through his hair. "Wooohooo!" he screams, and laughs out loud.

When they're like this, he and Toby, Alex actually forgets his troubles. There's no Mom or Dad, no Kevin or Christina or Kyla. It's just the two of them, the way it was when they were little. But on the way home while Toby is pushing and Alex's sitting behind the wheel, he hears the sound of a familiar engine. His heart starts racing. He prays to God again, *please*—but it doesn't help.

Kevin and Val slam on their brakes in front of the go-kart, staring at it. "What the hell is that?" Kevin snarls, but there's something else in his voice that isn't usually there. Interest?

"A go-kart," Toby states calmly.

They stifle a giggle. "Did you build it yourself?" Kevin asks.

"Yes."

Alex doesn't say anything. Maybe they haven't noticed him sitting there, crouched in a fetal position. Or don't they care?

"How the hell did you do that?" Val asks, climbing out of the car. "Where did you find the parts?"

So it *was* interest. Toby explains as if he were talking to someone besides Kevin and Val. As if he were explaining it to Alex, just as enthusiastic and eager—it's almost painful to hear. Alex notices Val watching him. The look in the other boy's eyes is candid and friendly.

"Sweet," Kevin says when Toby is finished. "I've built a bunch of go-karts too. But none of them were anywhere near as hot as this one."

Alex is astounded. Is Kevin human? Did he just say something complimentary? Has the guy done something in his life besides insulting people and swaggering around school?

Toby keeps pushing. Alex rolls along in the go-kart. Kevin's interest begins to wane. "Val, let's go. We've got other shit to do."

"Yeah, yeah," Val agrees. He studies Toby carefully. "Listen, I'm having a party on Friday. You guys can come if you feel like it."

Alex can't believe it. Toby turns around. "What?"

"Are you deaf? Or retarded? Party at Val's place!" Kevin yells.

"Oh, yeah . . . sure." Toby looks confused.

Alex pokes his head up from the go-kart, praying pathetically that Toby isn't the only one invited.

"Alex, we want you to come too!" Val assures.

What, is Val some kind of mind reader? "Us?" he asks. "You're sure?"

"Yeah! Val's parents take inventory before and after his parties, so you have to bring some booze," Kevin laughs. "See you later, NASCAR!"

Kyla can't help but love Koi, a stylish place on La Cienega and Melrose. There are aquariums everywhere—even in the floor. All kinds of multicolored exotics swim in them, swooshing around submerged Buddha heads and swaying plants. They play music that fits with the fish—something grownup and wispy. And the waiters smile at them respect-fully. It doesn't matter that they didn't want to serve her wine. She sips her soda and enjoys it anyway.

They each get a bright pile of fancy lettuces before the meal, which they eat off little plates.

Kyla feels something close to happy. When Lucas offered to take her somewhere nice, she'd immediately said she felt like sushi. And they wound up here, not just any old sushi bar, but the place her father brought her for lunch the last time he was in town.

"Do you want to taste my wine?" Lucas asks.

Kyla shakes her head. "You know how I get when I drink. I'd probably start dancing on the table."

Lucas grins. His whole body smiles when he looks at her. She can't help but be surprised: What's making him so happy?

"Lucky for me you finally gave in."

"What would you have done if I hadn't?"

"Kidnapped you."

"Yeah, right," Kyla laughs.

"That's the way I am. I don't give up that easily."

"But you should have respect for what other people want too."

"Well, you're sitting here now, aren't you?"

"So it pays to nag, you mean?"

"Exactly."

"We'll see about that." Kyla dabs her mouth with her napkin.

He doesn't tell her much about himself, just wants to talk about her, and all his attention makes her dreary life seem fantastically interesting. He rests his chin on his hand. In the end she can't help but giggle. She's never had such an intense spotlight trained on her. Not with the jerks she's hooked up with.

There's something about him when he talks. It's like they're from different planets. Not because of their clothes or how much older he is; there's something else. Something that makes her both nervous and curious.

She tries, but he refuses to let her pay for her half. "I'm not poor, if that's what you think," Kyla insists.

"It doesn't matter. I would never let a girl pay."

She doesn't have the strength to protest, knows instinctively that he'll never give in. Outside the restaurant she thanks him for what honestly was a nice evening.

He looks at her in surprise. "Aren't we going to go somewhere else?"

"Silly, I have to go home. I have school tomorrow! And I'm too young to get in anywhere."

"But I don't want to go out by myself," Lucas moans, pulling her toward him.

"Then call someone!"

He cracks a smile, holds her in a strong hug, and says into her hair, "You're not *that* young."

He goes for a kiss. She doesn't try to stop him. But there's something that feels strange when his tongue finds its way into her mouth. Something that makes her think, *That's enough, right there.*

She pulls away from him. "Take me home now."

"Sure thing." He sighs.

Alex can't concentrate on the dancing. He's obsessing over Val's party—should he even go? How's he going to get booze?

"Alex! Pull yourself together!" Paulina scolds.

Alex glances over at Christina. She's radiant as usual. The other girls fade in comparison. He hasn't dared approach her lately. When he stopped hearing from Kyla, some of his self-confidence evaporated. And Christina doesn't seek him out either—she slips into her mother's car right after class and hasn't done more than flash him the occasional secretive smile. Or were they just polite? Henning puts his hands around her waist and lifts.

Alex wonders what Christina thinks about drinking. Surely she's never done it. A dancer with her intense attitude would never. Surely she thinks it's stupid. Or how would she put it? That it's *wrong.* It's *wrong* to ruin your body.

"*Alex!* What did I just say?!"

He jerks his head toward Madame Paulina and mumbles an apology.

Later, in the changing room, Henning turns his pimply face toward him. "You seem a little, um . . ." Henning's cheeks redden slightly. "I mean, before. Are you not feeling good?"

Alex smiles, unconcerned. He suspects that Henning might *want* him not to be at his best. "I'm okay. I just wasn't really concentrating. I was thinking about something else."

There's disappointment first, then curiosity in Henning's eyes. "About what?"

Alex remembers the devout gaze in Henning's eyes as he lifted Christina. Then he understands. Henning loves her too. *Of course.*

"A party I'm going to go to," Alex says. He notices Henning get self-conscious. For a brief instant, the other boy's whole body indicates that he never gets invited to parties either. Alex slings his bag over his shoulder and slips out of the changing room. Henning follows close behind.

"So, are you going to try out for the part?" Henning asks.

"The part?"

"You know what I mean."

"Oh, yeah. San Francisco." Alex is just about to say that he doesn't really care, when Christina comes out of the girls' changing room.

"So, aren't you going to try out?" Henning repeats, giving him a playful punch. The punch feels far from natural—it's obvious he wants to impress Christina. "Maybe you're afraid of the competition," Henning suggests, puffing up his chest.

Alex hesitates for a second. Christina is listening. Then he smiles wryly, imagining he looks a little like Johnny Depp. "Don't think so."

"So you *will* be auditioning, then?"

Alex does something he never thought he would do: returns Henning's fake punch in the arm. As if they were buddies and did that all the time. "Of course. But you'd better work on that jump, otherwise you'll be in sorry shape." Alex nods his head at Christina. "Later."

When Kyla gets home, her mother is in the kitchen. She's sitting at the table, looking through a bunch of bills. Kyla's surprised; she's the one who usually pays them. And Mom looks upset.

"What are these, Kyla?"

"Bills."

"But for *this much*!?"

"Yeah, what do you think? It all adds up."

Her mom looks desperate. "I don't have enough to pay all these."

"Of course we do. I was thinking this month—"

"We're going to have to cancel the cable!"

"That's not even forty dollars a month."

"We have to start somewhere, and it's all crap on anyway."

"Says *you*. I'm not even the one on the couch all day!" Kyla exclaims. Where did this sudden attitude of motherly responsibility come from?

"Grow up, would you!" Contempt flashes in her mother's eyes. "You're so spoiled, you know that? You get every little thing you want from your dad. And by the way, we're selling your DVD player too. I'm sure we can get a hundred bucks for it."

Kyla's head is spinning. What's going on? When she left for her date a few hours ago, everything seemed fine. She feels the tears welling up.

"Mom, calm down. Tell me what the problem is— "

But her mom isn't listening; she's not even looking at her.

"Do you know what a materialist is, Kyla?" Her mom bolts up suddenly and leaves the room. Ten seconds later she's back with Kyla's new clothes, the ones she bought at the mall today.

"Let me tell you, I haven't bought so many clothes in the last two years combined. And you come home with a bunch like this every week!"

"Were you in my room? You can't go in there without asking!"

"And to think your father is off in New York enjoying his life of luxury while we can hardly make ends meet . . ." Her mom's voice is bitter. "How do you think I'm supposed to pay for your lifestyle?"

"I don't cost you shit! Dad pays for—"

". . . not without that job . . ."

Kyla just stares. Oh, no. Did her mom lose this job—already? Is that why she's raving? The tears are coming now. They won't be stopped. Kyla grabs the clothes out of her mom's hands. "Dad's money supports my *materialism*. And it supports you too, so just snap out of it!"

Immediately the underdog, her mom's chin folds down to her chest. Kyla almost enjoys it. "Don't you get it?" she whispers. "I've been using his money *every month for the past year* to make sure we were taken care of. They raised the rent six months ago, don't you remember?"

Her mom doesn't make eye contact. Kyla is quiet but ruthless. "Dad may have left. He may have fallen in love with someone else and you may have let that ruin your life, but don't make it ruin mine too."

This topic has always been out of bounds. But now that the floodgates are open, she can't stop what's coming out of her mouth. "You know what? I get why Dad ditched you. Because you can't deal with *anything*. Not working, not cleaning, not . . . not even buying bread. *Nothing!* You can't even take care of your own child! I get why you lie there in bed with your nose to the wall, because you can't stand being you."

She's quiet for a second, then goes for the zinger. "I wouldn't be able to either, Mom. I couldn't stand being you, because you're worthless. *Worthless!*"

Kyla tears out of the kitchen, slamming the door behind her.

i've been such an idiot. i'm sorry for everything. can u 4give me? there's so much i

117

want to tell you, but it would take all night. i thought i could get by without you, but i can't. can you forgive me, alex? i'm so alone and i need you. i'm going to tell the truth from now on. i lied to you too, u know. i pretended i was someone else. someone better. well, i hope ur ready 4 the real deal, cuz it's coming. my full name is kyla billings and i live in la. there is no house in joshua tree. in fact i've never been there. just heard about it on tv nature shows. i've got a facebook page that should tell u (and show u) pretty much everything u want 2 know. i hope that, after u see, we can still b friends.

Kyla,

I'm SO HAPPY to hear from you!!! You know, you're the only person I can be honest with. That probably sounds bizarre for a liar, but it's true. And everything I wrote about my feelings was true. Everything. It doesn't matter that you're not the girl on the horse in the desert, because I'm not a soccer jock either. Thanks for telling me about your Facebook page. I took a look and I think you must be some kind of model or something! ☺ I don't have a Facebook page, but I'll start one. I hope you're not disappointed.

thanx 4 the compliments. no photo shoots lately. but u r sweet. my mom is in bed as usual. we haven't talked since our fight yesterday. I *want* to hate her, but I can't help feeling sorry 4 her either. she says being depressed is like watching happy people through a window, while ur stuck behind a glass wall and u can't do anything. i'm sure i'll find out what it feels like someday... haha. soooo, facebook says you're into ballet. i've never met a dancer before! can you do the splits and all that flexy stuff? can you do a million pirouettes in a row? god, i wish *i* could do something. sometmz i want to b drunk a lot, since when ur drunk u feel good and 4get about everything and all the crap disappears. although i don't want 2 4get about u. ☺ listen, you don't really have a page unless you post a picture—so put 1 up! i want 2 see who i'm talking 2!!!

He slips downstairs. It's pitch-black. He sneaks into the living room. Where is it? Their living room looks like a little cultural museum with all the wooden knickknacks and hand-woven Russian crap. Ah, there's the liquor cabinet. It's full of bottles, so many that they'll hardly notice if . . . He scans the labels. What does any of it mean? *Vermouth? Bourbon? Bristol Cream?*

Alex hesitates. Should he take a whole bottle? And if so, which one? What if he picks the wrong kind? He can just hear them: "You brought *bourbon*? Only losers drink that!"

He decides to take a *small* bottle. That'll have to be enough. Besides, it hardly takes up any space in the cupboard, so it won't look like anything's missing. There are only two small ones. One is brownish and called Kahlúa and the other is clear, like water. It's tequila, and it looks more appetizing than the dark liquid.

On his way back to his bedroom, he slips into his father's office—pulls up Kyla's Facebook page.

There she is again. And God, she's gorgeous beyond measure. Some unholy combination of Scarlett Johansson and Aphrodite and the beach volleyball players he saw on TV during the last Olympics.

He'll never find a picture good enough to impress a girl like her.

Never.

I'm such a badass! I stole liquor from my dad . . . I've never done anything like that before, but now I'm sitting here with a bottle of tequila in my hand. There's a party on

Friday. I know this is going to sound totally lame, but what do I do, Kyla? How do I get these people to like me? I'm not kidding, I've never understood how. Something ALWAYS goes wrong. I'm practically a senior. It's TIME already! PS I'm looking for a picture to post. Haven't found the right one yet but don't worry. It's coming!

do a couple shots and forget who you *think* they think you are. it's all about *chillaxing*. go 4 it, baby!!! ps make sure pic is hawt ;)

It's Friday afternoon. She walks hurriedly across the school grounds, wanting to get out of there before Therese and Susanna come racing after her. Besides, she needs to go home; neither she nor her mom has said anything since the fight. Her mom has completely reverted to a bedridden zombie.

"Kylaaaaa!" Susanna yells.

Kyla stops. Why did she think she'd escape? She turns around, waits for them.

"What, do you have to get somewhere or something?" Therese demands.

"Yeah, I have to go home."

Susanna deflates. "Home? On a Friday? Aren't you at least coming to the café?"

"I have to study."

They laugh. "Study?" Therese jokes. "Want to be one of the *cool kids,* huh?"

Kyla just walks. Susanna grabs her arm. "Wait," she says quietly. "You don't have to go home alone. We can study together, right?"

"You guys are so boring!" Therese plows on. "Seriously."

"Listen, I don't want to," Kyla explains. "But my dad—"

"Hasn't he given up yet?" Therese asks. She's doing the worst of the three of them in school. She says she's got other plans besides sticking around and finishing high school. Since she gave up her modeling dream, just what those plans are isn't clear, but she claims there are lots of famous people who didn't even finish ninth grade and now earn boatloads of money. Kyla has to admit, in this town, Therese has a point. But Kyla can't help wanting something different, something that feels right to her, feels more . . . meaningful. Suddenly, Therese takes her voice down a notch. "Or is it your mom, Ky? Is she worse?"

Kyla's startled by the question, but sort of touched as well, even if she's not about to admit anything about her mom. She starts, "Thanks, but I—"

That's when Therese spots Elizabeth's new boyfriend, Erik, standing outside the school. He's wearing black clothes and his hair is cut in a hipster guitarist's shag; he plays in some band. Kyla pretends not to see him. But Therese whistles, elbows Kyla in the side, and says, "Come on!"

"What?"

"Elizabeth will be really pissed if she sees you with Erik. Go over there."

"And say what?"

"I don't know. Just look hot." Therese looks at her meaningfully. "Erik likes hot, and you're good at it."

What does she mean by that? Like "looking hot" is the best conversation Kyla's capable of? "No."

"What?"

"You heard me. I'm not interested in payback."

"So it's okay if she just goes around saying anything she wants about us?"

Kyla makes up her mind. She locks eyes with Therese and tries to make her words as loaded as possible. "I can't be bothered to care about every single person who talks crap about me."

Therese just looks puzzled. Whatever. Kyla turns on her heel and heads for the bus stop.

Feet on the floor, he can only see his upper body, so Alex stands on the toilet lid to check out his new jeans. It feels different wearing such baggy pants. And the polo-hoodie combo with the athletic-themed logo—it's like he's put on a costume. Everyone's going to think he's some kind of poser who went to town and bought himself a look. Which is basically what he did.

He turns around to see how he looks from behind. Right then the door opens.

Andrei is amused. "And what are you up to, little bro?"

Alex blushes. "Uh . . ."

"Are you going out for the varsity team or something?"

"Close. I'm going to a party."

"Seriously?" Andrei looks genuinely happy. "Dude, it's about time."

Alex swallows his pride. "What do you think?"

Andrei scrutinizes him carefully, from top to bottom. "Is that your style?"

"I have no idea. I kind of don't have a style."

"Come!"

Alex follows Andrei into his room. It smells faintly of smoke. The bed is unmade and there's hockey equipment strewn across the floor. Andrei rummages around in his closet while Alex contemplates his back. To think that it took a party for Andrei to show some interest in his lame little brother.

"Leather jacket!" Andrei exclaims gleefully, pulling out a hanger. On it dangles a garment Tom Cruise might have worn in his Top Gun days. Black with stripes down the sleeves—kind of Euro-racing inspired.

"Uh . . . I don't know."

"Chicks dig it. I promise you."

"Maybe if you ride a motorcycle."

"No, *always*."

Andrei forces Alex to try the jacket on, but it's too big in the sleeves. Alex is about to shrug it off, when Andrei stops him, chuckles, and starts rolling up the cuffs—just once underneath. Then he digs out a black leather belt and a fitted T-shirt. "Looking good, dude," Andrei pronounces when Alex's finally fully dressed. "This is really you, you know that?"

"*This* is really me?" Alex smiles.

"Yeah." Andrei smiles back. *Are they actually sharing something?*

"You've got great muscles," Andrei continues, with admiration in his voice. "You should show them off more. I'm too bulked up."

Great muscles? Obviously dancing keeps him in good shape, but Alex spends so much time drowning in the crap associated with it, he never much considered the perks.

Alex shrugs the jacket off and flexes in the mirror. "Thanks, man." He grins.

"Good luck, bro." Andrei winks and gives him a brotherly shove out the door.

Someone is standing outside the building when she comes back from the grocery store. She can't tell who it is until she's about ten yards away. She's struck again by the intense way he looks at her. As if his look were meant for someone else, someone imaginary. But there's no one on the street behind her.

She feels grateful for a second, takes his hand and exclaims, "Hi! What are you doing here?"

"Waiting for you. What do you think?"

She regards him in mock sternness. "But I can't get together today. Did I not say that yesterday?"

"Yeah, but I'm not okay with that."

"Well, I'm afraid you're going to have to be."

He pulls her to him. She puts her arms around his waist. Today it feels good to do that. Today since she succeeded in making it clear to Therese and Susanna that she wanted to go home and didn't back down. But what does she want from Lucas? What does he want from her?

"What do you want from me?" he asks.

She looks up at him, startled. Can he read her mind?

"Yeah. Obviously I know what *I* want from *you*, but what do you want from me?"

Kyla pulls away. "I don't know, Lucas. Do I have to know?"

"It's just that I don't get you."

She scoffs. "Join the club."

"This isn't going to be easy then." The corner of his mouth curls into a smile.

"Nope," Kyla agrees. She holds up her key to show him that she has to go inside now.

"Can't I come up with you?"

"Absolutely not."

"Why?"

"My mom is sick."

He gets serious, then looks suspicious. "For real?"

"Believe what you want."

She wants him to leave now. She's tired of playing games. She punches in the code and opens the front door.

He reaches for her arm and holds on tight. A little *too* tight.

"Hey, let go!" Kyla glances toward the doorman's desk. Sid's not there. He must be on break.

Thankfully, Lucas loosens his grip. "Sorry, but can't we just . . . I mean, it took me half an hour to get out here."

"How's that my fault?"

He looks down at the ground. Poor Lucas. "You can't just treat me however you want."

She softens. "Look, don't worry, okay? I'll call you."

"But when are we going to see each other?"

"I said I'd call you." Kyla's about to close the door, when he grabs her hand again.

"Can't we set a time now?" he pleads. "Otherwise I'll go crazy . . ."

She can't help but notice how cute he is with his out-of-control hair. And his wide eyes—so serious, as if their relationship were a matter of life and death.

"Saturday night," she tells him. His eyes light up like a little boy's at Christmas.

"And try not to go crazy between now and then!" She gives him a final smile as the door swings shut behind her.

So this is what happens at parties? In the movies everyone staggers around wildly, dancing, crying, making out. Beer cans fly through the air, stuff gets trashed. Here, everyone is kind of dressed up and nervous. Full of anticipation. Groups of people are standing around, quietly engaged in small talk. Val is more nervous than anyone. He's been laughing a little too loudly since they got here. When Val opened the door he seemed happy to see them, and here Alex had pretty much been prepared for a wad of spit in the face. But Val welcomed them inside like the man of the house. "Thanks," Alex had said. Toby just trudged right in.

Mostly Alex was worried about his outfit. It was as if he could hear people thinking, Leather jacket? That is just *so* wrong! But no one said anything. Toby's wearing his regular clothes, whatever T-shirt and cords he'd worn to school pretty much all week. When they walked into the kitchen, Alex couldn't help but feel embarrassed by his friend. Hot Muscle-Man Alex and Geek LEGO-Master Toby. But he lost that train of thought as soon as Amanda flashed him a big smile and giggled, "Whoa! Look how cute you are!"

He grew a couple inches and took off the jacket, showing off the tight top underneath. Amanda couldn't peel her eyes away from his six-pack, and the second Shauna came in she checked him out the same way.

The four of them form their own little group. All of a sudden they have a lot more to say to one another than they ever do at school. Alex must've gotten a little of Andrei's self-confidence along with the jacket. He even admits that he borrowed it from his brother. The girls laugh as he describes trying on all the other clothes.

"So, where's the booze?" Val asks, gathering the attention of everyone in the kitchen. His eyes light up when Amanda and Shauna present a small keg, courtesy of Shauna's older brother's fake ID, and everyone else dutifully holds up the bottles they managed to swipe in one way or another. Only Toby looks dumbfounded: "Booze? Uh . . . ," but Val quickly says, "That's okay." And then he takes Alex's bottle.

"What *is* this?"

Alex's spirits sink a little, but he won't let it show. "Tequila, dude."

"Oh, right, of course. Cool."

Javier and Anton come over, wiping their palms. "Tequila! Awesome! Do you have any lime, Val?"

Val opens the fridge and takes out two limes. Javier cheers, then stops and asks Alex, "Is it okay if we take shots?"

Alex tells them they can have as much as they want. Javier offers him some of their beer, but Alex sets the can down to follow along. Javier shows them how it's done. Alex enjoys being the center of attention, the one who brought the tequila, one of the ones everyone's watching. Could this party get any better? Javier pours the clear liquid into the Dixie cups they're using as makeshift shot glasses and measures out little piles of salt. They each get a wedge of lime.

Alex asks Javier where he learned how to do this and Javier says he's seen his parents do it. Alex's stomach clenches. What if he throws up just from the taste, right on the kitchen floor? He's only ever tasted alcohol one time. His father had smiled with delight when he spit it back into the glass, while his mother mumbled about how irresponsible it was to let a thirteen-year-old taste liquor.

They raise their glasses in the air. Everyone is dead quiet.

Javier has already explained what will happen: first the salt, then the liquor, then the lime. Alex repeats it to himself. "Bottoms up!" Javier calls. Alex quickly sucks up the salt. He manages not to think about the taste until he's opened his mouth and dumped the entire contents of the cup straight down his throat. He swallows and presses the lime wedge between his teeth, sucking like crazy. Only now does he look up at the others. Yup, they're sucking too, in a frenzy. Everyone around them waits, tense. Alex is keenly aware of the tequila taste welling up from his stomach and mixing with the acid from the lime. It tastes so horrifically bad, like the tequila is sitting in his throat, daring to fly out onto Val's kitchen floor for the whole crowd to see.

He concentrates and tries to breathe slowly. Gently but determinedly he urges the tequila back down into his stomach. He swallows and struggles until the pressure diminishes and he's finally put the alcohol in its place.

He's the first one to manage a smile.

"That was awesome!" he cheers.

She's made spaghetti and meatballs, lit candles, and tried to find plates and silverware that all match. And she bought Diet Coke, chocolate ice cream, and those yummy baked chips to eat while they watch *Project Runway* later. Down in the laundry room there are two loads she's already washed spinning around in the dryers.

Her mom sits there with her messy hair, gazing listlessly

down at the plate Kyla's served. She's wearing a tight old sweater and baggy sweatpants. Kyla hates those clothes, the sick clothes.

"Wow, it looks great, honey."

"I hope so!"

They eat in silence. Her mother pokes two strands of spaghetti into her mouth at the same time. She chews mechanically. Kyla can see right into her throat, the viscous saliva stretched between her upper and lower jaw. It's gross. She watches her mother as if she were a stranger and thinks: What a sad, broken person. Imagine if people knew. If Therese and Susanna, the teachers at school, Lucas . . . Suddenly her mother's eyes fill with tears. They drip rhythmically into her spaghetti, a concert of shame.

"Kyla, I'm sorry." She drops her knife and fork and puts her hands over her face. The table shakes. "What should I say? Is there anything I can say?"

Kyla just waits until the crying starts to subside. Her mom gets up and grabs the roll of paper towels, blows her nose loudly, and sits down again. She scans Kyla's face with small, red eyes. "My poor Kyla. You really don't have it easy."

Kyla starts clearing the table.

"You're much too young to have all these responsibilities."

Kyla puts things in the sink, item by item, clenching her teeth so hard that it hurts.

"I know," her mom continues, "because it was exactly the same for me. I did everything around the house when my Mom and Dad were . . . carrying on."

Kyla stops in mid-motion and looks at her mother. *Carrying on?* What does she mean by that?

"I know you think your grandparents were the greatest, but they really weren't. It's just as well they died." Her mom sighs. "Let me tell you."

Kyla has only faint memories of her grandparents, but what she remembers is all sunshine and bunnies. She remembers people whose laps she could curl up on, loving smiles, some semblance of true family. But apparently they were messed up too. To think she'd missed them so much.

Her voice is a whisper. "Why didn't you ever say anything?"

Her mom contemplates the tablecloth, rolling a stray thread through her hand.

"I didn't want to ruin it for you, Kyla. I mean, as if it weren't enough with . . . well, with everything else. It was never the right time."

Kyla feels her studied control fade. "You never tell me anything! As if I were too young to deal. But taking care of the whole house, sure, I can handle that!"

"It's not so easy to know how to put things."

Kyla sinks down onto a kitchen chair with the spaghetti pot between her legs, staring straight ahead. "Mom, what was wrong with them?"

"Wrong? It's not that. It wasn't that anything was wrong with them, but they were sort of . . . revelers. You know? In the end they were partying all the time, drinking every day. They were more or less *always* drunk."

Grandma and Grandpa—winos?

"That's why I left when I was fifteen, because I couldn't take it. I thought with my career that I could look after myself, but . . . Well, then I met your dad and we had you. Then for the first time I thought everything would be all right. And it was good too, for a really long time. But then things started to fall apart and I . . ." Her mom pauses. She straightens her back, stares her daughter in the eye, and continues, "I've really tried. You know that, Kyla, lots of times. But each time something happens." She slumps back down and peers searchingly at the fridge, as if the answer might appear in the shiny stainless steel. "I don't know why."

They sit in silence, each contemplating an opposite part of the kitchen. Then her mother gets up and walks around the table. She squats on the floor in front of Kyla's legs and the tomato-coated pan. "Do you want me to talk to Social Services, Kyla?"

What?

"I get that this isn't working. I'm not working. You could end up with some great people, not far from here. Just a few weekends a month, maybe."

Kyla jumps up so quickly that the chair topples over behind her. The pot crashes to the floor. "You're sick in the head!" Kyla's whole body is trembling. "Great people? I'm supposed to go live with some *great people* instead of my own mother?"

"But it's just that—"

"You can't force me. I *refuse.*"

"It'd be for your own sake—"

"*My* sake? It's obviously for your sake. Because you can't deal with me *and* your screwed-up self!"

Her mom looks profoundly exhausted. "No, I just thought that maybe you should meet some healthy adults. Role models. The kind of people who can give you what you need."

"I don't need anything!"

"You're not as strong as you think—"

"What? What can I not handle? I haven't started taking drugs, if that's what you think. I'm not mixed up with that kind of thing."

"I never thought you were."

"Then what are you going on and on about?"

Her mom gets quiet. She's sitting on the floor with her legs crossed, like a kindergartener. Her hands rest limply on her knees. "Don't you get it?"

"No," Kyla answers simply.

They stare at each other. Her mom's eyes well up again. Despite it all, there's so much love reflected back.

"What are you afraid of, Mom?"

The answer comes as a whisper, barely a breath. "I'm afraid that you'll turn out like me."

What if Christina could see him now? Or Kyla? It's like he was born to party. He's had just enough to drink: one and a half beers and a second shot of tequila. He felt like a

134

pro as he measured out the salt and poured the foul liquid down his throat.

Things are only spinning a little. Mostly he feels warm and mellow. Why has he always been so down on alcohol? This rocks. Everyone around him is smiling and talking to him, as if they were relieved that they turned out to have something in common. Was that what was going on the whole time? They thought he was so different, they didn't dare reach out? Did they think he was stuck-up?

He dances with Amanda. He just moves to the music, simply and easily. It isn't hard. Occasionally he exaggerates a turn a little, but he doesn't go overboard. He doesn't want to draw too much attention to himself. Amanda smiles at him. He grins back as if she were as beautiful to him as Christina, although he doesn't even feel that much like— flirting? It must be the booze.

He looks around. Several couples have formed around the room. Some are kissing. Alex doesn't dare stare although he wants to. Still, his eyes keep straying to the couple on the sofa; they're the worst. Billy has his hand up Vera's shirt. Toby is sitting next to them. He feels a twinge in his gut. Poor Toby. He'd been sticking like a barnacle to Alex all night until Alex was finally forced to put his foot down: "Can't you manage on your own for *one second*?" That was when he pulled Amanda out onto the dance floor. His friend's eyes had seemed to register some pain then.

Toby gets up and comes over to him again. Alex pretends not to notice, but his plan fails when Toby leans in and yells right in his ear. "I'm going home now. Are you coming?"

Alex jerks back, holding his ear. "Ow! What the hell?"

Toby shrugs guiltily. "Sorry."

Alex realizes how he's beyond irritated. He can't believe how clingy Toby is, how he didn't even remember to bring booze or make an effort to wear some decent clothes. "Go home if you want to," Alex hisses. "Seriously, get out of here! What do I care?"

Toby just stares at him. *Shame on him, shame, shame, shame!* But Alex just glares at his friend as he dances closer to Amanda, his arm wrapping around her waist. Toby retreats slowly from the room. Alex watches from the corner of his eye, and for a second his heart aches. Then Toby is gone.

A while later they're standing in the kitchen. Amanda and Shauna are still there. And Val, who's now happy and animated, clowning around and juggling empty cans and sponges. He keeps talking to Alex, clearly trying to sound impressive. *Why?* Is he going to break free from Kevin?

"So where's Kevin?" Alex asks, trying to make it sound natural.

Val shrugs, as if he didn't care. "He couldn't come. There's probably some trouble at home."

Trouble at home? Well, lucky for them anyway. Amanda and Shauna go off somewhere and the two of them are left alone. Leaning against the counter, they have a serious conversation, each with a beer in his hand, about school and where they live.

"I just don't want to turn out like them," Val says about

his parents. "They're so Jones. You know, a totally average, vanilla family. I hate it."

Alex smiles. "Enjoy it, man. I would *love* to be Aleksandr Jones. Or even better, something less Russian, like Bob. Bob Jones."

Val laughs. "You're crazy! Who wants to be Bob Jones? Imagine sitting around for the rest of your life thinking about mowing the lawn. And working down at the gas station or something, damn!"

They both make faces and then get quiet. Alex gulps down some more beer to fill the silence. Nothing is natural between him and Val despite the fact that they've been standing here together for half an hour. It's important that Alex not let his guard down.

"So have you given any thought to soccer?" Val asks.

Alex takes another swig of beer, to gain some time. "Er, um . . . I . . ."

"You what? What'd you say?"

"I don't know."

"You don't have to go to all the games if you don't want to."

"Yeah, you said that."

Then Alex catches a glimpse of someone behind a group of people chatting on the other side of the kitchen. A lone figure leaning in the doorway, eyes trained on Alex and Val: Kevin. Val strolls over to Kevin quickly, smiling nervously and holding out a can of beer. Alex abandons the scene.

They're lying on their own sofa, surveying each other. The TV is on, but neither of them is watching. They haven't said anything since the kitchen.

Kyla notices the clock on the DVD player and yelps, "Crap! The laundry!"

Her mom seems confused. "You're doing laundry?"

"Um, yeah. Obviously."

She doesn't want to go to the laundry room alone. It's always so creepy down there, especially in the evenings. It's dark and deserted, and the guy next door said he saw rats last week. Her mom pulls herself up with enormous difficulty, her hair flying every which way and her eyes in tired slits. "I'll come with you."

They're standing out in the stairwell, each holding a basket to put the clean laundry in, waiting for the elevator. Kyla is completely unprepared when the elevator doors open and Elizabeth is suddenly standing there. She's dressed up, and must have been to a party. Elizabeth glances at Kyla's mother, but not meanly. Her eyes linger. Kyla knows what she's thinking, because she would think the same thing. Scrub-brush hair and sick clothes. Kyla blushes.

Her mom says hello to Elizabeth when she gets out of the elevator. Is Kyla the only one who notices the hello sounds slurred? Elizabeth says a quick hello back. Kyla sees the other girl glance back at them before she opens her door and disappears into her apartment.

More and more people pile on the sofa. It's a regular schmoozefest.

"Why so much talking?" moans Javier, who's just come back from throwing up in the bathroom. He reclines and takes deep breaths. "I had no idea you were such a rock star."

Alex laughs. He feels dizzy and giggly. *If only Kyla could see me now!* But he doesn't dare stand up for fear of falling down.

"There's a lot you don't know about me," he answers furtively, pulling a cigarette out of Javier's pack. He lights it, sucks the smoke in, but keeps it in his mouth. He hasn't completely lost his good judgment—what if he started coughing like a fool?

"The tequila king!" Anton cheers, and then pulls Shauna up to dance. Amanda stays put—wherever Alex is, she's always right nearby.

Someone new plops down on the sofa. First he sees only her legs, gleaming white beneath her short skirt. When he looks up he recognizes her: Lottie. She's in the same grade but has never given him a second look. And yet now she's smiling right at him, her lips glistening like gold. What does she want? Amanda appears to be wondering the same thing.

"Heya, Alex," Lottie murmurs in a low, smoky voice.

"Hi."

Lottie leans her head back dramatically. "God, I'm so tired!"

Alex can't find any words. Lottie puts her hand on his thigh and lets it rest there. He immediately tenses. She looks startled.

"Oh, sorry!" Lottie pulls her hand back. "What *am* I doing?"

"*I* don't know."

"Yeah, it's hard to know."

They both laugh. Suddenly Alex has so much laughter inside him that the whole world seems funny. Amanda gets up quickly and stomps off into the kitchen. Lottie watches her go, surprised.

"Is your girlfriend in a bad mood or something?"

"She's not my girlfriend."

"Oh, really? She seems like it."

"Well, she's not."

"Good," Lottie coos.

Why is she saying that? Never mind. Now it's just the two of them. Javier seems to have fallen asleep at the other end of the sofa, and everyone else is dancing or making out somewhere else. Then he feels Lottie's breath against his cheek. He cocks his head and looks into her eyes. She moves closer. *Is she . . . ?* He follows her actions with astonishment. When she's as close as she can get, he closes his eyes in sweet anticipation.

Despite the fact that they've never said a word to each other before, this feels completely natural. He doesn't have to think about how to kiss. He slides one hand behind her head. She strokes his thigh.

"Ew, get a room!" he hears Kevin taunt. Lottie quickly pulls away from Alex and darts back over to Kevin, who's grinning triumphantly. Val and two other people are standing behind him. They seem drunk and confused. And behind them is Amanda, staring at Alex with utter disdain.

"So then he's *not* gay." Kevin studies Alex critically.

"I don't think so." Lottie smirks, smoothing down her hair.

"*Think?* He practically raped you," Kevin broadcasts loudly. "But maybe he was just faking?"

Lottie shrugs her shoulders. "Whatever. You owe me two beers."

Two beers. Alex rises slowly. He has to stand there for several seconds before he regains his balance. Everyone stares at him. Those twelve steps to the front door feel like a mile.

Kyla, why would you ever wish you were drunk??? Drinking SUCKS. Alcohol just makes people assholes. Alcohol is for weak and pathetic people who don't have the GUTS to do anything without it. Is that how YOU are? Do you drink and then treat everyone like crap?

"Breakfast is ready, *dorogoi,*" his mom calls up the stairs. "I have made blintzes!"

Alex slowly wakes up. His mouth feels dry and he's exhausted. All he wants is to go back to sleep. His mom's voice again, insistently, "Sasha!"

Leave me alone, please, Alex groans inwardly. She's always going on and on about the weekend family breakfast. Everyone is expected to treat it as sacred.

"Yeah, yeah!!!" Alex calls.

It's quiet for a minute, then she pops her head in his doorway, anxious.

"What is wrong, Sasha?"

"Nothing," he says scratchily, trying to wake up his voice.

When he trundles into the kitchen, it seems like there's more people there than usual. Everyone looks at him expectantly. Andrei is grinning. "So how are *you* feeling today?"

"Um, fine." Alex stiffens as he's about to sit down in the one empty seat. There *are* more people. *Katy* is sitting next to Andrei. Are they a thing now? For real? With this little window on his private life, she might report on his hangover at school. He can't even bring himself to say hello. Katy looks down at the table awkwardly.

"Would you like more?" his mom asks, holding the platter of blintzes out to Katy.

"Yes, thank you," she replies.

His mom serves their guest and then places the blintzes in front of Alex.

"Did you have a nice time yesterday?" She smiles without looking at him. Her eyes are scanning the table to make sure everything is picture perfect.

"Sure."

"C'mon, dude," Andrei pesters. "That was your first party. How was it?"

So harsh! Andrei just laid the bitter truth right out on the table for the world's entertainment. Now Katy will have Monday's best gossip: "Alex had never been to a party before! Can you believe that?!"

"How was it?" Andrei repeats.

"Fine," Alex sighs.

There's a giggle and a groan from Nina. Of course she has to get her two cents in. "What a boring answer!" Nina laughs. "Didn't you even talk to anyone?"

Alex shoots his *little* sister an angry look. "Of course I did!"

"How nice for you to go to a party," his mom chirps. "As long as it is not every night."

"Not a chance," Nina mutters.

Then his dad looks up from the paper. "I noticed this morning that the light was on in the office. Did you use the computer last night, Alex?"

The computer? Then he remembers . . . the e-mail to Kyla.

"Oh. Yeah."

"So late at night?" his dad continues. "Why?"

"Does it matter, Dad?" He only vaguely remembers what he wrote, but what he does recall isn't good. He took out a big load of misery on Kyla.

"Is it the girl you have been writing?"

His mom is startled. "What girl is that?"

Alex feels Katy watching him. Can't he have anything to himself, just something small, half an ounce of privacy?

"You have an Internet girlfriend?!?" Nina squeals. "That is totally cool!"

"He is writing to a girl he has never met," his father says, turning to his daughter expectantly. "Do people do this?"

She gives a know-it-all nod, and focuses on Alex again. "So who is she? I want details!"

"Yes, tell us about it, Sasha!" his mom urges.

Alex gets up to grab something from the fridge—anything will do—but he stops partway there. Maybe he can just leave the family torturefest and go e-mail an apology to Kyla.

"You have to tell us about the party!" Andrei insists, refusing to give up. "Did you dance? Did you talk to any *real-life* chicks?"

What can he say? That they only invited him to make fun of him? That he finally had his first kiss, but the kiss was a *joke*?

"Did the clothes work out?" Andrei asked.

"Well, who is she?" Nina badgers.

"Let's hear it, Sasha!" his mom pesters.

All their expectant eyes threaten to bore a hole in his head.

"Enough!" someone says, a blessed rescue. It's *Katy*. She smacks Andrei's shoulder crossly, challenging everyone. "He obviously doesn't want to talk about it, can't you see that?"

i don't get it! if ur so hell-bent against drinking, fine, but go unload ur crap on someone who deserves it, alex. it may be hard for u to understand how hard some people have it when u live such a cute little life with your cute family and your little dancing lessons. don't u even get how f-ing *minor* ur problems are? my mother is literally FALLING APART while you go on and on about yes booze or no booze. has it never occurred to u that maybe some people drink to FORGET? i know i shouldn't, but i do it anyway, it makes everything a little lighter. yup, so there it is!!! am i a horrible person now? i'm sure i'll become an alcoholic, but that's probably just as well. or maybe i'll just go crazy before i have to move into a cardboard box. u have no idea how good u have it. kyla

I am sooooo sorry, Kyla. Can you forgive me??? I hate myself, for more reasons than even my AWFUL email to you (which I'm sorry about again!). I was such a jerk yesterday to the only person in my life here who's a real friend, my oldest friend . . . how could I do that? What if he never talks me again?!? I wouldn't really blame him. You think my life is so great? I don't know. I don't know anything. But I do know you're not going to become an alcoholic, OK? And it's not your job to take care of your mother. Maybe she needs help meeting someone who can do that for you. I know it's easier said than done, but it's worth a try. People meet *real* people online these days . . . ☺?

—Alex

When her mom enters the kitchen at eleven o'clock in the morning, Kyla is already done with her yogurt.

"Good morning," Kyla says cheerily, presenting her mother with toast and a knife for the marmalade.

Her mother studies her with surprise. "What are you so happy about?"

"Nothing in particular."

Her mom pours the coffee with slow movements. "Have you thought any more about what we talked about yesterday?"

"You're not calling Social Services."

"Okay." Her mom turns around and smiles.

"I had an idea," Kyla announces. She takes her mom's hand and sits her in front of her laptop, set up especially for the occasion. "I've already found some promising prospects."

Her mother peers at the screen until it dawns on her. "A dating site? Kyla, you've got to be kidding me."

"You've got to do something eventually."

"I can't even handle going to the grocery store! There's no way I can go out and meet men!"

"You have to *try*. You have to make an effort."

Her mom seems to shrink. "But I *have* tried."

"You haven't tried this."

"Yes, but honey . . . who would want me?"

"Maybe not the way you look right now."

"No. *Exactly*."

"But I can fix you up. You can be as pretty as you used to be!"

"Honey, look at me! I have no desire to meet men. It won't work."

Kyla clenches her jaw. Should she? "I got an e-mail from Dad yesterday," she starts. "He said I could come live with him. I can move to New York whenever I want."

Silence.

Kyla continues, "If you don't agree to try this, I'm moving."

He hesitates at the gate. Stands there with his hand on the handle, unable to go any farther. But surely they've already seen him through the window, so it's too late to turn back.

He slowly enters and walks up to the front door. Rings the bell, his hand trembling. Before he can count to five, Toby opens the door. Alex doesn't know what to say.

"What are you up to?" Alex asks lamely.

"Reading."

"Am I disturbing you?"

Toby shrugs his shoulders. Then nothing happens. Alex fiddles nervously with the zipper on his jacket. Toby stares at the doormat, which says "Welcome." After a while, he's tired of standing there. "Was there something you wanted?"

"Nah . . . I mean, well, yeah," Alex stutters. "I just wanted . . . Um, it's just that it was all so dumb. I mean, I was dumb. Last night."

Toby looks right at him, waiting for him to continue. Okay, Alex thinks, so far so good.

"I don't get why I did that thing," he says. "I had a lot to drink, I guess that's why." What a lame excuse. Toby thinks so too.

"Which thing do you mean?"

I deserve this, Alex thinks. "Huh?"

"Which dumb thing?"

"That I was so rude."

"A complete jerk, you mean?" Toby looks determined. Alex has never seen him like this, never heard him talk with such resolve.

"Um, yeah. A complete jerk."

"So you're saying you're sorry."

"Yes." Alex nods. "I am."

"Sorry that you didn't even talk to me even though we went to the party together? Sorry that you moved away whenever I came over to you?"

Alex nods again.

"Sorry that you told me to get lost?"

It comes out as a whisper. "Yes," Alex begins. "Really."

Toby seems to have grown overnight; he's a different person. Alex's cheeks glow. This is torture, and Toby is holding the branding iron.

"Can you get the actual words out?"

"Um," Alex tries. "I was lousy to you . . ."

"And?"

"And I'm sorry, Toby."

Finally Toby relents. He studies the welcome mat again, scraping his foot while he thinks. "It's okay. But you really hurt me, you know? When I started thinking about it . . ."

So, Toby *does* think about how people relate to each other.

"I understand. I would have been really upset too. But can't we . . . I mean, we can still be friends, right?" Alex hears the desperation in his question, but he's pretty sure he spots some forgiveness in Toby's expression.

"I suppose we can e-mail."

What? What does Toby mean, *e-mail*?

"We're moving at the end of the month. My dad finally got a job. Up north in Portland."

She'd forgotten what her mother looked like underneath the pallor. She's beautiful, with the same thick hair as Kyla, the same green eyes. She still has a slight runway flair, some of the style and electricity Kyla used to love watching in old videos of her fashion shows. The whole kitchen table is strewn with eyeliners and compacts—and the woman sitting in the kitchen chair is ready for the catwalk again. No one would believe she's the same woman as last night.

Kyla holds up a mirror nervously. "What do you think?"

"Nice." Her mom smiles dismissively.

"You're still drop-dead gorgeous."

"Maybe."

"Well, it's a good start, isn't it? I hope it's inspiration enough to start searching!"

Her mom doesn't answer. She looks in the mirror shyly and arranges a stray hair, then pulls out a pack of cigarettes.

"You're ready to knock 'em dead, Mom!"

Kyla hears how forced she sounds. Don't they both know she can't camouflage despair with makeup? In all her beauty, her mom looks so unbearably miserable. And to think she's a victim of blackmail . . . Kyla steels herself.

"I'll only click on the ones who say they're 'nice.'"

Kyla begins to read aloud. About considerate, kindhearted, warm men, middle-aged men who are "better-than-average" or "very attractive." About men who like to laugh and enjoy the outdoors, who like books and theater and quiet evenings at home. Who want to hold someone's hand and feel close. About men who want to share their lives with a special woman.

Her mom doesn't make a sound. After each profile, Kyla tries: "What about him? He sounds good, doesn't he? He's cute, don't you think?" But it doesn't help. After every few lines, Kyla hoots with joy: "That's him! He's the one!" just to test her mom's response, but she never agrees or disagrees. Sometimes she offers a little smile or nods, as if to keep her daughter from feeling too disappointed.

Kyla finally settles on someone. He's older than her mom, forty-one, and likes to cook and hike. And then, of course, he's responsible and compassionate. The idea on this site is that you're supposed to call a mailbox and leave a message about yourself. Kyla knows her mom can't compose her own introduction, so she helps.

"And you like going to the theater, right?"

"I do? I never go to the theater . . ."

"Yeah, but when you weren't sick, you liked going, didn't you?"

"Maybe," her mom says quietly. "I can't remember."

She's hopeless.

"And you've got a good sense of humor. Definitely."

"No, I have no sense of humor."

"You used to! I mean, you used to joke around *sometimes*."

"Did I?"

If Kyla left it up to her mom to decide, she wouldn't say a single positive thing about herself. In the end, Kyla slams her head to the screen and demands, "So what do you want it to say? 'I'm a lazy, slovenly thirty-six-year-old woman who is interested in zilch and enjoys lying on the sofa feeling depressed'? You do realize that will never work?"

Finally, Kyla writes out something passable and her mom practices several times before calling and leaving the message. Kyla stands next to her, making faces to pep her up and get her to sound a little more energetic. Her cheerleading has only limited effect, but it's better than nothing. Her mom actually giggles after she hangs up.

"I can't believe you got me to do this!"

Believe it, Mom. At least it's a start.

> i'm a little happier today, alex! this has to work!!! thanks for the inspiration, and for being there 4 me. i thought again after looking through all those profiles...u still haven't put up a picture! i can't believe i've held out this long! heehee, kyla

He thinks about the picture all through Monday at school. He almost forgets to be nervous about seeing Val, Kevin, and the nauseating Lottie. And Amanda, whose scorn he deserves.

But nothing turns out how he expects. Kevin isn't at school, and the others pretend like nothing's happened.

They act totally normal: They ignore him. Worst of all, he lets them. Without Andrei's leather jacket and a bottle of tequila he's his usual nobody, too shy to strike up a conversation with Javier and Anton. Even though they were like old friends at the party. So he's shocked when he passes them in the hall and he gets a little punch on the arm.

"The tequila king," Anton says, smiling. Alex blushes, but smiles back—in on the joke. It feels good, but not good enough. He's still a long way away from being accepted.

In class, Amanda makes a point of turning around to talk to him. He's ready for anything. How pissed is she that he deserted her to flirt with Lottie? Or maybe she'll just glare at him and call him a fag.

"What a bunch of idiots!" she hisses. "That Lottie . . . is a total skank."

And then she turns back around again. *Hmm.*

It's impossible to listen to what the teacher is saying. Should he post his school picture from this spring? No, he looks too serious and his hair's totally flat. Then he remembers a picture Andrei took on the beach last summer: Alex in his swim trunks at Lake Tahoe. A cheerful Alex with wet, tousled hair and no shirt. No shirt and muscles.

Val comes over to him during the break. Alex moves closer to Toby. He's not going to let Toby down this time.

Val says hi. Alex nods.

"Thanks for coming on Friday," Val tells Toby.

"Thanks for inviting me," Toby answers.

Val continues smiling, a little anxiously, actually. "The party was okay, wasn't it?" His eyes roam.

"Yeah, totally," Alex agrees quickly. But Val is looking for something more. "I . . ." he begins.

This is how it must feel to have the upper hand. Alex and Toby against a solitary, skittish Val.

"Well, um . . ." Val continues. "That totally sucked, that thing they did."

That thing. Back to being the underdog. Alex's cheeks flush instantaneously.

"I mean, I just wanted to say that what Kevin did was totally messed up."

Is Val taking his side against Kevin? Isn't that a little risky? In a flash, Val is gone. Alex watches him walk away in astonishment.

Kyla imagines the scent of freshly baked cookies wafting through the stairwell when she gets home from school. She imagines the apartment sparkling clean, taking Sunday drives to Santa Barbara and big brunches that last all afternoon. She can't help but daydream about their new life after Mom meets Mr. Perfect. She's also trying to forget that Elizabeth is sitting at a table out in front of the café. But it's impossible. It feels as if there's a laser beam running from Elizabeth's body to hers.

Susanna and Therese won't let up.

"But you have to hang out with your friends *some* of the time too," Susanna says. "I mean, that's just wrong, having to stay home with your mom all weekend. I couldn't even deal with that!" Susanna's whining is piercing.

Therese wrinkles her forehead and asks, "Kyla?"

"Hmm?"

"Are you mad at us or something?"

"Why would I be mad? Do I have some reason to be mad or something?"

"Nah, I just mean that you sounded mad," Therese says. "When I called."

Kyla sighs deeply. "We can't hang out twenty-four/seven."

"You're ditching us for that Lucas guy, right?"

"No, it's my mom. I told you that."

"Kylaaa!" Susanna moans. "What is so wrong with your mom?"

She says it so loudly that everyone hears. Elizabeth's eyes meet Kyla's for a fraction of a second, then Kyla looks back to Susanna. "Shhh!"

"Okay, sorry, but what is it?" Susanna continues in a heavy whisper. "I really don't get it."

"It's nothing in particular."

"Well, *something* must be wrong if you have to take care of her all the time!"

Out of the corner of her eye Kyla can see Elizabeth looking her way again. "Shut up!"

"What the hell? Just tell us!" Susanna whimpers. "We're your friends, Kyla. It's not as bad as cancer, is it?"

Knowing that Elizabeth is watching them is painful. Her look is hard and penetrating. Elizabeth saw, Elizabeth *knows*.

Kyla gets up and puts on her jacket. "No, it's not cancer!" She's too angry to keep her voice down. "Why did you have to . . . never mind. I can't deal with you guys anymore!"

> hi, alex! it feels so weird to know i'll see ur face soon—it's like it makes everything different. sometmz i just wish u were here w me, that we could see each other in person, however often we want. i put up some more pix right from before christopher's party, in case u didn't notice. i might look a *little* trampy with the lipstick. ;) but whatevs . . . waiting to see u is torture!!!

He loves all the pictures of Kyla. How can she be his closest friend? He can only imagine Andrei's reaction: He'd hoot and whistle and ask for her number. She's so gorgeous it scares him.

He can barely stand waiting for her reaction to his . . . which is surely why he waited so long in the first place. Now it's out there; his bare chest is available for all the world to see. Maybe she's sitting there, staring at it and, well . . . and at least thinking something positive?

The guy in the picture has just come out of the water after swimming. His tan body—thin but still muscular—is glistening. He's smiling at the camera, a wry smile—shy? His teeth gleam white against the dark, wet hair that helmets his head, his features are stately, sharp. He looks *good*. His body is amazing. *This* is the dancer who doesn't have any friends?

She feels a weight lift from her chest. He's not a freak, hooray!

Christina is so pale, you can almost see through her. She's wearing leg warmers over her toothpick legs, and her eyes are wandering nervously around the room. Alex fights the urge to go over and wrap his arms around her. Her long-necked hardheaded mother is hardly someone to lean on. She seems even more stressed out than his own mom, if that's possible.

Auditions always create such hysteria. Everyone is gathered here in the same room and they all want the same thing. *The part.* They're standing around in their practice clothes, warming up. One by one they get called in. Their parents give pep talks. His mother sizes up Alex's competition, scrutinizing them as they bend and stretch. Then she smiles at him.

"You'll get this *easily,*" she assures him.

Alex doesn't respond. He waves to Henning, who's standing at the other end of the room with his parents. Henning waves back and smiles, does a little air boxing to remind Alex they're competitors. Henning has been training hard lately. He really wants the part, and he really wants to beat Alex. Alex has no idea what *he* wants. He hasn't been concentrating on dancing at all lately. He certainly hasn't told his mom that Paulina took him aside the other day to ask if anything was wrong. He blamed it on a cold.

This is a big party for his mother. She's wearing globs of lipstick and has her hair up elegantly. She squeezes Alex's hand, eyes gleaming.

"I am so proud of you!"

"I haven't gotten the part yet," Alex reminds her.

"Not yet, but *still.*"

What does she mean? That she'd be proud of him regardless of how he does? That he'd still be her pride and joy? Would that be true?

On the other side of the room, Christina suddenly puts her hand on her forehead and falters. Instinctively Alex jumps up, but he stops himself from rushing over. Christina's mother helps her onto a chair. Someone brings a glass of water, which Christina drinks as if in a trance. Her mother's mouth moves urgently, but Christina seems frozen.

"Sasha, look!" In her ecstatic visions of his big debut, his mom obviously hasn't noticed what's going on.

"Huh?"

"At my arm," his mom exclaims. "Do you see my goose pimples? Feel! I love this!"

"Love what?"

Her laugh comes out like a snort. "All of this! The big atmosphere. All the dancers gathered together, because they really *want* this."

Henning has closed his eyes and is concentrating hard, is totally off in his own world. His parents stand a bit away from him, watching with reverence.

"Alex, you must concentrate now!" His mother's voice is stern.

It's impossible for him to care when he's concerned about Christina. She stands up with her mother's help. But as soon as her mother lets go, Christina collapses headlong onto the floor.

He's there in a flash. He takes her hand in his. "Christina, what happened? Are you okay?" Her mother is at a complete loss. In a panic, she tries to wrench Christina's hand from Alex's, hissing, "Excuse me, but do you know my daughter?" As if they'd never met before.

"We dance in the same group," he explains, watching how Christina's eyelids slowly flutter open. And then she looks him right in the eye.

Her look says all those things Alex has thought so many times: Please, can't we get out of here? He really wants to say, "Of course, come on," but he doesn't get a chance before her mother takes over.

"Are you okay? Oh, Christina, darling . . . let's go outside and get some air. Do you think you can walk? I'll help you."

Alex goes back to his mother, who is staring. "What happened? Was that . . . ?"

"Christina."

His mom looks sad. Seconds go by. Her eyes are troubled. "Poor Christina," she says. But the next second, she claps her hands together excitedly and exclaims, "Oh, Alex, now there are only two dancers before you!"

Her mom holds out her freshly painted nails, smiles flirtatiously at the wall, and quips, "Hey, baby."

Kyla cheers, hoping their girly giggles will ease the fog of tension. But her mom shakes her head and makes a face. "I don't know, Kyla," she says quietly. "I've forgotten how to do this."

"You have not."

"I can't flirt. I don't think I ever could."

"Don't give me that! Flirting was your *job*. All you have to do is act a little, like you were trained to do. Act *cool*."

Her mom furrows her eyebrows. "Cool?"

"Like you're self-confident, even though you're not."

"Like how?"

"Like *acting*. Act mysterious, and you will be." Kyla winks and her mother snorts, then rolls her eyes upward, as if remembering something.

"And then you have to *tease* him, Mom. Talk back a little.

Contradict him, be a little full of yourself." Kyla stops for a second, then breaks into a grin. "That's what *I* do."

Her mom is quiet as she studies Kyla, as if she's never seen her before. Smiling wanly, she sighs, "My little Kyla."

Kyla is embarrassed; she has no idea what to say. Perhaps thankfully, the doorbell rings. It's *him*. Him—Richard, who's forty-one and likes hiking and barbeque. His voice sounded warm, her mother had reported after their conversation. But she was really nervous about his owning his own Web business.

Now her mom is frozen. Her hand—bright red nails already chewed off—trembles slightly. Her eyes move around anxiously. "Kyla, what do I say if he asks?"

"About what?"

"Anything about computers!"

Kyla takes her mother's hands to reassure her. "You don't have to tell him you don't know anything about computers. It's okay to lie a *little*. C'mon now."

But her mom still won't budge. Her face is numb. "What are we going to talk about? I mean, I don't have anything to say . . . "

The doorbell rings again. "Well, come on, answer it!" Kyla says. "Okay, fine. I will."

Kyla doesn't know what she expected, nothing special, just someone who looked "nice." She's surprised when she opens the door. This guy is really good-looking. Not hip, but still. The way you would imagine a dad. Short, dark hair, coat, black shoes.

Kyla smiles at him and holds out her hand. "Hi. I'm Kyla. It's nice to meet you."

He returns the greeting. His hand is slightly damp and he smiles apologetically. "Yeah, I'm here to meet . . ." he stammers. His eyes dart past her into the apartment.

"Mom, Richard is here!"

Kyla asks Richard to come in, then she goes to hunt for her mom. She's in the kitchen.

"I don't want to go."

Kyla feels her irritation rising. "He actually seems super-nice."

"Yeah, but I feel . . ."

Now Kyla's just mad. Mad that her mother is too chick-enshit to do anything. "It doesn't matter how you feel. You *promised*. Otherwise . . ."

That does the trick. Her mom swallows and checks her hair, then cautiously steps out of the kitchen. Kyla sticks her head out to follow what happens. She sees Richard's face as her mom approaches him, how it changes from anxious to relieved. He thinks she's pretty. *That's half of it right there.*

"Sasha!"

It's dark and foul in the parking garage. His mother scur-ries after him like a persistent puppy. He hears only the clicking of her footsteps. The smell of urine is bordering on the intolerable.

"But you must be able to tell me something!"

"No," Alex says firmly.

He's at the car, staring into the dark while he waits for her to unlock it. She groans, *"Ohhh! Why do you not speak to me anymore?!"*

"What?"

"Nothing."

It's been a half hour since he emerged from his audition. His mother was standing there outside the room waiting, of course, but he just walked by without looking at her. He went straight to the showers with her desperate voice trailing after him: "How was it? Did you dance well?"

And the voice is still going. In the dark parking garage. Amidst the urine.

"But, *dorogoi,* you must have a *sense* about your dancing, yes?"

"I don't sense anything. Aren't you going to unlock the car?"

She sighs, rummaging around in her purse for the car keys. "I cannot understand."

He climbs into the backseat. She's more exasperated now. Why can't he sit up front? He doesn't want to. What happened, really? Did it go *that* badly? Why is he acting so strange? How? What? On and on with the questions.

"As a matter of fact, she's my friend."

He can see his mom raise her eyebrows in the rearview mirror.

"What are you saying? What are you talking about?"

"Christina! It really sucks for her."

"Don't speak this way, Sasha. What *sucks*?" Then she gets his reference. "Oh, yes. I am sure that it is simply that she could not handle the pressure. Not everyone is strong enough."

"Exactly. *That's* what sucks. That it has to be that way." Alex sighs, hunching into the seat.

His mom drives quietly. The next time she speaks, her tone is mild and instructive. "I do understand how you feel, Alex."

Yeah, right.

"You believe the world of dance is difficult and elitist, yes?"

He doesn't respond. She thinks some more, weighing her words carefully while driving calmly and methodically, for once.

"I cannot deny that this is true. But it is simply the price you must pay. Even if you do not approve."

"So to hell with anyone who can't cope?"

"No, you never say this 'to hell' with a person you care about. But it may be better for some people to stop. Before it goes too far."

Their eyes meet in the rearview mirror. "Maybe Christina does not have what it takes."

"Christina is the best."

"No. *You* are the best."

"Stop it, Mom."

"You know this is true! You have everything it takes."

"But—"

His mother can't take it anymore. "No!" she yells, and quickly softens her tone. "I *know* you do."

Then it's quiet. Her eyes in the rearview mirror fill with tears.

"It *does* suck," she continues, more to herself than to him. "If you love to dance. And don't have the opportunity to *do* it. This . . . this is terrible."

The highway ahead seems endless. The only sound in the car is the purring engine. It's like that for several minutes. He almost forgets his mother is there.

Then she says, "I should remind you. We're going next Friday."

Alex is startled. "Going where?"

"To Los Angeles. You didn't forget?"

hello there, mr. hottie! j/k ☺ but seriously . . .
nice. thanks for the picture! i'm the only one
home. this is wonderful, sucky loneliness. wish
u were here, but no one else. i even turned off
my cell phone. can't deal with a bunch of jerks
calling me. i'm going to stay up until mom
comes home, if she does! ;)

It's eleven o'clock. Then twelve. Then twenty to one. Then she hears a key in the lock. Kyla is lying in bed watching MTV. She gets up quickly and practically runs to the front door. Her mom is fiddling with the buttons on her coat.

"Hi, Mom!"

Her mom looks up. Is she happy or disappointed? Oh, she's *drunk*.

"Hi," she gurgles. She goes back to her buttons, breathing and then groaning. "Couldn't you . . . Could you help me with this?"

Kyla undoes the buttons and helps her mom off with her shoes too. Then she takes her by the arm and leads her to the sofa. Her mom's body plops down with a soft thud. Kyla snuggles up next to her.

"How are you doing?"

Her mom leans back, closes her eyes. "I don't know. Tired, I guess."

"Are you going to be sick?"

"Maybe."

"Do you want me to help you?"

Silence. Kyla gets impatient.

"So, how did it go? What was the magnificent Richard like?"

"He was . . . nice, Kyla. Actually, he really was."

Yippee! Kyla has to stop herself from dancing around the room like a little girl. She pictures the three of them sitting in a meadow with a picnic basket as Richard pulls out one delicacy after another: spareribs dripping with BBQ sauce, chicken, potato salad. He whispers something and winks at her mother, who collapses back into the grass in a fit of laughter.

"He paid for everything! He treated me to a lot of wine. Jesus, did we drink!"

Kyla's vision of Richard in the grass disappears immediately.

"So when you say he was nice, that's what you mean? That he bought you a lot of wine?"

"I don't know, that's just what he did. At the restaurant. He bought food too."

"So what did you talk about?"

Her mom takes a deep breath, scrunches up her forehead. She's trying to remember. "Yeah, what *did* we talk about?"

"Well?"

She struggles, lips pursed, eyes squinted. In another situation, her expression would almost be funny. "Oh, now I remember. We talked about him."

"What about him?"

"About his job and his ex-wife." Her mom holds her index finger up in the air as if remembering something else. "And, oh right, about his kids. Eleanor and Ma . . . Marcus? No, Matt." She sighs. "Whatever the hell their names were. God, it was so uninteresting."

"Didn't he ask anything about you?"

"Hmm?"

"Wasn't he curious about *your* ex-husband and *your* kid?"

Her mom thinks again. "No, I don't think so . . . Maybe I didn't seem willing to . . ." She rolls her eyes and looks at Kyla as if seeking support. "You know how I am—just not a chatterbox, I guess. So when he got going I just, well, drank my wine." She laughs. "God, that was a *lot* of wine."

Kyla feels a wave of rage surge through her. She can imagine the entire scene: Richard, squirming in his seat, trying desperately to get her mother to say something—anything—while she sat across from him, ignoring him and drinking like a fish.

And after Kyla had arranged everything! All her mother had to do was say thank you and be a little bit nice, but no. So much easier to ruin everything by not even trying.

Kyla leaps up. "What is *wrong* with you?"

Her mother looks at her as if she's just woken up, her eyes foggy. "What? What do you mean?"

"Maybe he was just nervous! Have you thought of that? What could he do when you just sat there guzzling wine and not saying anything? No kidding he talked about himself. What else was he supposed to do? Put on a puppet show?"

"But, honey . . ."

"You . . . You . . ." Kyla has a hard time getting the words out. "You don't care about me. You don't care about anything. You don't give a shit about my feelings! You never did."

Her mom's lower lip is quivering. It doesn't matter. Kyla grabs her jacket and lets the front door slam on her way out.

Christina.

He hasn't stopped thinking about her since the audition.

That look in her eyes as she gripped his hand, he knew it too well. It's haunted him. He has to talk to her. He looks her up in the online studio directory. Sits there tossing his cell from one hand to the other.

But she hardly knows him. What if he's just a random guy from dance to her? His heart is pounding.

Screw it, he has to find out one way or the other. He dials her number and waits for an answer. One ring, two— he's on the verge of hanging up when he hears a click.

"Hanson residence."

Christina's mother. Her voice has a hard edge. She might as well have said "Who's calling to disturb us?"

"Um, hi. This is Alex Borodin, from Christina's dance class."

"Hello." The woman's voice is completely deadpan.

"I, um, I was just wondering how Christina's feeling."

The woman emits a brief sigh. "Well, she's not well."

"What's wrong with her?"

"She's very tired."

"Could I speak with her?"

God! What is he thinking? Even if she does come to the phone, what would he say to her?

"She's *very* tired."

He feels almost relieved. "Yes, of course. I under-stand . . ."

Then, sounding uncertain, she continues, "But . . . I'll ask her if she's feeling up to it."

Alex swallows. "Uh, thank you."

He hears the sound of footsteps retreating. He can't believe this is happening! He hurriedly maps out a con-versation in his head. If he says "How are you feeling?" and she answers "So-so," then he'll say "I'm so sorry, but the important thing is for you to get some rest." And if she responds "I know, but right now everything just feels so hopeless," then he'll say "Don't think that way. You'll be back on your feet in no time . . . "

"Hello?" A high, gentle voice asks. Christina. His mouth is as dry as Kyla's faux desert.

"Hi. It's Alex."

"Oh, hi."

"How are you feeling?"

"So-so."

Crap, what was supposed to come next?

Silence. Then he hears himself ask, "What happened?"

"I don't know. I just fainted. I'm so tired, Alex."

I'm so tired, Alex. It sounds so intimate.

"That happens."

"Hmm."

Oh, God. He could kill himself. *That happens? Way to be supportive, dumbass.*

"I mean," he corrects himself quickly, "I mean, I feel like that too. All of the hysteria that comes with dancing— sometimes, I can't cope with it."

"What do you mean?"

He gulps. Does she really have no idea what he's talking about? "You just have to ask yourself if you really want to be part of all that. If it's worth it."

Whoa. That sounds so wise, like something he'd say to Kyla.

Christina doesn't have to think about her response. "I know what I want," she says. "I want it so much."

He hears sobbing. "Christina?"

"Maybe that's the thing. Maybe I want it *too* much."

His heart aches for her. "Don't cry, Christina. It'll be all right. You'll get stronger if you just rest."

"That's not it."

"What is it then?"

"The part. My mother said it was made for me." She cries, louder now. "Oh, God. She'll never forgive me. I'll never forgive myself."

> What am I going to do, Kyla? It's driving me crazy! Why can't our moms get that we're human beings, not some puppets they can use to act out scenes in the lives they want?
>
> I have to do something . . . I'm thinking, maybe I should quit dancing. I mean, I know I'm good, but how much of wanting to dance is my mother and how much is really me? I can't tell anymore. I'm not sure any of us at the studio really know—and I need to find out. I have to figure out what I want—on my own terms.

She's been wandering around for quite a while looking for the right address, but finally she's here, standing outside the door of a large house in the Hollywood hills.

She didn't know where else to go. The first person that came to mind was Alex, but of course, he's in Oakland.

She scoffs. Oakland—what good does *that* do her? It'd

probably turn out like Richard in the personal ad—perfect when you imagine it, but in reality, a totally different story.

It wasn't hard getting Lucas's address. She just called information, and the rest was cake. Now she's here in this fancy neighborhood, ringing the doorbell. The only lights on are upstairs. Maybe he's not here. But then she hears footsteps approaching and the door opens.

He looks out without seeming to see anything, expressionless, wearing really fashionable jeans and a T-shirt with a little logo on it. He's practically standing on her feet, he's so close. Then he breaks out into a smile.

She throws herself into his arms. Breathes his scent in deeply, curls into him like a small animal.

He invites her in and offers her a real cappuccino from a machine. He maneuvers around the kitchen nervously, asks if she wants cinnamon or cocoa on the foam. She shakes her head; she just wants *him*. No sign of his parents.

They don't drink their coffees. After a few sips she eases herself onto his lap and kisses him. He eases his hands beneath her shirt and she stops him, leans back, and pulls the whole thing over her head.

In seconds she can feel how much he wants her. He'd beg like a puppy now if she asked him to, and the thought nearly makes her laugh out loud. Every molecule in his body is focused on her, and she is in complete control.

He kisses her harder, pulls her closer. It's a little awkward and for a moment, he looks like he's going to say something. But she puts a finger on his lips. *Oh, no, don't talk, Lucas. Don't ruin it!*

She doesn't need to say it. He understands, does any-thing she wants him to. They're a perfect match.

He's going to get his bags. As he passes Andrei's room he hears a sound. The door is ajar. Anyone walking by can see what's going on in there, so he peeks in.

Andrei's lying next to Katy, leaning over her with his hand inside her sweater. *No way!* As they're kissing each other, his other hand pulls down the zipper on her pants, starts searching inside her jeans. *Dude!*

Alex is transfixed. It's like a porno in his own house . . . or what he imagines one to be like. It makes him think of Kyla. It feels like his whole body is calling out for her.

Wait—why is he thinking about Kyla and not Christina?

He turns his head. What is he doing? This is no better than those dorks who sit around at home and jerk off to the Internet. Actually, he's *worse*. And yet he can't move from where he's standing by the door.

"Sasha?"

That does it. His mother calls from downstairs, and he jumps. In a tenth of a second he's away from the doorway, pressed against the wall, holding his breath.

"Sasha! You are ready?" his mom yells. "We leave in ten minutes!"

A second later he hears Katy's voice. "Shut the door, Andrei!"

It closes with a thud. Alex sneaks slowly and silently into his room. He sits down on his bed and feels his pulse slowing and his breathing calming. Only the sense of loneliness remains—an ache deep inside him.

His door swings open and his mom is standing there. "What are you doing? You have packed your things, yes?"

Alex picks up his bag and heads downstairs. "I'm just going to go say good-bye to Toby. I'll meet you outside in five minutes."

There's a moving truck in front of Toby's place and the whole yard is full of furniture and boxes. Alex has a lump in his throat. He can't believe Toby's leaving already. Part of Alex feels he's being abandoned, left behind—alone again.

He spots Toby surrounded by armchairs, lugging a potted plant. Alex goes over to him. Toby sets the plant down on the ground.

"Hey," Alex says.

"Hi."

Alex knows his next line. This is where he's supposed to say "Good-bye, I'll miss you." But the words just won't come.

"So, um, you're leaving."

"Yup, I am."

"What's it like in Oregon?" Alex imagines the distance, for the first time really thinks about how far away Toby will be. "A, wet, B, rainy, C chilly, or D—"

"All of the above." Toby laughs quietly. "Yeah, D."

Alex offers a small smile in return. He wants Toby to understand that he's sad.

"Well, I guess all that's left is to say good-bye. I have to go. We're going to Los Angeles for the weekend."

Toby nods. "Okay."

Alex holds out his hand. Toby takes it. "We'll e-mail."

Toby nods. But they both know it won't be the same. They're letting each other go. Alex turns and slowly walks toward his parents' car. He feels the tears coming, doesn't understand why—it's not the end of the world. He tries to pull himself together for a few seconds. But then his legs stop as if on their own. Toby is still standing there watching him. Alex turns around and jogs back. He flings his arms around Toby's neck and buries his face in that old Toby jacket that's starting to be too short in the arms.

At first it's like hugging a floppy doll, but after a while he feels a response; Toby's arms steal around his body and hug him back.

"Yeah," Toby chuckles. "I'll miss you too."

Lucas comes and picks her up. He's standing outside the school when they emerge from the doors. *God,* he's so hot!

Kyla stands up straight, proud. Seeing him perks her up. Or is it having everyone else see him? She skips down the steps in front of Therese and Susanna and hurls herself into his arms. He kisses her deeply. His hands circle around her back and move down to her skirt.

"Now, now," she scolds. "Save that for later."

He lets her go, grinning like an unrepentant child.

"Jesus, get a room." Therese giggles. But a second later she and Susanna fawn all over Lucas. They want to ride in his car and ask him thousands of questions. It's embarrassing, how ridiculous they can be.

Kyla's feeling indulgent, so they get a ride from him today. Susanna jumps up and down; she's never been in a Porsche.

Therese is cooler. "This is awesome."

The music is booming. They sit in the back and push at each other, each of them trying to stick her head between the front seats. "Oh, you have a built-in MP3 player! That is so cool!"

But how is it that he has time to pick her up so often? Kyla wonders. He's going to school full-time; he must have a hefty course load.

She's asked him about it, but he brushes aside her questions: "Don't worry, baby. *You're* my first priority."

It bugs her when he says stuff like that. But why? Isn't this exactly what she wanted?

Her mom is back in her own little world, lying in bed again. But Kyla doesn't care anymore. Lucas drives her to Santa Monica and takes her to expensive fusion restaurants and comes home with her and lies there in her bed smoking one cigarette after another. Her mom has only said hi to him briefly. Kyla told him that her mom works nights and has to sleep during the day—that's why she's always tired.

Kyla looks out the window. A billboard with a woman in a ballet outfit sweeps past—she only eats I Can't Believe It's Not Butter. The picture makes her think of Alex. It's been a while since she wrote to him. Of course, she thinks about him almost every day, but lately when she feels the need for someone, she just turns to Lucas. They don't exactly *talk,* but Kyla can't let that matter.

After her mom's online dating debacle, the whole Alex thing has seemed more and more impossible. What hope was there that their friendship could survive if they'd never even meet each other in person? And what would be the point of having a friend who couldn't actually *be there* when you need him?

Therese laughs loudly at something Lucas says. She only laughs like that when there are guys around. "But anyway, you can't go to Kyla's tonight because it's *girls' night!*"

Girls' night? Did she really agree to that?

Lucas smiles wryly. "Girls' night? Well then I'm definitely coming."

"We won't let you in," Therese assures.

"What do you guys do at those things anyway?" Lucas asks. His hand reaches across the seat and finds Kyla's upper thigh. "Tickle fights? Stress-relieving massage?"

Kyla gives an exaggerated sigh. "We take quizzes from trashy magazines and try out eye shadow." She pauses. "You should be glad to get out of it."

It's quiet in the car. Kyla feels her friends glaring at the back of her head.

Lucas glances at her and smiles. It's the two of them now, the two in the front seat, the ones who are a little more mature. Kyla turns her head to look at the children in the back and asks, "What's so special about girls' night?"

No response. She knows what they're thinking. That she's uptight and full of herself and her *relationship,* and not being a good friend. That she thinks she's all that since she got together with Lucas.

Therese is going to talk behind her back even more now, maybe even spread rumors about her at school.

Oh, Kyla will sleep with anybody as long as he's a little older.
She doesn't care about her friends once she meets a guy.

Blah, blah, blah. She's heard it all before. Still, someone has to be grown-up in her life.

"Hello?" Kyla says cheerfully. "I was kidding! We're going to have a blast."

They look at her distrustfully.

"I mean it. The only downside is that we have to do it at my place. Couldn't we go to your house instead, Therese?"

"Your place is best. You know that. Your mom doesn't give a crap what we do."

Kyla turns to face the road. Therese doesn't mince words.

Alex gets the window seat. His mother insists—as if he were five years old and really, really wanted it. But whatever.

The three of them sit in a row. The trip will only take an

hour and twenty minutes, according to the voice over the PA system. He's only an hour and twenty minutes away from Kyla. He's never thought about it like that before, that they're so close to each other. The flight attendant shows them where the exits are and explains that a lighting system along the aisle will direct them in the event of an emergency.

His mother and father are beaming, their chests puffed up with pride. They enjoy being able to afford this. Being able to take a plane from Oakland to L.A.—that's luxury. They used to drive. He used to live in the backseat of the car with Andrei and Nina, until Andrei got older and was able to get out of it and Nina began to just flat-out refuse. Alex wonders, How long until *he* gets out of it too?

Alex's mom holds his hand as the plane takes off, as though that's something they do in their family, touch each other all the time. He looks down at the San Francisco bay, which is little and getting smaller, while Kyla is getting closer and closer.

He hasn't been sure, but now it seems obvious, even required, that he find her. He takes out her picture. He's ashamed of the way he printed it to carry with him because, seriously, how *lame.*

"Who is this?" his mom asks.

Alex blushes and tries to stuff the picture back into his pocket.

"Who is this?" she repeats. "Is this someone you know?"

"Yes, *it's someone I know.*"

His mom refuses to give up, snatching the photo and looking at Kyla. She raises her eyebrows. "Hmm."

"What do you mean 'hmm'?"

"This is quite a girl. Who is she?"

He tries to yank the picture out of her hand. "Give it back!"

His father is distracted by the bickering. "What is happening over here? Why are you arguing?"

"We're not arguing," Alex says.

"Alex has a picture of a girl, but he won't tell who she is."

His father looks at him in surprise and then at the picture. "Maybe she is the one he's been e-mailing. Is this her, Alex?"

Alex sighs, irritated. "Maybe."

"Oh, her." His mom sounds sulky, as if she's jealous. She examines the picture again. "Now I understand why she seems familiar. She looks like Andrei's Katy."

His father studies Kyla and doesn't seem to approve of what he sees. "Yes, it's true. She's very similar."

"She is not!" Alex protests. "They're completely different!"

His mom just looks at him, astonished. "Why do you say this? There's no reason to make a fuss. The resemblance is very clear. They're both equally . . . swanky."

"*Swanky?* What does that mean?"

"You know." She shifts in her seat. "I am sure you can see what kind of a girl she is. Is this really someone for you?"

Not *swanky,* Alex realizes. *Skanky.*

He bristles on Kyla's behalf. His mom doesn't know her. And when they finally do meet, she'll eat her words.

Kyla lugs along the beer that Lucas bought, and the can of Pringles and Milk Duds—Therese's favorite candy. *I have to be nice to Therese and Susanna tonight. I have to try!*

She made Lucas go home. He was pouting when she said good-bye, and she had to promise seventeen times that they would see each other tomorrow and several evenings next week. Sometimes she doesn't get him. What did he do before he met her? Didn't he have a life?

She takes the elevator up. Before it comes to a stop, she sees Elizabeth standing there, waiting to go down. Elizabeth in tall boots with a helmet and a riding crop under her arm. Kyla is surprised. Elizabeth dressed to go horseback riding? Doesn't she play the cello or something else geeky? Of course, at *this* moment she has to be carrying a case of Budweiser.

They stare at each other. Elizabeth looks down. As if she finds it embarrassing to be caught in her riding clothes. Kyla's glad for the reprieve, though she knows the embarrassment should go the other way.

The clothes look brand-new. The boots are gleaming. Is today her first lesson? Kyla wants to put down her party fare and go to riding class—yes, even with Elizabeth. That's how much she wants to break free, how little she wants to have girls' night with Susanna and Therese, how little she wants to go into the apartment and see her mom lying there, drenching her pillow in drool.

Kyla gets out of the elevator. Elizabeth gets in. Her riding crop brushes against Kyla's arm as she passes.

Alex is sitting in the backseat in between his mother and father. Vladik and Eva, who picked them up from the airport, are sitting in front. Vladik speaks quickly, probably telling childhood tales about his dad. The mood is upbeat, exhilarated. Everyone is speaking loudly in Russian and laughing. Alex understands what they're saying, but he doesn't speak much Russian himself. What would be the point? He's lived in California his whole life.

They're so happy! Yes, even his dad—his face is relaxed and animated and full of laughter. Maybe he's bored at home, where nothing ever happens. His parents don't have many friends. Just like him, Alex realizes.

Alex sits quietly and looks out the window at Los Angeles. He is struck by how it seems just like San Francisco with less hills, even though L.A. is two or three times as big. He hadn't been expecting that at all, that it would feel so familiar. So what *did* he expect? Maybe that her world would be different, something he had never experienced? But it feels just the same. As if their lives could be intertwined without much difficulty at all.

Her mom appears as if out of nowhere, standing in the doorway of the kitchen with her tired, shifty eyes. "Hi."

"What are you doing here?" Kyla hears how harsh she sounds. She feels her hard gaze destroying her mother.

"I'm sorry to interrupt. I mean, um, I'm heading to my room."

"Good."

Her mom looks even worse than usual. And to top off the nasty hair, she has a canker sore. Kyla, on the other hand, is the pinnacle of perfection. She's spritzed herself in trendy perfume and is wearing a new dress her dad sent her from New York. She continues her preparations at the kitchen counter: dumping the chips and chocolate candy into bowls, getting out ashtrays and glasses. She takes a beer out of the fridge and opens it with a hiss, making a show of it for her mom. She swallows big swigs and sets the can down with a slam.

Her mom watches her uncertainly. "Are you going out tonight, honey?"

"Does it look like I am?"

"No . . ." She's *so* cautious, walking on eggshells. "Is someone coming over? Maybe Lucas?"

"*No!* Do I have to spend all my time with him?"

Then there's silence. Kyla gets out a tray and arranges everything on it. She lights a cigarette, sticks it in the corner of her mouth, and strolls past her mother and off into her room. She sets the tray down on the desk and then hears footsteps behind her. But before her mom gets to the door, Kyla slams it shut. She turns on the stereo and Madonna fills the room.

The door opens cautiously. Her mom's face is troubled.

"You're supposed to knock!"

Her mom says something. Kyla groans and turns down the volume.

"What?"

"I knocked."

"And?"

Her mom looks as if she's about to cry now. Kyla doesn't want to go there, not right now, but it hurts so much to see her mom like this.

"Was there something you wanted?"

"I was thinking . . ."

"Yes?"

"I was thinking about what you said. About moving to New York to live with your dad full-time. I mean, after you said you *wanted* to stay, now I can't imagine the thought, I can't bear . . . I do actually have custody of you, you can't just . . ." She sounds so scared, her whole body is shaking.

A part of Kyla wants to throw her arms around her mom and say, "Mom, you know I would never leave. How could I?" But someone else inside her wants the opposite.

"Actually, I can. If Social Services finds out about you. I just haven't made up my mind yet." Kyla turns away and cranks up the volume.

His parents and their friends get all dressed up. His mom's makeup has reached critical mass, a mark of how meaningful this evening is. She's wrapped in a sparkly gown. This is Olga Borodin at her best, on her way to a party in glamorous L.A. She's assured him twelve times that tomorrow night they'll see *Swan Lake*.

Alex sneaks a peek at Eva, who's giggling as she puts her earrings on in front of the mirror—a plain Jane by comparison.

"Excuse me, but do you have a phone book?" Alex asks before they leave. He knows they don't have a computer, but the old-fashioned way might still work. "I'm thinking about ordering some pizza."

"Just in the drawer beneath the microwave," Eva says.

Eva asks for the third time if Alex has everything he needs. He assures her that he'll have a great time watching TV. "The cable must be better in Los Angeles than it is at home, right?" They laugh and head out. Alex goes into the kitchen. There are bags of corn chips and Russian candy out for him on the counter.

He looks up "B" in the phone book and starts systematically going through all the Billingses in Los Angeles. One of them must be Kyla, that's all there is to it. And it works! After two pages full of Billingses, he finds it: Marie and Kyla Billings.

Now he's not sure what to do. In all his daydreams about this trip, he never really played through this scene. He flips open his cell. The numbers on the keypad are blurry. He puts his finger on the three anyway. His heart is pounding. He's sweating. Blushing even.

Slowly he folds up his phone again and opens the chips. Mechanically he stuffs them into his mouth and chews like a motor, without tasting anything.

"Hiiiiii!" Susanna and Therese squeal.

They greet Kyla by kissing her first on one cheek, then the other. They look around curiously; it's been a long time since they were here. Kyla has cleaned and straightened up. She aired the place out all afternoon. Does it still smell like sickness? They peer into the apartment.

"So where's your mom?" Therese asks.

"In her room. She doesn't want to be disturbed."

Therese and Susanna exchange knowing looks. Therese stops outside Kyla's mom's bedroom door. "What do you mean? Is she still sick or something?"

"No, she's not." Kyla pulls Therese along by the arm to keep her moving, but Therese resists.

"Well, it seems like we ought to at least say hello."

Susanna nods in agreement. "Yeah, I haven't seen your mom in ages."

Kyla feels the panic spreading through her body. What are they doing?

"I said don't bother her!"

Therese quickly pulls her hand back from the doorknob. Kyla knows her mom heard every word, but that's no big deal. She waves her friends along and they head off to her room, where she shuts the door behind them. She opens a beer to win herself a little time. Chugs it down until she feels like she might be sick, then lights a cigarette. She hands beers to Therese and Susanna, who are eagerly awaiting an explanation. Kyla takes a deep drag and slowly exhales.

"She's doing yoga," Kyla says. "That's her latest thing."

They make faces like they've never heard of yoga.

"Anyway, she has to have quiet while she's doing it because she concentrates like crazy. She goes nuts if you disturb her."

Will that satisfy them?

Susanna giggles and says, "Parents do the weirdest things."

Therese looks pensive. "Maybe my mom needs that," she says. "Her job always has her running around like a whirlwind to meetings and stuff."

Kyla laughs and says, "You should tell her about it."

Then the subject is forgotten. Therese pulls out a lemonade bottle full of malt liquor and the party begins. Kyla cracks open another beer. Maybe girls' night isn't such a bad thing.

There's one of those homicide investigation shows on. Gritty New York cops grab life by the balls as they solve the case. Nothing scares them.

And here sits the wimpiest guy in California, sitting on a couch pigging out in an exciting city full of opportunities. He's disgusted with himself. How can he be such a coward? Andrei and Nina both do what they want. And Kyla only lives a little ways away. Maybe she's sitting at home alone too, and would like nothing more than to see him.

He opens his phone again. It's make or break time. *Just do it.*

They're clicking through the pictures from Christopher's party, laughing at all the drunk shots and complimenting each other's outfits. Therese has the mouse; she spends an extra-long while at a picture of her and Jake. In it, Kyla's glad to see Jake is smiling. Maybe there's hope for the two of them after all? Kyla's about to ask what happened, when Susanna grabs the mouse away and clicks to the end of the album.

"Whoa! Who do we have here?"

"Let me see." Kyla turns back to the computer. It's the picture of Alex. She totally forgot she downloaded it and stuck it with the party photos. She feels a twinge in her heart, embarrassed.

God, that wry smile of his. She misses him more than she wants to admit. But maybe that's just the alcohol.

Susanna doesn't give up. "Well, hello? Let's hear it."

Therese double clicks the picture and suddenly Alex fills the whole screen. "He's cute!"

Kyla raises an eyebrow. "You think so?"

Therese stares at her in surprise. "Hey, you're blushing! Susanna, look! Kyla looks like a tomato."

"Shut up. I do not!"

Susanna looks delighted. "So who is it? Why didn't you tell us you have a secret guy on the side?"

"Hello? I can't have anyone *on the side*. Lucas and I are a couple!"

"Okay, but then who is this?" Therese prods. "A *lov-ah*?

You have to tell us so we won't think you're being unfaithful or something."

Kyla concentrates. She takes a drink from Therese's lemonade bottle. The alcohol makes her shiver. What does it matter if they know?

"It's this guy I used to e-mail."

"Get out!!!" Susanna squeals. "What do you mean? Did you meet him, like, on Facebook or something?"

"In a chat room."

"No way!" Therese's mouth is hanging open in a big oval.

"But why didn't you say anything?" Susanna asks.

"I don't know. I guess it didn't seem that important." Suddenly Kyla realizes that they're jealous. In their eyes, of course it's cool to e-mail a cute guy.

Therese's eyes are glued to Kyla. "Watch out, he's probably a sex maniac or a pedophile or something."

Kyla can't help but laugh. "Alex is *hardly* a sex maniac."

"What do you mean?"

"He's . . ." Kyla hesitates. She doesn't really want to rat Alex out, it feels wrong. But what does it matter? He'll never find out. "He's never done it before."

Therese's eyes widen. "Wait." She studies the photo again. "He's a virgin? *This* guy? I don't believe it."

Kyla gives a quick summary of Alex while her friends sit there listening in amazement. They ask a ton of questions. She answers as little as possible, just enough to make them even more interested.

"So what kind of person is he?" Susanna wonders. "Is he a bad boy or, like, a jock or what?"

Kyla tries to think it over before she answers, but the alcohol is definitely starting to take its toll, and it's getting harder and harder to keep secrets.

"You're not going to believe it."

"What?" they answer simultaneously.

"He dances ballet."

Therese looks disapproving. "Isn't that sort of lame?"

Susanna shrugs her shoulders. "It could be cool, I guess."

"Don't you think that seems a little, well . . . like there's something wrong with him?" Therese's comment sucks all the warmth from the room.

"No. He seems totally normal to me."

"A virgin who dances ballet? Sorry, honey, but he's gay. Totally. One hundred percent."

Kyla stares at Alex's picture.

"Oh, dear." Therese's tone oozes faux-sympathy. "You didn't think he was *interested*, did you?"

Susanna laughs, stuffs a Pringle into her mouth. "Oh my God! Kyla! How does it feel to be a fag hag?"

Kyla scowls. Why did she have to talk about Alex? Why did she think she could be honest?

The landline rings. Irritated, she snaps, "This is Kyla!"

Her voice is so different from how he'd imagined. It's dark and powerful, with a commanding presence. Alex can't get a single word out.

"Hello?" Kyla urges.

This isn't working. What if she isn't . . .

"Lucas? Is that you?"

Lucas? Who's Lucas? She's never written about a Lucas.

"Asshole," Kyla says. And then there's a click.

No damage done. Now he knows she's home anyway. He stuffs the keys into his pocket and heads out the door.

Therese and Susanna have tried on almost everything in her closet. Kyla generously lends them everything they think is cute just to improve the mood a little. It works. Even Therese hugs Kyla tight and squeals, "God, you're so sweet!"

All is well again in their little corner of the world, and all it took was a few shiny objects to distract them. Now it feels like it used to, like they really have been close since Mrs. Olsen's fifth grade.

"You guys, I have to tell you something." Kyla swallows pointedly, picking at her green painted nails. "It's weird that you don't know. But, it's really hard to talk about."

Her friends nod somberly. Kyla takes her time.

"Well, you know, about my mom . . . " She stops. Should she really? Yeah. "My mom is, well, she's *depressed.*"

They both nod slowly. It's too late to take it back.

"Not the these-jeans-don't-fit-anymore kind of depressed. The doesn't-get-out-of-bed-ever kind."

"Oh crap," Susanna says, exhaling. "Poor you."

"Is it really bad?" Therese wonders. "Is she, like, *clinically* depressed?"

Kyla nods. "It feels that way, yeah." They hug her tight. Kyla's eyes well up.

"But promise not to tell anyone," she mumbles, a little choked up. "Please . . ."

They promise.

Therese looks at her tenderly. "I want to give you something," she says. She digs around in her bag and takes out a cigarette. "It's from my brother, actually, but now it's yours."

Then Kyla realizes that Therese is holding out a joint. Susanna puts it together herself and squeals with delight. They've smoked a few times before, with Adam and Jake and that crew, but not regularly.

Smoking pot in the house—yikes! What would her mom think . . . ?

Kyla scowls. *Her mom wouldn't* think *anything.* She tosses Therese the lighter. "Well, what are you waiting for?"

He's sitting on the bus as if he's done it a million times. No one seems to think he looks out of place. A group of guys about his age are messing around with each other, but they don't pay any attention to Alex. He hops off and starts walking, emerging on a street where taxis are ferrying people back and forth and the restaurants are close together. He asks for directions. The building is only three blocks away. *Kyla is three blocks from him.*

He makes his way there, asking one more time before he finds the residential street and then counting his way along to number 8236. He stops outside the main entrance of a big glass and steel building. He looks up at the windows. Kyla is in there somewhere, inside one of them.

Through the wide glass panes he can see a doorman sitting at a desk near the elevators. Alex freezes in place. *This* he hadn't counted on. Should he just stroll up, like he knows what he's doing? *Evening, my good man. Just going up to pay a visit to Miss Billings.*

He looks down at his now-sweaty palm. Yeah, that won't work. He needs a code to get in. He punches in some random numbers and then stands outside for a good ten minutes without knowing what to do. But then a girl his own age approaches. She's wearing some old-fashioned outfit, made for horse polo or something. Her hair hangs like a curtain, covering one of her eyes. They look at each other. She reaches for the code box, but then stops as if waiting for an explanation. He gets nervous.

"I'm, um, going in to meet a friend," Alex says.

"Who?" She doesn't sound suspicious, more like curious.

"Does it matter?" He tries to be hard, mysterious, but immediately backpedals. "Um, Kyla Billings?"

The girl looks surprised. "Kyla? I know her. She's my neighbor."

Alex nods and gestures to the box. But she still won't budge.

"How do you know each other?"

"What?"

"Excuse me for asking, it's just that I've never seen you here before."

"No, I don't live in Los Angeles."

She smiles. "I can tell. So are you a relative or something?"

"Not really." He doesn't want to say anything more. She begins to poke in the code. The door opens and he tries to nudge past her, but she won't have it.

"I'm afraid I can't just let any old person in. You can't even tell me who you are."

"I . . . " The eye that's not hidden by her bangs squints, sizing him up. "We met in a chat room."

The girl's pink lips fall open in surprise. "Really?" she asks. "That's cool."

He shrugs, flustered but triumphant. She pushes her bangs behind her ear and holds open the door expectantly.

Madonna strikes a sluggish pose, swaying and shaking her hips, gyrating sensually for her audience. She flips her hair back and flies her arms slowly through the air, dancing a bit like she's swimming. Although she's got to look ridiculous, she enjoys the rapt attention of her fans.

They sit on the bed clapping to the beat. They cheer and sway, and Madonna is starting to feel dizzy. Her head is spinning and her body feels heavy. She collapses onto the bed and joins her audience. They explode in laughter. They laugh for several minutes even though they don't know what they're laughing at—everything is just super-hilarious. Especially when Susanna says she has to pee. They're writhing with laughter. *Pee*—what a funny word! In the middle of their giggle fit Kyla hears ringing and slowly comes back to reality. It's the door buzzer. It must be Lucas, back even when she told him to scram for the night. Who else?

Kyla sobers up and turns down the music. It wouldn't be good if he saw how wild things got here at these girls' nights—something tells her he wouldn't approve. She shushes Therese and Susanna, whose grins are so wide, they're threatening to break again. She can hardly hold herself together either, but she has to: Lucas cannot know they were smoking.

She looks sternly at the giggle twins on the bed. "Now, you guys stay in here! Do not come out. Promise me!"

A new explosion of laughter.

"Shhh!"

Kyla steps out into the hallway on unsteady legs. Her walk to the front door is long and wobbly. She hangs on to the wall as she makes her way down the hall. The buzzer rings again. Stupid Lucas, why can't he stay away for a single night?

She yanks open the door.

The girl peers at him, seems to snicker. As if he were interrupting something. She's leaning against the wall. Her pants hang off her hips, a pierced belly button is visible between her waistband and her top. Her hair is long and wild. There are beads on some of the strands of her hair. She's even more beautiful live than he'd imagined, if that was possible.

Those eyes. What are they saying? He raises his hand in greeting, cheerfully, trying to project a calm that's ready to break any second. "Hi."

She doesn't respond. *Is this really Kyla?*

"Alex," he clarifies. Her eyes widen immediately, but she stands there as if frozen. Her mouth opens slowly, but then closes again. He feels the panic spreading through him.

"Um, I was . . . Well, not me," Alex falters. "My parents were coming to Los Angeles to meet some people and they dragged me along to go to the ballet, but tonight they're out and anyway since I'm here I thought, well, I mean, I found your address . . ."

She doesn't do anything. Doesn't even say hello. They're strangers. Maybe Kyla has a secret twin, one who *wouldn't* be happy to see him?

She hates her head. She can't think, can't talk. And her body won't do anything until her head asks it to. *Oh my God.* This

196

is Alex standing in front of her, *her* Alex. He's a little shorter than she thought, but otherwise everything matches.

There's so much she wants to say, so much she wants to ask: What is he doing here? Why? She only saw his mouth moving, doesn't know what he said.

She has to find out if he's real. Now. Slowly she reaches out and takes his hand. Yes, he *is* real. She pulls him toward her into the apartment and closes the door. Then they stand there facing each other in the hallway, hand in hand. She wants to cry. She has no idea why. And her head is spinning. She tries to smile at him, really wants him to understand how glad she is, but the tears come instead.

"I'm sorry," she sobs. "I don't know what my deal is. Sorry I'm so weird right now."

His Kyla is standing there in front of him sobbing, wiping her nose on the back of her hand as if she were three. What does this mean? He puts his arm around her, it just happens. She smiles through her tears. It doesn't matter at all that she's a supermodel with a piercing. He laughs.

"Well, this was weird. . . ."

"Yeah, it sure was." Kyla laughs.

Then he smells it and pulls back instinctively. Right away he understands why everything is so muddled. She's wasted. She must have had quite a lot, to judge from how confused she seems. She looks at him, her eyes scared.

He hears a sound from inside the apartment. Two figures appear. "What's taking you so long, Kyla?" one wonders.

Kyla turns to them quickly. She yells, her voice harsh. "I said you were supposed to stay in my room!"

"Yeah, but who is it?" the other girl asks.

The catastrophe is unavoidable. She really wants to explain to Alex, explain what happened tonight, tell him that she doesn't always . . . Suggest that they could meet tomorrow. But there's no time, no chance.

Her friends are standing there staring like idiots.

"Hey, aren't you . . . ?" Therese begins. "Isn't that him, perverted e-mail guy?"

Susanna bursts out laughing. "No way! It *is* him! What is he doing here?"

"Go away!" Kyla tries pushing Therese and Susanna. They resist, laughing the whole time.

"But he doesn't *look* gay." Susanna giggles. "He's really cute."

"Come on. Let's take him back to the bedroom!" Therese can't contain herself. "We'll turn him straight!"

"Knock it off!" Kyla pleads.

She makes one last attempt to push them on their way, and then gives up. She just can't do it anymore. Alex looks baffled. And hurt. Therese takes his hand and tries to drag him back toward the bedroom.

"Come on, big boy! We need a guy to have a little fun

with." And then she stops. "Oh, *right*! You've never done it before!"

Kyla sinks down onto the floor, her hands over her face.

"There's no need to be afraid. We'll be nice to you. Won't we, Suze?"

"Oh, yeah!"

Kyla's going to die. Alex will never speak to her again. She hears his voice say, "Cut it out!"

"Cut it out!" Therese mocks.

"Chill out, dude, we're just messing with you!"

Therese falls into another fit of laughter. Susanna hangs on to her, barely able to stand up. Nothing else can be heard besides bubbling laughter. Then something remarkable happens: Kyla can't stop herself. Something is boiling inside her, like the carbonation in a bottle of soda, and soon her whole body is shaking. The laughter is so intense, it's almost violent as it seems to explode from her pores.

"STOP!!!" a voice screams.

He just hears the voice. He doesn't know where it comes from. The girls shut up immediately. He makes out a woman in a nightgown a bit behind them. She looks exhausted and insane. Insane with anger.

Kyla is slumped on the floor, hands still covering her features. Only small giggles erupt from her, the aftermath of her laughing fit. She doesn't look up at him.

I didn't say anything before I left, but IT'S ALL SCREAMING INSIDE ME. So I'm going to say it now. Fuck you. And your friends. Maybe it's just as well that I found out who you really are. That you're a deceitful, spiteful bitch who talks about people behind their backs and betrays their trust. Even with all the crap I take at school, I have never felt as bad as you made me feel. You're pathetic. I don't know if I hate you. I just know that you're not a friend. You're not good enough for me. This is good–bye.

🖱

Her mother is sitting across from her. That look she's giving her, it's so serious.

Kyla slept at Lucas's place to avoid just the kind of look her mom is giving her now—to elude phrases like Alex's: *You're pathetic* . . . She just ran last night, away from her mom's anger, and the echoes of her own ridiculous laughter, just calling home briefly to say where she was.

Now she's finishing her coffee and getting up to leave.

"Kyla. We need to talk."

"I have a test tomorrow."

"It will wait. I have a couple of things to say."

Kyla makes a face and sinks back down onto the chair.

Her mom doesn't know where to start. She sits there

fidgeting with her fingers. Her lower lip moves as she thinks.

"I know that you guys were smoking. I know *what* you were smoking." She looks right into Kyla's eyes with a look that says everything—a look that is penetrating and not to be defied. "I don't approve. But then, neither do you, when you think about it."

Her mom fidgets a little with the edge of the tablecloth and then goes in for a new attack. "You know that you and your friends were horrible. And I'm not just talking about the drugs."

Kyla winces. As if she didn't already know what a bitch she was. As if she hadn't spent every second since being tormented by the memories from that night. As if it hadn't taken all her energy this morning just to get out of bed.

"The way you treated that boy, it really makes me wonder . . ." Her mother pauses. "You're not like that, Kyla. Not really. Maybe Therese and Susanna aren't the best influence."

Kyla lifts her chin, defiant. "You don't get to pick my friends."

But her mom doesn't back down. She raises her voice. The words flow fast and heated. "You should never do things you don't want to do. I know that it's hard to break patterns, especially ones you've been in for a long time. But if you're not being true to yourself, then there's really no other choice."

Kyla raises an eyebrow. "What is that? Did you finally seek out some kind of self-help consultation?"

"At least now you know how I feel."

Kyla feels her head spinning. Has the whole world turned upside down? How did she get to a place where *her* mother, the most pathetic and pitiable person she knows, is lecturing *her* on her behavior?

The words from Alex's e-mail echo in her head. Oh, yeah. She's the pathetic one now.

Kyla tries to ward off her mother's sad, disapproving stare. "Just so you know, I'm not planning to go live with Dad. But I can't live like this anymore. So I'm moving in with Lucas instead."

Alex runs into Henning in the dressing room. Henning's whole body lights up, even his fingers stretch happily. "Alex!" he calls.

There must be a good reason for Henning to look so happy, even though Alex can't think of one right now.

"Hi."

An apologetic look comes over Henning's face. "I hope you're not bummed."

"About?"

"I got the part!" Henning is bouncing on the balls of his feet with excitement. He's obviously more thrilled than gloating. Alex can't find it in him to be disappointed, or jealous. Henning worked hard. He deserved his success.

"Congratulations." Alex offers a high five. "I really mean it."

"Thanks, man."

They go into the studio together, where Paulina is waiting for them.

"Henning got the part," Alex announces, being generous. Paulina looks at him for a second, surprised, then turns to Henning and congratulates him. Then she gets serious again and looks out at the class.

"I have some bad news."

It's Christina. Alex knows it, even before Paulina manages to say her name.

"Christina is not doing very well. She's in the hospital."

Murmuring. Then Paulina suggests that they send a bouquet of flowers. She asks if there are any volunteers to deliver them. Henning and Alex are fastest. Paulina hesitates. "She's only up to one visitor at a time."

"Alex can do it," Henning offers, smiling. Now that he has the part, is it okay for Alex to get the girl?

Henning dances like a god for a whole hour. Just watching him gives Alex the energy to do his best. It's been a long time since he enjoyed dancing. It lasts a few minutes. Then he thinks about Kyla again.

Paulina grabs him on his way out. "That part should really have been yours, Alex."

"I tried."

"Not hard enough. Henning is very good, but he doesn't have your gift."

Alex looks away. "It doesn't matter. I guess I screwed up."

"*Why* did you screw up?"

He shrugs. Paulina reaches for his arm so he won't run off. "You're not taking your dancing seriously."

He feels the blood rush into his cheeks. What right does she have to interfere? As long as he's paying tuition and is good *enough,* why should she care?

"I didn't want the part!"

"*The part* is not what this is about," she insists, her eyes boring into him. "I see what's going on inside you. Believe me, I understand. But think about it, Alex, that's all I want to say. It's not so easy if you want to come back in a few years."

He tears himself away from her and practically runs out the door.

They've apologized a thousand times for the whole thing with Alex. They actually seem honestly ashamed—which, of course, they should be. Kyla shouldn't forgive them, but she's weak right now. They're all she has. Them and Lucas. She hasn't called her mom since she went to Lucas's place five days ago, and she knows that that's wrong too. She looks down into her cup. The shape in the foam reminds her of old Gypsy ladies who like to read tea leaves. Sigh . . . what would her non-fat foam foretell, exactly?

"So . . . what are you saying? That you're, like, living there with him? For real?" Susanna's eyes are wide.

"I'm not sure. I'm not sure of anything anymore."

"Don't worry." Therese takes over. "I totally get it. I want to move out too. All my parents do is fight and get on my case about how often I go out." She gets up for more silver tea.

Susanna moves her chair closer to Kyla's and whispers in her ear, "So, do you guys have sex all the time?"

Kyla rolls her eyes. "No, we don't."

"But every night, right?"

"Not exactly."

Susanna looks disappointed. "But what do his parents say about your being there?"

"They don't really know. He has the whole upstairs to himself."

She hears how it sounds. Like a dream. But it isn't. She isn't happy at all.

"No way! They must be filthy rich!"

"I guess." Either way, it doesn't impress her the way it seems to impress Susanna.

Therese comes back with her water. "So, have we invited everyone?"

Susanna is instantly nervous. She's having a party on Friday. They've been planning it for ages. Her parents are going out of town and taking Michael with them.

"I think so."

"Kyla, did you tell all the guys?"

Kyla nods, wishing Therese would have taken some initiative. She's never going to get the guy without the pursuit. "*Jake* is coming. But Lucas can't. He's going to some kind of *guys' night.*" She makes a face, trying and failing to push away the image of Alex at her front door.

"Dude, that sucks," Susanna answers immediately, clearly

not getting the reference. Therese is disappointed too. "And here I was thinking he could bring his hot older friends!"

"Afraid not."

"Then, Suze, you've got to take a chance and invite some people we don't know already."

Susanna is uneasy. "I don't know. I don't want there to be too many people."

The door to the café opens and Elizabeth's boyfriend, Erik, walks in with a buddy.

Thank you, God. Thank you, thank you that Elizabeth isn't with them.

Erik nods at Kyla, who nods back.

"Him!" Therese hisses. "Let's invite him! Go for it, Kyla!"

Kyla shakes her head. "Do it yourself."

"I don't know him."

"So what?"

Silence. Everyone reaches for their cups. Therese sets hers down on the table decisively and gets up. "You've got to try new shit sometimes!"

Kyla and Susanna watch her in surprise. She goes over to the guys' table with a stiff smile and engages in a few minutes of nervous conversation. When she comes back, she's glowing.

"They're coming."

"That was crazy!" Susanna squeals.

"He asked if he could bring Elizabeth too."

Kyla stands up, startled. "Are you insane?"

Therese backs up. "Take it easy. I did it for you."

"For *me*? What are you talking about?"

"I just gave us the chance of a lifetime. At the party, you can finally get back at her!"

He can't shake the thought of Kyla. She follows him everywhere. The images of her, his *friend,* who took his hand and smiled through her tears. Then the drunk, cruel girl who laughed at him—the two-faced bitch. He can't reconcile the two. The best and worst in the same person. He tries to banish her from his brain, but stubbornly she sticks around, even now as he's on his way to see Christina.

She's lying in a hospital room with her parents on either side of her. Her mother, always so cool and collected, is completely discombobulated. Her face is gentle and unsettled with worry. Her movements are disjointed, her eyes full of apprehension. Christina's father sits in a plastic chair like a statue, as if locked inside himself. Christina herself is hardly recognizable. Her long hair is spread out, covering the whole pillow. Her face is pale and doll-like with dark shadows under her eyes. There's a needle in one of her arms that's channeling clear liquid into her veins.

Not even her eyes move—it's like she's Sleeping Beauty, nearly dead for hundreds of years, and just waiting for her Prince Charming to arrive and dazzle her awake.

Alex quickly scolds himself for the fantasy. He stands there with yellow roses in one hand and his bag of sweaty dance clothes in the other. He could still turn around and leave—they haven't noticed him yet. But then her mom glances up.

"Oh, Alex!" She gazes hopefully at Christina. "Alex is here, your friend from dance class!"

Christina turns her face toward him in slow motion. He fumbles with the paper around the flowers as he walks over to her. She smiles a shy Christina smile. He smiles back.

"Sorry it's so late, but I came straight here."

He gets the paper off and holds out the bouquet.

"Here," Alex says. "They're from everybody."

She can't even lift her arm to take them.

"Thanks."

Her mother takes the flowers and goes to look for a vase. Her father stands up and takes Alex's hand. There's something terrifying about him. His handshake is dry and firm.

"Maybe my wife and I should wait outside?" Alex is about to say that it's all right, he won't be staying, but Christina beats him to it.

"Yeah, thanks, Dad."

And then they're alone. He sits down on a chair next to the bed. Neither of them knows who's going to speak first. Christina's mother comes back and sets the vase on the nightstand, then hurries out. Then they're on their own again. There's so much he wants to ask, but he hasn't prepared anything. She takes charge of the situation.

"Tell me *everything*!"

"What do you mean?"

She looks at him expectantly. "Tell me about class, what you guys practiced."

For some reason, he can't think of anything.

The he remembers something. "Henning got the part."

Christina's mouth hangs open. Then she looks down at the covers. Her cheeks turn pink. "I thought it would be you and me."

The idea that she thought about him feels unreal.

"I sucked." He looks at her hands resting, thin and white, on top of the covers. The needle is attached to her skin with a piece of tape. His eyes linger over her tiny, thin arms; it seems as though her skin can barely contain her bones.

"How are you doing, really?" He quickly moves his eyes to her face. "What happened?"

His eyes wander back to her arms. Who did that to her? Did she . . . ?

"Everyone keeps asking that." Her eyes fill with tears.

"I'm sorry."

She shakes her head. "No, that's not what I meant. It's just me." It's as if she can hear his questions. She whispers the rest: "It's in my head. That's what's so incredibly freaky."

She takes a tissue from the nightstand and blows her nose.

"They're going to move me later. I'm going to a special clinic for people like me. I just have to get strong enough first."

He takes her hand. He hadn't planned to do that. The tears stream from her eyes again. She gazes at him intensely as they flow.

"They're not sure if I'll be able to continue dancing. Can you imagine, Alex?"

Her face is so full of anguish that he's at a loss. There aren't any words that can help. He squeezes her hand.

It's the first time she's had a drink since that night. The more she drinks, the further away Alex and her mother get. She enjoys feeling them slip away. It's a party. She can have fun. She's the prettiest one there; she knows it. All the guys are looking at her, all the girls too, although in a different way. For a second she wonders: Which is more important?

Susanna circulates, talking to all the guests. People are still trying to get a feel for one another. Everyone is waiting for the alcohol to take over and make the nervousness disappear. It only takes about an hour to get to that stage. Kyla is working on the bottle of wine Therese's sister got for them. At any second Elizabeth could walk in the door, and it's important to be prepared. She will not let it affect her; she will not be made to do something dumb.

An hour passes. Kyla has almost forgotten to be anxious, when suddenly Elizabeth is just standing there. She looks pale and lost, and is sort of hiding behind Erik. Kyla feels sorry for her; it's so obvious that Elizabeth doesn't want to be there. Susanna glides over to them. Therese joins her, smiling so hard she's unrecognizable. Elizabeth relaxes the slightest bit, seems happy to be welcomed so warmly. This is *so* screwed up—Therese and Susanna making Elizabeth feel wanted and forgiven. What if she knew it was all a trick? Elizabeth turns her head and their eyes meet. There's no hatred in Elizabeth's gaze, nothing disparaging. But Kyla still looks away and heads off upstairs.

She winds up on a sofa with Jake the skateboarder. They drink beer together and then he rubs up against her, but not enough to really bother her—unless she wanted to get bothered for Therese's sake. Which she doesn't. Too bad going back downstairs is out of the question.

Susanna comes up every once in a while to check on what's going on. After a few hours, Therese appears. She's visibly seething. "What are you guys doing? Are you going to sit here all night or what?"

Jake offers her a sip of his beer. "Chill out."

"It's just so boring when people sit upstairs."

Jake gets irritated. "I don't know why *you* care. You've been ignoring me all night."

Therese looks away and focuses on Kyla. "Did you forget what we were going to do tonight?"

"I'm not going to do anything. Why do you keep going on and on about it?"

"What is it with you? You've got to get back at her. She dissed us!"

"Why don't *you* do it, Miss Try New Shit? Does it look like I care?"

Therese sits down on the arm of the sofa and smiles sweetly at Jake. "I'm sorry about tonight, Jakey. I *do* want to hang with you. But first I just wondered—have you heard about Kyla's mother?"

An ice-cold lump forms in Kyla's stomach.

"Heard what?" Jake asks, curious.

Kyla subtly shakes her head. *Don't.*

Silence. Therese raises her eyebrows expectantly.

"What about Kyla's mother?"

Alex stands up when Christina's father comes in, embarrassed by Christina's admission. Her mother says it's late and that Alex will have to get going. She walks out to the corridor with him.

"I think she was really happy to see you, Alex."

"Is it really serious?"

Her mother looks down at the floor. "Yes. And truthfully, it's not just one thing—there are so many problems that she . . ." She pulls herself together, puts on a smile and says, "Thanks for coming, Alex. Thank you so very much."

Kyla is talking to Erik. She's so *totally* interested in hearing about the band he plays in and really *everything else* that has to do with him too. She nods enthusiastically, hanging off his every word, interjecting little playful comments, tossing her hair. She has him already. It wasn't hard, only took half an hour. What a pathetic, cheating moron.

Elizabeth is standing a little ways away, distracted by Susanna and Therese. Every once in a while, she glances over. Kyla can feel her glare, but she feels it less and less the more she sips her Super Susanna Punch.

Kyla tries to believe that she hates Elizabeth, that Elizabeth looks down on her, but it doesn't help. All she sees in her once-friend's eyes is despair.

Kyla asks Erik if he wants to dance. He nods and they walk by Elizabeth on their way to the living room. Erik quickly rests his hand on Elizabeth's arm and drivels, "I'm just going to be gone for a sec."

Kyla raises her arms and transforms. He can't take his eyes off her. Neither can Elizabeth. Kyla's hair whips around in her face. She closes her eyes. Forgets for a few wonderful minutes what she's doing. For those few moments, everything feels good. Then the song is over and she opens her eyes. Sees the hungry look in Erik's eyes.

Next comes a slow song. They turn down the lights. A few other couples are making out. She doesn't need to do anything. He pulls her to him. She dances pressed up against him, her nose against his throat. Therese and Susanna are grinning. Elizabeth watches in panic and hopelessness. Kyla keeps going, letting him stroke her back down over her jeans and kiss her ear.

God, just get it over with! The next second they're kissing in front of everyone. His kiss is deep and demanding, she feels his hard-on pressing against her stomach. It's time. She takes his hand and leads him off the dance floor. He follows her like a shadow. Everyone watches as they walk through the open door into the bedroom.

He gets her down onto the bed, pulling at her clothes.

The only thing she can think about is Elizabeth. Elizabeth, who actually thought she was welcome at the party, who might have thought they were leaving the bullshit behind. And she feels an intense hatred toward the guy lying on top of her panting. What kind of guy lets some girl pick him up right in front of his girlfriend?

She tries to push him away. He doesn't respond, just keeps fervently tearing at her clothes.

"Stop!"

He stops, confused and breathing heavily. "What?"

She wriggles out of his grasp. He's still lying on the bed like a fool, holding out his hand to her. "You know you want it, so come and get it."

She can't look at him. Feels the tears coming, the lump settling like an abscess in her throat. She mumbles at the wall while she buttons her clothes. "I'm sorry. This wasn't about you. But for the record, you're an asshole."

She quickly leaves the room. Steps out in a fog. Doesn't see the people, zigzags past them out to the front hall. She digs frenziedly in the big pile on the floor for her jacket, finds it, and is right about to leave, when Therese shows up, all out of breath.

"Well, that was what you would call a quickie!"

Kyla stops, her hand on the doorknob. "What's wrong with you two, anyway?"

"What are you talking about? That was the plan perfectly executed."

Susanna chimes in. "What's wrong, Kyla?"

Then it comes, like an angry roar from down in her stomach:

"You can go to hell, both of you! I never want to see either of you again."

She runs out into the windy night, quickly storming away from the house. She hears their voices behind her. "But, hello? You were the one who . . ."

First her face contorts. Then comes the sound: a primitive howl. And finally the tears.

The only thing she wants is her mother.

There's a whole bunch of people at the bus stop. Alex can tell who they are even though it's dark: Kevin, Val, Anton, and a couple others from school. They're holding beers and are obviously buzzed. They've probably been roaming around Lake Merritt trying to pick up girls. Normally he would hide until the bus came, but today he does the opposite: He walks right up to them with his bag slung over his shoulder.

"Well, if it isn't our little dancing queen!" Kevin chuckles.

A couple of the others join in.

"Hi, Alex," Anton says. Alex nods at him. Val greets him too.

"Was it a tough workout?" Kevin tries to get more laughs, but Alex just stares him down. It works. Kevin breaks his gaze and starts kicking at a fallen can.

The bus comes and everyone except Alex pushes their way in through the doors in the middle. The driver shouts that the middle doors are for exiting only, but no one pays any attention to what he says. Alex goes through the front like a good boy, then goes to the back, where the guys are throwing playful punches at each other. He approaches slowly and sits down next to Anton, as if that were the obvious spot. Val looks at him with amazement. Kevin too.

"That's messed up."

"It is?" Alex asks, pretending not to hear the threat in Kevin's voice. Alex turns to Val and asks, "Can I have a taste?"

Val holds out the beer can and Alex takes a swig. The beer is warm and tastes terrible. But he takes another.

"Had any tequila lately?" Anton wonders.

"Nah, no luck in that department."

"Bummer."

"Yeah, but I'll let you know if I get ahold of some."

"Yeah, man, definitely call me. I'll be right over." Anton smiles.

"Hey, no fags allowed back here!"

No one pays Kevin any mind, but that doesn't stop him. "Do you smell that? The whole bus reeks of fairy!"

Alex looks out the window, ignoring him. Kevin slugs him in the arm.

"Didn't you hear what I said? Get lost!"

It's now or never. "Oh, did you mean me? I'm sorry. I didn't realize."

"Are you out of your mind?"

"No, I don't think so," Alex says. "And actually it can't be me who reeks, because I'm not gay."

Kevin clenches his fist and gets right up in Alex's face, but no one makes any attempt to help or even cheer him on. "So, you're saying that you're a ballerina who hops around queering yourself out, but you're not gay? Yeah. Right, I believe you."

"Oh, it's the dancing you're talking about!" Alex smiles. "In that case I can tell you that I don't 'queer myself out' anymore." He pauses for effect. "Didn't you know I quit?"

Kevin gapes. Val's eyes widen.

"Right. What's in your bag then?"

"Workout clothes. I was lifting weights."

Alex is cool, but his brain is screaming, *Please don't open the bag!*

"Does that mean you want to start on the soccer team then?" Val really seems sincere.

"Maybe."

"He's not going to play with us!" Kevin sputters. "I'd make him regret it—or I'd quit." His eyes narrow menacingly.

Anton mutters, "It's not like you're the best forward ever."

Alex gets offered more beer and Anton says that Alex should play defense, he needs help back there. Val begins to chatter with them both, and when Alex gets off the bus he's a new person. He's part of the team.

Mom! Kyla scolds silently in her head. The door is unlocked as usual. Kyla inhales the familiar Mom-scent. It doesn't feel suffocating today, just homey. She calls out as she kicks off her shoes, and gets no response. Goes in with her jacket on, looking around quickly: No one in the living room or kitchen.

Kyla peeks through the doorway to her mom's bedroom. There she is, sleeping with her face to the wall. She feels a wave of tenderness wash through her body. God, she's been so stupid.

Kyla flings her jacket on the floor as she walks over to the bed, carefully lifts the covers, and crawls in. She puts her arm around her mother and pulls her up against her, buries her nose in her mom's matted hair.

"I'm sorry," she whispers.

Her mom's lying totally still. She's dead asleep. Kyla shakes her a little.

"Mom, I'm back, and I'm not planning to leave you ever again."

Still no response. She pulls her mother's shoulder so she falls over onto her back. Her eyes are closed. She probably took a sleeping pill. Kyla sighs in disappointment—she wanted to talk about everything tonight. She strokes her mom's cheek and tries to comb her hair with her fingers. Then she stiffens. Something isn't right. Her mom is unusually pale. Kyla puts a hand on her mom's chest. It isn't moving. She leans over the body and tries to hear if her mom's breathing.

An unfathomable cavern opens up in her chest as panic wells up. Kyla shakes her mom, hard.

"Mom, wake up!"

The silence is deafening. Kyla slaps her mom's face. She

screams. Shakes her again. *Please, say this isn't real! It's my fault! Mine! Mine! Mine!*

She falls off the bed and fumbles toward her jacket. Grabs her phone and dials 911.

Alex knows his parents are still up, they never go to bed before midnight. But he doesn't try to sneak in tonight. It's the new him walking into the house. As expected, his mother is waiting in the entry.

"How did you dance?"

He smiles at her, but doesn't respond. She takes that as a positive sign.

"You're so gifted." But then she gets worried. "Did you hear about the part today?"

Alex walks past her into the kitchen.

"I will call them tomorrow."

"That won't be necessary." Alex opens the fridge.

"Why not?"

He pours a glass of milk and spoons some Nestlé Quik into it. She waits for an explanation.

"Did you find out?"

"I've known for a while. I just haven't said anything."

He hears how different the new Alex sounds, so calm and self-confident. His mom is so excited, she's about to burst.

"Haven't said . . . ! What are you talking about?"

He stirs his glass.

"I couldn't say anything. Didn't want to alarm you."

In an instant her face changes, going from glee to despair. "You don't mean—"

"Yeah. Henning got it."

Her hands fly up to her cheeks as she stifles a scream.

"Calm down. God, it's just a part."

"I don't know if I can accept this, Sasha."

He takes a gulp of chocolate milk to see if it's strong enough. "I'm sure you'll manage."

"But Henning . . ." She makes a face. "He is not half as good as you. There is nothing unique about his dancing, no charisma."

"Well, he got it anyway." Alex drinks in deep gulps, then sets down the empty glass. He wonders if he has a chocolate milk mustache but keeps himself from smiling at the thought for his mom's sake. "Where's Dad?"

His mom is frozen against the table, panting and speechless. Alex finds his dad—where else?—in the office. The new Alex doesn't ask if he's interrupting anything.

"I wanted to talk to you. And Mom."

His father looks up, irritated.

"Then you must wait. I have quite a bit to do here."

"On a Friday night? Do they need the code on Saturday?"

"No, but—"

"Then you can listen *now*." Alex doesn't even wait for his father to go back downstairs. His mother has pulled herself together. Her eyes are hopeful when he walks in.

"We are not going to let this get us down, my Sasha. That's important." She makes a pointing gesture with her arm. "Think toward the future. You understand? We will start extra lessons on the weekends."

Alex sits down across from her at the kitchen table. "I have something to tell you."

His father walks into the kitchen. Who knew it was that easy to get him out of his chair? They are focused on him. His nerves pinch on the inside, but this Alex doesn't show it.

"I'm going to stop dancing. Or, actually, I have stopped."

Silence. His mom is too shocked to say anything. Alex can't even look at her. Instead he looks to his father, who gently places his hand on his wife's shoulder.

His father turns toward him. "Have you thought very caref—"

"Yes."

And the discussion is over. Alex leaves the kitchen. He's never felt so strong.

Kyla sits in the corridor instead of the waiting room while they pump her mom's stomach—she insisted on being as close to her as possible. There are only a few yards between them.

The wait in the apartment was unbearable—she paced back and forth between the window overlooking the street and the bed, until they finally got there. The EMTs lifted her mother's eyelids and checked her pulse. The way they looked at each other said it was serious. She suppressed the scream in her stomach while they prepared the stretcher. They'd turned on the sirens and shot through all the red lights. Her mom's eyes remained closed the whole time, a plastic oxygen mask over her mouth.

No one can tell if she's going to make it yet. She swallowed a lot of pills. Soon Kyla will find out if she stayed at the party too long. She can't imagine having to live with that—with what she was doing while her mom was *dying*.

People in white coats rush past her. Two of them snap at each other in irritation. A man who's bleeding screams that he needs help. Some super-drunk girls are sitting on the floor crying.

The door opens. Kyla doubts for a second that she has it in her to turn around, knowing that the answer will be evident in their faces. But she does, and calms down when she sees them. The nurse squats down on the floor in front of Kyla, like an angel, taking her hand.

"She'll be okay."

Kyla flings her arms around the woman in white. Hugs her so tightly, the woman emits a squeak.

"Thank you."

"She won't wake up for several hours. And you absolutely can't be alone while you wait. Do you have anyone you can stay with? Your father? Your grandmother?"

"I don't . . . I'll be fine."

"No you won't. I need to call someone."

Kyla shakes her head. "I have my boyfriend."

"You're a minor, honey."

Kyla looks down at the floor and gives the number for Mr. Chow's. She promises to sit where she is while the nurse makes the call. But as soon as the woman disappears behind a door, Kyla hightails it out of there.

Alex *so* wants to tell Kyla. She would be so happy for him. It all feels kind of unreal. To think—he just did it! He wants to tell her that he's discovered the secret of happiness: All you have to do is make a decision and jump. But they don't have each other anymore. Now who will he tell?

He walks past Nina's room and, on impulse, he knocks. She's sitting at her desk painting her fingernails dark purple. She turns to look at him and doesn't seem annoyed, just surprised. "What's up?"

He sits down on her bed. "I quit ballet."

She stops in mid-motion. One hand extended with the dark purple on the tips of each finger, the other holding the brush.

"You what?"

"It's true. I told Mom and Dad."

She gasps for air, opening and closing her mouth like a fish. "You didn't!" She starts to laugh. "Oh my God, I can't believe it!"

"No one knew. Though Kyla might have suspected. The girl I was e-mailing with."

Nina stuffs the applicator back into the glass jar. She

stands up and starts wandering around her room, waving her hands as she speaks. "Alex, this is incredible! I have to tell you, it was the best thing I ever did. Mom was just constantly hounding me and I couldn't take it and——" She stops short. "Poor Mom."

"I know." Alex gets a lump in his throat. Nina sits next to him. But she can't touch him—the nail polish isn't dry yet.

"It's not your fault. You can't live your life for her. You have to live it for yourself."

"I guess I just figured that out." He smiles at her and feels the connection he's been longing for—now they have something in common. He leans his head on her shoulder for two seconds. There's nothing more to say. Alex is going his own way, just like his sister.

She's sitting on the sofa with her coat on. The silence echoes through the hall. Not a car can be heard from the street below, not a footstep from the floor above. Rarely is she totally alone in the apartment.

The thoughts are spinning in her head, mixing with the rampant guilt. That her actions made her mother . . . that it's her fault. There's no one she can tell this to. Alex is the only one who would understand. And she screwed that up.

She flips open her phone and dials her father's home number. What time is it on the East Coast? She can't figure it out. Just hits the number she has on speed dial, even though she rarely calls. Madison answers and Kyla immediately stiffens. It's been so long since they've seen each other, she doesn't even know if her half sister remembers her. Then Camilla picks up another line. Clever Camilla, who went to NYU film school and worked as a production intern for her father until she'd swept him off his feet, he divorced her mother, and she began producing perfect progeny. Whereas Kyla and her mother—they're too imperfect to fit into his new motion-picture-perfect life.

Camilla says he's working late and that she can call him on his cell. Is it anything in particular? Kyla says it isn't and hangs up. She's not planning on calling her dad on his cell phone, doesn't want to hear a stressed-out, guilty-conscience voice that says they can have a *super-long* conversation another day.

To think that Mom was prepared to leave her all alone . . .

The buzzer rings. Its long, whiny tone cuts through the apartment. Who can it be, so late at night?

She goes to the door. It buzzes again. Someone pounds repeatedly. "Open up! I know you're in there!" It's *Lucas*.

She looks through the peephole. He's taking aim to kick. *Bang*. His coat is unbuttoned and his hair is all messed up. Only now it's not sexy—it's as crazy as the look in his eyes. He's sloshed.

"Open up already, you little slut!"

"Lucas, stop! What do you want?"

"What do you want?" he mocks. "What do you think?"

"I don't know." Kyla can feel her fear rising.

"You think I don't know what you're doing? You think I don't know about you cheating on me? I'm not gonna put up with this. Open up!"

She doesn't dare. He's lost it, and everything is way too much already. She sinks down onto the floor. She's freezing. Her whole body is shivering.

"I know all about what you did tonight!"

Then it's bitch this and whore that and all the stuff he's going to do to her. She holds her hands over her ears to try to block it out, but it doesn't help. She starts screaming to drown him out, goes farther back into the apartment, but he's still there, pounding incessantly and screaming. She trembles, sobs. She's never been so scared, never felt so alone.

She grabs her phone and dials 411, trembling. "Oakland, please? Borodin?"

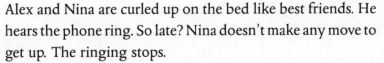

Alex and Nina are curled up on the bed like best friends. He hears the phone ring. So late? Nina doesn't make any move to get up. The ringing stops.

From downstairs someone yells, "Alex!"

He and Nina glance at each other, surprised. Then he gets up and leaves the room. "I'll get it up here!

"Yeah? This is Alex."

There's massive background noise, and then a faint voice. "It's Kyla."

226

He's totally unprepared. His back stiffens. He has to be on the defensive.

"I . . . I . . . I had to call someone, I don't have anyone else . . ."

Her voice sounds so fragile.

"What?"

It's quiet for a second. She breathes into the phone, sniffles. Does she have a cold? "Oh God, Alex . . . Help!"

Help with what? Is she crying?

"I don't know what to do. He's crazy! And my mom tried to . . . Do you know what she did?"

Something must have happened. Her betrayal pulses in his mind, but somehow he knows now is not the time to punish her.

"What is it, Kyla? What happened?"

"And she . . . it's my fault. When I left . . . I almost . . ."

It's so loud in the background. "Is there someone with you?"

"He keeps pounding on the door and screaming!"

"Who?"

She whimpers, and then the crying starts again.

"Lucas. This guy I was seeing. He says he's going to break down the door!"

"Where is he?"

"Out there!"

"Out where?"

"In the hallway pounding on the front door!" She's screaming now.

"Kyla, are you home alone?"

She says nothing, but he can imagine her nodding tearfully on the other end of the line.

"Calm down. He's *not* going to get inside. Take the phone into your room. Can you do that?"

"I think so."

"Keep talking to me while you're on your way in there."

She does what he says. Tells him about each step she takes, her voice trembling. When she gets to her room, she goes in and locks the door.

"Now he can't get to you. There are multiple locks between you and him. You'll stay there until everything has calmed down. Now click over to the other line and call down to the doorman."

"Sid?"

"Yeah. He'll handle that creep. And I'll be waiting for you when you click back. And we'll talk for as long as you need. I promise, Kyla, I'll be right here when you get back."

How long has she been huddled on her floor? Long enough to tell Alex everything. About what happened at the party, about her mom's suicide attempt, about Lucas, who presumably found out about what happened with Erik. Alex hasn't said much, besides that it's okay, that *she's* okay, that what her mom did isn't *her* fault.

She told him about that night too. About how they'd been smoking pot and how they'd ended up talking about him. About how it was just too much when he showed up at her door that night—too hard for her to get everything together. She apologized, and he listened. He didn't get mad, just said afterward that it sucks how nothing is ever simple.

Now she slowly stands up. With the phone still in her hand, she unlocks her bedroom door, sneaks silently over to the front door, and peeks cautiously out. The hallway and stairwell are empty. Sid might have called the cops an hour ago already.

She lies down in bed with the phone. Now it's Alex who's talking. He says she has to get a handle on things: Apologize to Elizabeth, dump her "friends," break up with that creep . . . She laughs because he sounds like he's a hundred years old and spouting a self-help book and how is she going to be able to do all of that? He says she has to, that eventually it's just inevitable. That's how it was for him.

With pride in his voice, he tells her how he quit dancing. She wonders if that's really the best thing. Doesn't he love dancing? He says he's not sure anymore, that he wants to make his own decisions about his life and this is just a start. She listens to him until he starts rambling and her eyes begin to close.

Alex slowly hangs up. Kyla is going to visit—everything is decided. She can come in a few months, when her mom is feeling better. It's pitch-black out his window. All the lights are off at the neighbors' houses. His bedroom door is ajar. Then he notices movement on the other side of the door. He leaps up and flips on the light. His mom jumps back, discovered. A wave of anger rushes through him.

"Why were you eavesdropping? It's the middle of the night."

"Yes, it is. Who have you been talking with for so long?"

"She called us, so it didn't cost anything, if that's what you're wondering."

"Was that that . . . *pen friend* of yours?"

He calms down, trying to remember that her world collapsed tonight. How could she be generous on a day like this?

"It's none of your business, Mom."

"It *was* her, yes? That . . ." She makes a face.

He decides to ignore that. *"It's none of your business."*

"Before you began with this . . . this *computer* friend, everything was perfect."

"No. It wasn't." He turns out the light again. "I'm going to go to bed now."

"Fine, Sasha." Her voice echoes in the darkness. "But I know what I know."

Kyla's mom has to stay in the hospital for forty-eight hours for observation. She has to talk to a psychologist and arrange to keep seeing someone even after she's released. Kyla convinced her father and the hospital staff that it wasn't necessary for him to fly out to L.A. just for her. She told them she was going to stay with a neighbor, that everything was under control.

Her father's relief was obvious as he swallowed the lie. No need to disrupt his ideal existence. Besides, Kyla really *could* take care of herself for a couple of days. She'd talked to Sid, made sure he wouldn't let Lucas anywhere near the building.

She and her mom hold hands. Minutes pass.

"There's nothing I can say to defend what I did."

"You don't have to." Kyla sounds more confident than she feels. "The important thing is that you're alive."

Her mom's face twists in anguish. "Leaving you alone . . . I don't know what I was thinking."

Kyla mobilizes all the strength she has to force back her own tears. "I don't get it either. But that's how it is, isn't it? People do all kinds of things without understanding why they do them." She gulps. "That I just left, for example. That was a totally nasty way for me to treat you."

They look at each other.

"We're not going to do stuff like that to each other anymore, right?"

Kyla shakes her head. "No, we're not." She smiles. "Hey, I have an idea."

"What?"

"Something we can do when you get healthy."

Her mom looks interested even through her exhaustion.

"We'll start going horseback riding. You and me."

Her mom is amused. "Aren't I too old for that?" But a second later she changes her mind. "No, I'm not too old at all."

"Good. Is it a plan then?"

"It's a plan."

But as Kyla leaves the room and walks down the corridor toward the exit, her stomach is clenched and queasy. Can she really count on her mom?

It's not really the weather for soccer practice. They're squishing around in the mud and falling into big puddles. But it doesn't matter. They scream with laughter every time someone takes a tumble. In the end practically everyone is covered in mud. Only Kevin is bitter. He doesn't want to play with "fags," and of course he refuses to be on the same team as Alex. He makes sure to tackle hard when he gets the chance. It doesn't accomplish anything. The others are on Alex's side. They boo and hiss at Kevin and cheer encouragingly to Alex even though he's just playing okay today. Afterward Kevin rushes off in a huff.

On the way home Val reveals that everyone has had it up to here with Kevin. He's just getting weirder and weirder, gets mad for no reason these days.

"I must be totally stupid or something," Val continues, sighing.

"What do you mean?"

"I can't believe I just did whatever he did all the time. I've been acting like a dumbass."

Alex can only agree. "Yeah."

"I've been a jerk to you . . . because I was, you know, jealous."

Alex is stunned. "What do you mean, jealous?"

"I mean, you always had your dancing and to hell with what everyone else thought. And I . . . I just wanted to get in with the varsity guys."

"But you have a ton of friends."

"Well, yeah."

"I don't."

"Not yet." Val smiles a little. "But it's just that . . . Everyone thinks I'm just like them." He looks at Alex, as if it's important that at least *he* understands that that's not the case.

"Aren't you?"

Val smiles wryly. "You have no idea."

They each come from a different direction on the street, approaching their building. Kyla can tell from yards away who it is and she's instantly anxious. Elizabeth knows too, it's obvious. But neither turns around and heads the other way.

They meet at the front door. Elizabeth punches in the code, pulls it open, and just lets it go behind her. While they wait for the elevator, Elizabeth stares at the wall. When it comes, they step in. It takes forever for it to start moving.

Kyla knows what she has to do. She has maybe a minute, but the words are buried so deep inside her.

"I understand if you hate me."

Elizabeth emits only a short sigh.

"*I* would hate me. And I *do* hate myself."

Elizabeth keeps staring straight ahead, seemingly indifferent.

"I'm sure there's no point in saying I'm sorry."

"No, there's not." Elizabeth's eyes shoot darts.

"I know."

Silence. Does Elizabeth understand even a little? Kyla has to keep trying, no matter how humiliating it feels.

"But, like I said . . . I'm so ashamed."

The elevator stops. Elizabeth steps out. Kyla follows her.

"Jesus, Lizzie, I'm so, so ashamed!" She uses the nickname she had for Elizabeth years ago—before her father left, when the two of them were still close. "And I'd take it back if I could!"

Elizabeth hesitates for a moment. Then she closes her apartment door behind her.

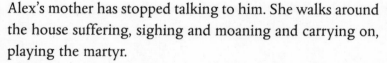

Alex's mother has stopped talking to him. She walks around the house suffering, sighing and moaning and carrying on, playing the martyr.

Now they're sitting next to each other on the sofa watching *America's Funniest Home Videos*. Alex laughs at the proper intervals, keeps glancing at her hopefully, but her mouth is pursed in anger. His father comes in wondering if she wants a cup of tea, but she shushes him as if he were interrupting something important—Alex is not the only one who has to pay for what happened.

Alex's eyes meet his father's over his mother's head. His father looks at him like a grown-up, an equal.

He blinks. Can it be that his father actually, *finally* gained respect for him when he put his foot down?

it's driving me crazy, alex. i'm terrified of what they're going to say. i'm sure everyone hates me after what i did and they should. they'll call me all kinds of names. i know how it will go. i'm going 2 have to confront therese and susanna on monday. and who am i going to hang out with now that i don't have them?

You've got to just suck it up, Ky. You don't want those girls back. Take a deep breath, and jump in. I'll be thinking about you all day.

It's like the first day of high school, she has the same shaky legs. There's no sign of Therese or Susanna. She's paralyzed,

235

her clothes soaked in cold sweat. It feels like everyone is staring. Or is that just her imagination? She passes a group of kids she doesn't know, notices them checking her out. As she passes them she only hears scattered words.

"*Slut . . .*"

"*Tramp . . .*"

"*Whore . . .*"

She doesn't turn around. She still can't explain, can't defend herself. But her suspicion is true—the whole school knows. Now she's the megaslut. Most Likely to Contract an STD Before Graduation.

She slips around a corner and collects herself. Swallows, blinks back tears, and takes a deep breath. She will not play into the role.

She runs into them in the library. Susanna is doing Therese's hair.

"Hey!" Kyla's voice is clear. Susanna smiles nervously. Therese just nods and peers into her compact mirror.

"No, not like that!" Therese hisses, shaking her head. Susanna has to start over again.

"You didn't call." Kyla is almost surprised at how calm she sounds.

"Didn't you say you never wanted to talk to us again?" Therese doesn't even take her eyes off her own reflection.

"Oh, right, *that's* why. I thought maybe it was because you were ashamed."

Therese sets the mirror on her knee. "I'm sorry, what did you say? What do we have to be ashamed of?"

Kyla is amazed at Therese's attitude. There isn't a hint of

guilt or self-doubt. All her fear disappears, replaced by the confidence Alex believes she can have.

"That you forced me to seduce Elizabeth's boyfriend at the party."

"How exactly did *I* force *you* to do anything? Did I make you stick your tongue down his throat? Did I hold a gun to your head and march you to Susanna's bedroom?"

"You threatened to tell Jake about my mom."

"That? Oh my God, I was just kidding." Therese opens her purse to take out some gum. "You did exactly what you wanted to do—what you *always* do—get smashed and screw someone else's boyfriend."

Susanna begins the style again, her hands shaking. "Uh, this hairdo is just going to be *so* cool."

Kyla won't allow the distraction. She sees a hint of stress in Therese as she stares at her intently. "How did Lucas know what happened at the party?"

Susanna's fingers freeze. Therese buries her head in her purse again.

"I said, *how did Lucas know about what happened?*"

"How should *we* know? You're the one with so many guys you can't keep track." Therese jumps up. "This is just *too* much. Come on, Suze. We're outta here."

Susanna fumbles to pack up her barrettes.

"I know it was you. You were the only ones at the party who knew Lucas."

"Whatever." Therese just walks away. Susanna stumbles after her.

Kyla feels a big, empty hole inside her. She can't believe

they could do something like that. But then again, it's about time she found some new friends.

"Therese! Since we're laying it all on the table here, I thought you should know that I know you've been saying this crap about me for a *long* time. That I'm a stuck-up slutty bitch who steals all the guys."

Therese's mouth opens. And then closes. "How do you . . . ?"

Kyla stares pointedly at Susanna. "Let's just say a little birdie told me."

Susanna turns beet red.

"Damn, that's cold," Therese hisses.

Silence all around.

"Next time, bring a sweater," Kyla calls cheerfully. She leaves them to each other and heads to her locker to get her books. There's no question now: She'll survive today, which will make the next day that much easier.

Sometimes Alex goes down to the mini-mart in the evenings. The guys hang out there and shoot the breeze, maybe nurse a forty someone managed to scrounge up, but mostly they just talk.

When Kevin is there he pretends Alex doesn't exist, which suits them both just fine.

Alex never says that much. He doesn't have much to contribute, but sometimes, if they're talking about how stupid their teachers are and that kind of thing, he joins in: "Oh, yeah. She's *awful.*"

Sometimes he thinks he'll never really fit in. But then it strikes him that Val feels the same way. Maybe everyone goes around feeling like an outsider, even though they never let on.

Tonight he says good-bye early, at around nine o'clock. On the way through downtown someone comes racing past him in high heels. He recognizes the short leather jacket. Isn't that . . . ?

"Katy!" Alex yells.

She turns around. It *is* Katy. Her face is red from crying. The makeup under her eyes has run. She's sniffling and shaking.

"What happened?"

She shakes her head. "I don't know. I'm sure it's my fault, but it's just not fair . . ."

Her sobbing is slowing down. Alex waits for it to stop.

"He doesn't believe me! Is he always like that or what?"

"Who? Andrei? Did you guys have a fight or something?"

She nods, standing there shivering in her tiny outfit.

"Well, what did he say?"

"He just went off on me." She gestures back the way she came. "At the pizza place. He started tripping about how a friend of his saw me with *Marcus*! I couldn't care less about Marcus, we were together a thousand years ago."

She takes a cigarette out of her purse and lights it. Her hands shake as she brings it to her mouth. She inhales deeply.

Then she continues. "And I'm like, 'What do you mean,

Marcus? I've told you a zillion times that we're just friends,' but he was just like, 'You slut, you're so full of it, you want me to just believe that?'"

Alex is surprised. "Andrei said that? He called you a *slut*?"

She starts sniffling again and brings the hand with the cigarette back up to her face. "Yeah."

Alex puts his arm around her. For one second it's like he's looking at himself from the outside: big, confident Alex comforting an unhappy girl. The next second, that's who he is. "What a jerk."

"I know," she sniffles, "but I'm totally in love with him. That's always how it is. I always fall in love with jerks."

"Then maybe you're a jerk too?"

She smiles. "Maybe so."

She looks so pitiful. He tells her to go home and she nods gratefully, as if everything were already settled: Alex will get Andrei to apologize and take her back.

He goes to the pizza place without any preconceived plan. Alex can see them through the window, Andrei and two of his buddies at a table. They're holding big frosty glasses of beer and Andrei is laughing loudly. He looks drunk and happy. Alex doesn't know where he gets the courage from, but in a flash he's there inside the restaurant, like the hero bursting into the saloon to teach the villain a lesson.

The villain spots him right away. He lights up and waves his hand. "Alex!" He turns to the others to explain, "My brother." They show no interest. The villain offers Alex a seat at the table.

The hero declines. "Nah, they won't serve me beer anyway."

The villain takes a swig out of his mug and wipes the foam from his upper lip. "What's up? Is Mom having a fit at home or something?"

The hero is stony, ignoring the question. "No, it's Katy."

Andrei's face changes. "What about her? What's her problem?"

"Oh, so now *she* has a problem?"

"What's wrong with you?"

"I don't think you should call her a slut." *Just keep going,* Alex thinks to himself. *Before you lose your nerve.*

Andrei's buddies get quiet. Andrei sighs, a condescending smile spreading from cheek to cheek. "Little Alex, go home. This is nothing for you to trouble yourself with." Andrei looks to the others for support, but they don't seem to know what to think. Still, the hero has no intention of leaving until he's said his piece.

"Don't treat her that way. She doesn't deserve it. And she didn't do anything with that guy. She's in love with *you.*"

Andrei gets up from the table. "It's time for you to head on home now, Alex."

The hero doesn't want any trouble, so they walk over to the exit together. The villain holds the door open, then begins to speak in a low and urgent voice. "Don't ever insult me in front of my friends. Okay there, little bro? Not *ever.*"

It's interesting that Always-Cool Andrei is as worried about saving face as the rest of the world, but Alex won't be drawn in. "Katy is really upset. I think you should call her."

"Come back in a few years with your opinions and see if I'm interested."

But the hero perseveres. "Dude, tell her you're sorry. Don't be an asshole."

I'm crazy. I don't get it. What happened to me? What made me think I could go up against my brother like that? Do you have any idea how BIG he is? He could have squashed me! ;)

Maybe it's because I knew what you were going to do. But I'm so tired of people screwing each other over just to make themselves feel powerful. And this time, I did something about it.

—Alex

i'm proud of you. and proud of myself. it's so weird that we met, that we had a real friend out there all along. & i can't believe we're really going 2 get to b 2gether for a whole weekend! it's not long now. can't wait. kyla

Lucas was waiting for Kyla outside the school. It only takes a second for him to drag her into his car—she doesn't even have a chance to feel scared. Her arm hurts where his fingers dig into the skin.

"Stop it, Lucas! Let me go!"

But Lucas is determined and clearly unstable. She decides it's best to stay calm.

"Maybe you have something to say to me," he hisses.

"Nothing besides what I already said on the phone."

"That it's over?"

"It's over," she confirms.

"Slut." He says it calmly, as if stating a fact. There's something comical about it even though it's awful.

"You said that already."

His nostrils flare. "Then I'm saying it again." Then he grabs her arm again. Hard. And shakes her whole body. She gets scared against her will, thinks about how he sounded outside her door that night, all the things he said he would do to her.

"Let go of me," she says as gently as she can.

"First you have to explain yourself!"

"You're hurting me, Lucas."

The tears are close, but she doesn't want to give him the satisfaction. It's obvious he's struggling too.

How could she have gotten together with him in the first place, or even worse, have *slept* with him? And who does he think he is, coming here like some crazy kidnapper and shoving her into his car by force?

"Do you think I should stay with you just to be nice? Is that what you want? For me to *pretend* to be in love with you?"

He lifts his arm wildly. She has time to think about how she'll disguise her black eye before school tomorrow; there's foundation in her makeup bag that will surely cover it. But the blow never comes. Lucas squeezes his eyes closed and his hold on her arm relaxes. When he opens his eyes, they're full of tears. The lunatic who was beating down her door just nights ago now seems like a small and heart-broken boy.

"But you made my life different, Kyla."

She doesn't get it. He'd spent most of his time pursuing her with phone calls and flowers. They were only actually together for such a short time.

"I was just a screw-up, doing a bunch of stupid stuff, not giving a damn about school. But then you came along."

"I'm sorry." She looks at him a moment without saying anything, then slowly opens the car door and gets out. This time, he doesn't try to stop her.

She slams the door shut, then leans in the window. "And if you *ever* try anything like that again, Lucas, I swear I'll call the police. Do not come to my house. Do not try to talk to me. Unless you like L.A. County lockup. Understand?"

He sits motionless, his head hanging from his shoulders. She turns to go on her way and finds Therese standing a little ways from the car. She's clearly been following the drama from a distance.

Kyla refuses to acknowledge her presence. Therese makes a little noise in her throat as her old friend passes—maybe the beginnings of an apology? But neither of them will ever know, because Kyla keeps on walking.

He must have changed his clothes seventeen times, switching back and forth between outfits until he finally just settled on a dark tie and jacket with jeans. He bought a bunch of new clothes, and not just because Kyla was coming.

The new stuff isn't extraordinary, but it isn't knock-offs Abercrombie either. According to Nina, if you dress mainstream, you project that you're insecure and boring. So she helped him find his style. He even bought a pair of black Converse to mark the new him. Nina said they were sexy. And shoes make the man, or whatever they say.

Her train arrives at 4:12 p.m. He's been chewing up a storm during the twenty minutes he spent waiting at the station, stuffing stick after stick of gum into his mouth; he went to the newsstand three times to study various packets of cookies. But now the train finally rolls into the station. He scans all the people pouring out and is suddenly afraid that he won't recognize her. But of course he can pick her out when she's still at least fifty yards away. His heart thumps. It's unreal that this gorgeous girl is actually scanning the crowd looking for *him*.

He makes his way through the crowd of people. She looks small surrounded by all the adults with briefcases and suit-cases. He doesn't yell her name. He just waits until she spots him too. And when they're about ten yards apart, she does, and bounds over to him with a smile lighting up her face.

Alex doesn't know what to do. Shake her hand or hug her? Or maybe neither.

"Hi," he says.

She throws her arms around him. He's taken by surprise, but quickly regains his composure and hugs her back. He breathes in her warmth and her perfume, which smells exotic and sensual. He hopes someone he knows will walk by and see them together.

"Wow, this is weird," she says.

"I know," Alex agrees. "Totally bizarre."

Then he takes her bag for her. She looks at him in surprise. For a second he feels embarrassed—was that too much? But then she thanks him and they head off, side by side. He doesn't know what to say. Even if he wanted to, he's never been able to just talk and talk.

Things between him and Kyla will have to flow naturally, the way they have from the beginning.

Even though she's spent more time at the café than at school in the last few years, going to a similar place with Alex feels unfamiliar and festive in some way. Just ordering while he listens—as if she were revealing something about herself through her selection.

A cappuccino, please—what does he think about that?

Then it's his turn. He orders an Italian soda and a blueberry muffin. Crap, she didn't order anything to go with the coffee. Does that make her seem like she's one of those girls who constantly thinks about her weight? They sit down at a window table. He offers to share his muffin. "Would you like some?"

She decides to tell the truth.

"No, I don't think I could actually eat anything. I'm way too nervous."

He watches her. That smile, so understated it's practically imperceptible—what does it mean? That he likes what she said? Is he shy or is he just acting? She ought to know. God, they've told each other almost everything there is to tell.

On the train she was scared about what would happen on the platform. What if it felt wrong right from the beginning? What if he were way lamer than she remembered— and she instinctively thought *NO*. Then, when she saw him, she was so happy, it startled her.

She forgets that her drink is hot and burns her tongue, but doesn't say anything. He sips his soda. How long has it been since one of them said something—half a minute? Two minutes? Shouldn't *he* get the conversation going? She *did* have a long trip.

"So, things kind of suck at home," Alex begins.

She jumps, startled, and spills some coffee on the table. He pulls his fingers through his hair.

"My mom is still pissed. I hope you can put up with it." His voice is anxious.

She smiles as warmly as she can. "Are you kidding? You know how *my* mom is . . . " She makes a face. "I'm pretty sure that after her, I can handle anything."

"How's your mom doing?"

"A lot better. She goes to that psychologist and is starting to actually go out." Kyla sits up straighter, proud. She'd actually been planning on saving this, but she can't wait any longer. "We went to our first lesson!"

Alex shows a whole row of teeth, he gives her such a big smile. "Really?"

She nods. "On Tuesday." And then the words start flowing.

"I was terrified at first, I didn't dare get up on that hairy beast for half an hour. He had these totally wild eyes, like I imagine in some crazy rodeo bull or something. But my mom—she just swung herself up on the other horse as if it were nothing! And finally I got so fed up with myself that I just thought, it's now or never. The worst that could happen is that I get thrown off and hit my head. But I was wearing a helmet, so my brains would be protected and it couldn't be *that* dangerous. Especially not since the horse was practically standing still and was, you know, like the nicest horse in the world, which is what they said."

Alex laughs. She's never thought of him as a laugher. But his whole body sort of twinkles, mostly through his eyes, which she discovers are so beautiful, they're bordering on divine. Is he laughing because she's funny/crazy or funny/funny?

She decides to go with the latter.

"And then what? Did you actually ride?"

"Oh, yeah. It's easy." She tries to seem nonchalant.

"You just galloped away?"

"No," Kyla admits timidly. "I'm kidding. It wasn't easy at all. The next day my butt was so sore!" She giggles. "Actually all I did was go out on that, what do you call it, that little sandy area they have? My horse walked around for about five minutes with me on top. It wasn't very wild or crazy, but that's okay. I'll build up to my cowgirl gallop across the desert plain."

It's just so strange. That he and Kyla are sitting in a café in San Francisco. That they're chatting like regular people. That they know each other, although not really. He wonders what the people around them would think if they were eavesdropping. That he and Kyla had once had a summer fling?

Occasionally he forgets to listen to her and just looks— at her face that changes expressions so quickly as she talks, at her fingers with their chewed blue nails, playing with her napkin on the table. Sometimes she moves her long hair to one side, as if to put things in their place.

She asks him a million questions—asks about *everything*. No one has ever done that before. She asks how he feels about one thing or another, what he thinks. It's like she wants to drink in all the thoughts and opinions he has. He tries to answer as truthfully as possible, though it's beyond tempting to say what might sound cooler instead.

They take the bus to his neighborhood. On the way he tells her how depressing his part of town is, which makes it so that she's pleasantly surprised when they get there: "This isn't *that* bad. Actually, it's really cute!"

They walk by the apartment buildings and townhouses

and single-family homes. In a few minutes, they're there. The light is on in the window at number three. He knows everyone is home. They're all waiting to check Kyla out. But she doesn't know that.

She hears him saying hi. It seems like someone is standing in the entryway waiting for them. When she peeks around from behind Alex, she sees a woman who's presumably his mother. She doesn't even get to digest an impression of her before another face appears, a dark-haired girl about her own age. A second later she hears footsteps on the stairs and another person appears, a guy several years older than her who's not shy about checking her out from head to toe. Finally Alex's dad shows up. His curly, grayish black hair is like a wreath around his face. She's never felt like such a curiosity before. Alex shuts the door behind them.

"This is Kyla," he announces.

The guy gets to her first, holding out his hand. "I'm Andrei," he offers, glancing at her chest in that familiar way. Kyla knows exactly who he is: The one who called his girl-friend a slut, the guy who plays hockey and thinks he's the biggest player in town. She takes his hand without looking him in the eye. "Hi." Then the sister comes over.

"Nina," she says. "How cool. I mean that you came. Really."

"Thanks. I'm really happy to be here."

The father's critical gaze makes her feel small and insignificant even though she's the center of everyone's attention.

"I am Aleksandr's father. Welcome." His voice is authoritative, with an obvious Russian accent.

Instinctively she curtsies and thanks him. Where did *that* come from?

The only one left is the mother. She's standing a bit away from the rest of them, watching Kyla with nothing welcoming in her eyes, nothing warm. It makes Kyla feel like an alien intruder, so much so that she almost wonders if she's grown green antennae and a third eye. She wishes she'd put a little more thought of this moment into wardrobe selection, maybe worn a baggy sweater and long pants instead of the little pink dress and heels she thought made her look sort of dancerly. Now she feels kind of ridiculous . . . and exposed. Still, she goes up to the mother, smiling.

"Hi. I'm Kyla."

"Yes," the mother replies icily.

"It was, like, super-nice of you to let me come."

Like? She can't believe she said that! What's wrong with her?

Alex gives his mom a scathing look and then takes Kyla by the arm. "My room is upstairs. Come on."

"But there is food on the table," his mother protests. "Aren't you hungry?"

He can't believe his mother. She didn't even smile. As if Kyla weren't feeling vulnerable enough with a totally strange family miles and miles from home.

"You see?" he hisses into Kyla's ear as they walk into the kitchen.

"It doesn't matter," she whispers back, smiling, even though he can tell that it does.

His mom set another place at the table and got out the extra chair. Kyla stands there at a loss while everyone else scurries around the kitchen. Alex sits down and gestures for her to follow. He feels bad. It's like all of her spontaneity and self-confidence are gone. She looks small and shy.

It's beef Stroganoff and boiled potatoes. His mom loads up Kyla's plate. She tries to stop her, saying, "Thanks, that's plenty," but there's already a mountain of food. His dad asks if she had a good trip. Kyla answers, "Yes, please" and then blushes and tries again. "I mean, yes, thank you." Andrei scarfs down his food at record pace while continuing to size up their guest. Alex is embarrassed—after the whole mess with Katy, his brother's been acting like an insufferable jerk. Kyla slowly chews and looks around with a hesitant smile.

"It's delicious."

"How nice," Alex's mother answers.

"So you're from Los Angeles," Andrei says.

She nods.

"This neighborhood must really look like crap to you, huh?"

Kyla shakes her head fervently while she finishes chewing. "No, I was just telling Alex that it's really cute here."

Andrei laughs. "Cute? Well that's a new way of looking at it."

"Do you live in downtown L.A.?" Nina wonders. Kyla nods.

"Wow, so you must go to a ton of concerts and stuff all the time!"

Kyla notices Alex's mother staring at her intently, and shakes her head. "Not that many."

"Imagine going out on the town in *Los Angeles*," Andrei snorts. "Just a bunch of shallow, stuck-up, Hollywood snobs everywhere."

Kyla looks down at her plate.

"I'm sure it's not like that," Alex protests quickly, glaring at his brother and trying to keep his cool. "It's not like everyone in Los Angeles is the same. Are *you* the same as *me* just because we both live *here*?"

"No, and thank God! But then, you're also a little . . . odd."

Alex blushes even though he doesn't want to. Nina steps in, fixing her eyes on their brother. "Well, I think anyone who doesn't want to go to L.A. sometime in their life is a moron."

"Nina!" his father chastises, then turns to his older son, carefully dabbing the corners of his mouth with his napkin even though there's nothing there. "We must never generalize, Andrei."

Andrei scowls and helps himself to another serving of rice.

"So," his father continues, leaning back in his chair

and looking at Kyla. "How *do* you pass your time in Los Angeles?"

Alex wishes the earth would swallow him up. Is this really his family? A bitter shadow of a mother, a pervy flirt of an older brother and a snobby, overcompensating father?

Kyla fidgets. "Um, I go to school."

"Yes, we should hope so." Alex's father laughs. "I meant . . . well, Alex has his dancing. *Had,* I mean. I'm curious about your interests."

"My interests? Well, I do all kinds of things." She flashes Alex a desperate look.

"She goes riding." He steps in like a gallant knight.

"Yeah, I do! I ride horses."

Alex's father doesn't know anything about horseback riding. Alex can tell what he's thinking: Horses, well, that sounds harmless. His father nods and pronounces his satisfaction: "That is good." Then he gets up and takes his plate to the sink. "Now, unfortunately, I must retire."

Meals. Families. She wishes she'd paid more attention at Susanna's; she just has no experience with this kind of dynamic. And she can't run home or go out if it bugs her.

Kyla feels the sweat under her arms. She stares down at her plate, where big pieces of creamy, stringy beef loom large. She really wants to score one against Andrei. And she just wants to straight-up demand of Alex's mother what the hell her problem is. Instead, Kyla glances over at

254

Alex. Their eyes meet and he smiles at her, somehow comfortingly, which makes everything feels easier. She chose Alex after all, not his family. And Nina, at least, seems completely normal.

When his mother gets up to start clearing the table, Kyla still has half of her food left. Alex takes her plate and scrapes it all right into the trash with the napkin on top before his mother has a chance to comment. She watches them in amazement as they leave the kitchen.

Alex gives Kyla a quick tour of the rooms. Only the living room shows any evidence that his parents are from another place. "Russian style, totally nuts," Alex says, rolling his eyes at the embroidered cloth panels.

They walk past his father's office and peek in the door.

"That's where I would sit at night," he says, his brown eyes twinkling.

She can picture him in his father's chair, his face lit up by the computer screen. It feels unreal to think that *that's* where it all happened—like a field trip from school to some historical site.

They lock themselves in Alex's room. He puts on some music that she's never heard before, but that she likes. When she asks what it is, he says it's a really cool band from Brooklyn. She's impressed—is he into the indie scene?

Then he admits he discovered them on an Apple commercial and she smiles—appreciates his sincerity.

He sits on a beanbag chair on the floor. She sits down on the bed. Then they pick up where they left off at the café, as if nothing had happened. It's like they don't want to talk about how wrong everything was at dinner. They talk about everything except that.

She glances at the poster on the wall. An attractive, muscular man in a tank top and tights posing barefoot in a dramatic pose.

"Who's that?"

"Hmm?"

She points.

"Oh, him." He sounds self-conscious. "I haven't taken that down yet. Rudolf Nureyev. This old Russian dancer. He was the best."

"Then why do you want to take it down?"

He brow is furrowed, and he looks confused. "I—well . . ."

Kyla decides to rescue him. "He's sexy!"

Alex lights up. "You think so?"

"Yeah, totally hot," Kyla assures him, laughing.

As Alex contemplates Nureyev wistfully, Kyla studies her friend. There's something about his demeanor that makes her curious. She suspects that there's another Alex behind the façade, one that she'd definitely like to see more of.

"Won't you show me something?"

"Show you what?"

"Some ballet steps or . . . I don't know. Any dance move."

But he's bashful. "Nah, I quit."

"So? That doesn't mean you've forgotten everything, does it?"

"No, but you would think . . . In this tiny room?"

"You have no idea what I'll think!"

He gives her a pleading look. "If it's okay, I'd rather not."

"Okay." She relents—the time just isn't right yet. She hopes someday he'll trust her enough to show her what's buried inside.

There's a knock on the door at eleven o'clock.

"Children?" It's Alex's mother. "Aren't you going to bed now?" She must have been pacing around in the kitchen for several hours wondering what they were doing up there. Maybe she'd even been standing outside the door listening.

"Just chill," Alex yells. "We're going!"

Her footsteps recede.

Now there's a new tension in the room. Kyla gets up from the bed and stretches. He can't help but notice her chest, which stands out so prominently under her sweater. Then she crosses her arms and huddles over. Did she see him looking? He curses to himself: He shouldn't think about her like that, especially after everything she's been through. He and Kyla are friends, nothing else. He can't go leering at her like some dirty old man.

She looks at him nervously. "Um, where should I . . . ?"

"God, I'm sorry." He trips over the words. "I don't want you to think that . . . um, I mean, you don't have to sleep here. Mom made up the sofa for you in the office."

She smiles, suppressing a chuckle.

He relaxes, smiles back. "Follow me."

257

Kyla puts her bag in the office, and he tells her to use the bathroom first. While he's waiting in his room he listens for sounds. When the bathroom door opens, he knows it's his chance to say good night. He sneaks out to her and sees her from behind, in just her panties. A second later she pulls on a T-shirt and crawls under the covers.

"Good night," he whispers.

She turns to look toward the hallway and smiles warmly. "Good night."

As he lies there waiting to fall asleep he pictures her again, almost naked in the darkness. He can't feel guilty. Things like that make an impression, that's just the way it is.

She wakes up because someone is staring at her. Scared, she bolts up in bed.

"It's time to get up. If you're going to get there in time," a strange woman says.

Then she remembers. She's at Alex's house.

His mother goes over and knocks on the door of Alex's room, calling out, "It's seven o'clock!"

It's like starting over again from the beginning. She has the same sense of insecurity at the breakfast table. She doesn't know if it's okay to help herself before Nina tells her to dig in, or if she dares ask for chocolate milk. It doesn't seem to be a chocolate milk family. They put muesli on their yogurt and only eat whole grain bread.

Thankfully it's better when it's just the two of them, on the way to school. She starts talking again: about playing hooky and hanging out in the café and how she might not get into the AP courses her father wants her to take, how he'd be mad if he knew she was taking a few days off to visit San Francisco. Alex doesn't say much. She sneaks a glance at him and then realizes that he's nervous.

What's he nervous about? About going to school with *her*? And what everyone will say? She wants to tell him not to worry. She won't embarrass him. Not after all the ways he's helped her.

It's the least she can do: Make him feel proud.

He spots Kevin, Val, Anton, and Javier in a cluster in the schoolyard. They haven't noticed him and Kyla yet. Kyla is rambling, "What a clean school! You should see mine, it's totally old and trashed . . ."

She's wearing different clothes today—something stylish and expensive-looking—and more makeup. He wanted to warn her in advance, point out that she's in a place where everyone who sticks out gets punished, but he stopped himself at the last second. It's really up to her how she wants to look.

They're not far now. He sees that Anton has noticed them and is standing there staring. He says something to the others. Maybe, *Who is that chick with Alex?*

And then they've reached the group. Everyone stares at

Kyla. They don't seem to understand what a girl like her is doing at their school, or what she's doing there with him. He hasn't mentioned a thing about her. He just told the teachers that he would be bringing someone with him today.

Anton snaps out of it first. "Well, hello, Alex!" His enthusiasm is comical.

Kyla smiles candidly. Alex introduces her. One after the other the guys in the group awkwardly mumble their names. Even Kevin seems off kilter, but he's still the first to ask, "So, uh, how do you two know each other?"

Alex is instantly afraid that Kyla will give away the truth, but she just smiles. "Some people sure want all the dirt!"

Dark red patches spread across Kevin's cheeks. All the anxiety and fear inside Alex instantly vanishes. He's simply grateful and proud of Kyla, who's able to do what so few succeed in doing—put Kevin in his place.

The others pick up where Kevin left off, bombarding them with questions. Where's she from? Has she been to the Bay Area before? What's she doing this weekend? Kyla answers with a minimum of words. As she flings her long gold hair back, they gaze at her admiringly.

"Well, new girl! Someone had better look after you today." Javier seems to be offering, but Kyla shakes her head.

"Alex will take care of me."

And then she takes Alex's arm and leads him away.

"See ya," she calls back to the group, leaning in against him.

He can't believe it. It's taken her five seconds to accomplish what he never dreamed he could do in a lifetime.

She's left them all utterly speechless.

She sits next to Alex in his classes as if she were auditing for some government agency. She's quiet, professional, studious.

The other students are obviously affected by her presence, constantly sneaking glances in her direction. It makes her feel important.

She looks around and after a while she's struck by how similar everything is: the classes, the students, the teachers—it's just like home. Alex's friends remind her of guys in her class, all acting so similar, they're hard to tell apart. And most people seem just as afraid of doing or saying anything original.

Alex doesn't make a sound. It's as if he tunes out. First she's afraid she's done something wrong, but when he whispers a tongue-in-cheek comment in her ear, she understands that it doesn't have to do with her; it's just the way he is.

The girl who sits in front of Alex keeps turning around all the time. She studies Kyla from head to toe with Elizabeth-like criticism. Kyla stares right back, that familiar anger bubbling up inside her. She wants to say something nasty but manages to restrain herself. The girl, whose name is Amanda, asks Alex about some group project.

She gets a pang in her heart when she sees them chatting with each other, though she doesn't understand why.

Obviously he can do his project with whomever he wants.

Kevin gives them a ride home. Kyla's in the front with him, Alex and Val in the backseat. Alex notes how Kyla leans in close as she chats with Kevin, who's trying to get his cool old Saab up to racing speeds. Kyla screams in delight, and turns to laugh with Alex, who grips his seat belt tightly. She grins and tells Kevin to slow down.

They hang out by the mini-mart. More and more people join them, all in higher spirits than usual. Guys are talking over each other, competing to see who can be the funniest. Kyla is the center of everyone's attention. Alex stands off to the side and watches. He really wants to show Kyla that he has a natural place in the gang, but every time he goes to say something, he gets so self-conscious that he only manages to say half of what he meant before someone else takes over.

Kyla has no problem holding her own. She laughs loudly and tosses her hair so much that it feels overdone. She looks at Alex a lot, a whole lot, with a sort of questioning look, and he's so embarrassed to be such a wimp that he avoids making eye contact. It's like she belongs to everyone else now; they've taken her from him. The more time passes, the more desperate he feels.

Now she's engaged in some banter with Kevin, who's egging her on with all of his L.A. stereotypes.

"So that makes all you Oakland guys straight-up gangster, just like the stereotype? Because you look sort of wussy to me." Kyla laughs.

Alex feels painfully excluded. He's just about to say that he has to go, when Kyla turns to him. "Alex, I'd like to go now. Is that okay?"

And he nods. He can't help grinning, he feels so warm from her attention.

He wants to take her out to eat. She says that really isn't necessary, but he insists. She paid for the train trip, it's only fair, blah, blah, blah . . .

There's something touching about how he is in the pizza place, his nervousness when the waiter comes and how he says the order wrong even though he repeated it beforehand. Fortunately, he laughs at himself.

"I'm really cool, eh?"

"Absolutely! You're so smooth, you might just be too smooth for your own good."

"What a joke." He sighs, looking down at the checked tablecloth.

"Hey," she says softly. "It's *not* a joke."

She glances around the restaurant with its tiled walls, cheesy light fixtures, and plastic-upholstered booths. It's no Koi, but there's no question that she'd rather be here, with Alex, than just about anywhere else in the world. She smiles at him, debates bringing up what's on her mind, then decides that that's exactly what she should do. Their relationship is based on being honest with each other.

"So, actually, I was wondering something. You don't show your friends the real you, do you?"

He just stares. Oh, no. Did she hurt his feelings?

"I mean, you just stand there and . . . I'm not sure. Obviously it's hard with them, right? To get a word in edgewise?"

"Maybe I'm not like that at all when you're not there."

"No, obviously. I'm sorry."

Alex fiddles sulkily with his napkin. She makes an attempt to patch her last effort.

"Maybe if you put some effort into it, if you just tried . . ." She trails off when she hears how that sounds, like some corny bullshit from a parent or teacher.

"That's easy for you to say."

"What do you mean by that?"

His posture is almost hostile. "Just because you're so over the top . . ." He stops and looks away.

"What is that supposed to mean? Over the top like how?"

"I don't know. You just say whatever you want. I'm not like that."

Says whatever she wants? What does he think of her? That she's some blabbermouth airhead?

"Well, how should I be then? I mean, if everyone were like you, they might as well just stay home."

He sips his soda slowly, refusing to look at her. Kyla hates herself. How did they end up arguing? Thankfully, the pizza finally comes and they can focus on wrangling long strands of cheese. Minutes tick by without a word.

Finally she asks, "What are you thinking about?"

"Christina."

It's like a slap in the face. *Christina? The anorexic dance girl he fantasizes about? He's thinking about her now?*

"I'm going to visit her in the hospital on Monday. I'm worried that she's gotten worse."

And what's she supposed to say to that? This is not exactly the time for a stinging retort. That poor girl is lying there in the intensive care unit starving herself to death.

"Oh."

Alex sighs, and Kyla takes that second to compose herself. "Are you still, I mean . . . are you still in love with her?"

He looks right at her.

"I don't know," he answers, his eyes unwavering. "Maybe I am."

He thinks about that the whole next day, about how everything got weird, and about how much Kyla hurt him with what she said. It's not exactly a newsflash that he has a hard time speaking up for himself—but still, to hear it from her . . .

She was quiet after their conversation at the pizza place. They'd gone home and watched TV, then gone to bed early without exchanging more than a few words. He'd lain there in bed for hours wondering: Did he overreact? Or just stand

265

up for himself? And why did he have to bring up Christina? To make Kyla jealous?

He's not sure of anything.

Kyla borrows Nina's bike. They ride a ways and stop by the edge of a forest preserve. The tension from yesterday slowly fades.

Kyla's cheeks are rosy. She's wearing his dad's big Windbreaker and no makeup, which changes her features. She isn't prettier without makeup, but her face is more regular. He likes seeing her this way; the beautiful girl is transformed into an almost-normal person.

She asks about various things they see, the redwoods and little animals, but he doesn't know the answers. For him this park is just a backdrop to his childhood. He tells Kyla that that was why his family moved to their neighborhood, to be close to "nature opportunities." "Not that we've come here since I was ten or something!" he adds, grinning.

Kyla laughs. She says she likes it out here, that maybe she was a redwood fairy in a previous life. She sits down on a rock and looks out over a small stream. The only sounds are the wind and the lull of quiet water.

"I could stay here. Forever."

He looks over, surprised.

"What do you mean? Stay in Oakland?"

"No. Here. On this rock."

He can't tell if she means it or if she's being sarcastic. Her eyes are fixed on the horizon.

"Imagine not having to deal with anything." She sighs happily. "Imagine the freedom!"

He follows her gaze, takes in the green ground cover and the bright purple flowers dotting the bushes, and feels a calmness spreading through him. "I know just what you mean."

She turns to look at him, an almost imperceptible smile tugging at the corners of her mouth. And they sit there in silence for the next several minutes, bodies so close they can almost feel each other's breath moving, but not quite.

It's been ages since she was this relaxed. The tiredness from walking around feels heavy, like cement in her body, but it's a nice feeling. They haven't talked about yesterday, but it seems cleared up, at least almost.

She still has a nagging sense of apprehension about Christina, but she tries to dismiss it and think instead about the stream. Not because they talk much; she just wants to focus on the feeling—the feeling of belonging together.

The house is different from this morning too. No one is home. His parents probably went to the city. Nina is rehearsing for a performance tonight and Andrei has a game. Just like Alex, Kyla hurries in the door and kicks off her shoes without setting them neatly in the shoe rack. "I'm *dying*," Alex groans, and runs up the stairs. "I have to lie down if I'm going to be up to going out tonight."

"I'm coming," she calls after him. "I'm just going to get a glass of water first."

Kyla jumps when she notices Alex's mother is sitting at the kitchen table, completely silent and motionless.

"Did I frighten you?"

"Um, yeah." Kyla goes to the dish drainer and chooses a glass, self-conscious. She fills the glass with water and feels Alex's mom watching her while she drinks. The water tastes metallic, but she finishes it to be polite.

"Weren't you guys going into San Francisco?" Kyla asks as cheerfully as she can.

"I am not feeling well."

Kyla washes the glass, and puts it back in the dish drainer carefully. She's on her way out of the kitchen when Alex's mom speaks again. "What exactly do you want with my Sasha?"

Kyla freezes. "What?"

Alex's mom sneers. "What do you share with him? Why do you want to be in his life?"

"I—"

"He is so different since he met you. So . . ." She stops and stares out the window. ". . . *contrary*. Not at all like he was."

Kyla reacts instinctively. "And what exactly does that have to do with me?" She hears how desperate she sounds.

"No, you don't understand, do you? You have no idea how gifted Sasha is!"

Kyla doesn't respond, just summons all her strength to try to look calm and unaffected.

"He could be the very best. Do you understand?"

"Of course." Kyla feels a lump forming in her throat. She's praying that Alex will walk in and rescue her.

"And he *loved* to dance. We had so much to talk about, Sasha and I. But one day it was over, he quit. I want you to tell me—what led to this?"

The tears are burning behind Kyla's eyelids. "I don't know," she whispers. "I don't see what *I* had to do with it."

"Alex never cared to go out, drink, all that you young people will do these days. But *you* thought he should be like that, didn't you? Like any of the boys on the corner."

"No," Kyla says so quietly it's almost inaudible, "that's not true."

"Isn't it?"

It's dead quiet. Kyla watches the woman's eyes fill with tears.

"It is a game to you? You come in his life and . . . and suddenly he wants to be a silly teenager—just like *you*."

Kyla slowly shakes her head, because it *isn't* true, none of it.

She runs out of the kitchen.

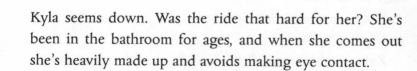

Kyla seems down. Was the ride that hard for her? She's been in the bathroom for ages, and when she comes out she's heavily made up and avoids making eye contact.

"Is something wrong?"

She shakes her head. "Should we go?"

They meet the others at the bus stop. Everyone brought something to drink. Alex stole a bottle of cognac from the cabinet. The bottle was so dusty, his parents would never miss it. He'd decided to show Kyla his other side tonight. He took his first drink right out of the bottle and even managed to avoid making a face—he's no wimp.

He takes an even bigger swig as Anton and Javier approach, whistling appreciatively at Kyla.

They take over the back of the bus. Even Alex yells, "Hey, send the beer this way!" He thinks Kyla is looking at him strangely. But then, she's not looking at him much at all right now. A bunch of bands are going to be playing this concert; Nina's is just one of them.

They stop at a park beforehand to get buzzed, and by the time they finish drinking everyone is starting to freeze. Kyla is standing there shivering. Javier pulls her in against him. Alex tries to make eye contact with her, but she looks away and lets it happen.

What's wrong with her? She's so far away from him again, messing around and showing off for the others and drinking *a lot*. Their moment in the redwoods starts to feel like it must have been a dream.

They pull themselves together and manage to get into the concert. He loses Kyla in the crowd, and everyone else too, except Val. Alex searches desperately for her in the mob, takes a spin around the room. Val sticks close by and tells him not to worry, they can look more after the first set.

For a little while, he forgets everything else. It's a revelation to see his sister so cocky and self-confident up on the stage. It takes his breath away. He's never seen her like this before, never realized how good she is, and it's as if everything falls into place. She's singing about things he knows: being hounded and bossed around, the desire for respect, resentment and frustration . . . He suddenly realizes that Nina is *really* doing something, carving her own way in the world. Suddenly he feels small and anything but cool. What is *he* doing?

After Nina's band plays, he finds everyone else again. It hurts him to see her; Kyla is teetering around with her eyes misted over and Kevin has his arm around her. She doesn't light up when she sees him, just demands, "Where the hell have you been?" He decides she looks cheap. After watching Nina perform, Kyla just looks like any other girl with her vacant stare, her shrill voice, and her bare midriff. She holds out a bottle of beer to him. He shakes his head.

"Come on!" she yells. "What's with you?"

"I don't want any. I think everyone's had enough to drink already."

Kevin brightens up. "Little Alex always drinks just the *right* amount, of course."

Alex just sighs.

Kevin tries to pull Kyla out onto the dance floor. She squeals and resists, but he succeeds in getting her to go. Alex watches from afar how Kyla barely moves while Kevin shifts from foot to foot rigidly, like a statue trying to bust a move. Then Kyla closes her eyes and starts slowly coming alive. First she just stands there swaying, then each part of her body starts gradually moving back and forth in time to the beat, her arms moving upward, her hips swaying. She loses herself in the music with such seriousness that he's amazed. It's nothing like his or Christina's technical grace; it's free and unrestrained and completely erases the side of her that went out there with Kevin in the first place. He can't take his eyes off her, wants to run up to her and whisper in her ear, "Come on, let's get out of here, away from all these people, because we belong together. It's simple as that."

When the song ends she opens her eyes. She looks around for him and when their eyes meet through the crowd of people it's as if they agree. But the spell is broken in the next second, when Kyla gives Kevin a drunken smile as he puts his hands around her waist.

Everyone else wants to dance with her too. Kyla is basking in the spotlight, teasing them and toying with them. After two more dances she comes over to Alex. "Shouldn't we dance?"

He shakes his head.

Her eyes narrow into slits. "No, right, of course. I'm just one of those people who runs around getting drunk and stuff. *A silly teenager.* God, how disgusting!"

"Knock it off."

But she stares at him defiantly. "Maybe you should just keep dancing with, you know, those *nice* girls . . . like whatever-her-anorexic-name-is . . . Christina?"

He doesn't respond. Just stares at her, tries to will anger onto his face. Inside it burns.

Kevin is tugging and pulling at Kyla.

"I can tell what you're thinking, Alex!" she shouts. "*God, she's a bitch!* Why did I even invite her here?"

"Shut up! All you do is . . . is just talk shit!"

"Well, that's better than *being* shit!"

What does she mean? What did he do? Why is she so angry? He stalks to the front of the crowd. Screw her. How can she talk to him like that when . . . Just screw her.

The only thing she wants to do is wreck as much as she can, make everything impossible between them. He's in love with Christina. She screwed up his life. It already is impossible, so what's the difference anyway?

It's just as well that Alex's mom pointed out how they have nothing in common. That she just drags him down. She was totally right. Kyla is a drunken, slutty mess—and little *Sasha* deserves better.

She lets that guy lead her around. It doesn't matter. Everything starts to get foggy and blurred. She drinks some more booze in the bathroom and she almost gets into a fight with a girl who gets in her face. "Bitch!" Kyla hears herself yell before someone pulls her away.

She ends up in a corner with the same guy. She feels his arms around her, his hands on her body, but doesn't care. Suddenly his tongue is in her mouth. It feels gross, but she lets it stay there. All she thinks about is how wrong it is, but after all, this is what she wanted.

She feels someone grab hold of her. She only sees his eyes through her haze, those divine eyes. There's no anger in them, just pain.

"I'm leaving now," Alex tells her.

She wants to scream, "I have to go with you. Please, I'm sorry, I suck, please, Alex, let me come with you." But her thoughts never turn into action. The guy who had his tongue in her mouth shoves Alex.

"What the hell?" Kevin shouts.

The other guys are drawn to them like flies. They come over with curious looks, wondering if there's going to be a fight.

"Didn't you hear me, loser?"

Alex looks completely deadpan and expressionless. Then he gets shoved again, for real, and loses his balance. Lightning flashes in his eyes.

"I can't take this anymore," he murmurs darkly.

Kyla sobers up instantly. The others stop too, and an "Oooooh" runs through the crowd. Now there's really going to be trouble. But Alex just stands there, as if turned to stone, fists clenched.

"Oh, so you're a tough guy, huh?" Kevin taunts. "Are you showing off for the girl? She doesn't want to be with a fairy fag, don't you get that?"

Then something happens to Alex. It's like he turns into a wild animal, ready to pounce.

"Fuck off." Alex snorts, spit spraying. The next second he punches Kevin right in the face. Hard. Kevin topples over onto the floor, his mouth bleeding.

Everyone trades astonished looks, staring at the boy crumpled on the floor. Kevin slowly stands up, bewildered, as if he doesn't get what just happened. He moves his lips, looks at his hand, makes a face at the sight of blood. Then he snaps out of it and turns slowly toward Alex, who's still standing in the same spot, motionless. With lightning speed he grabs Alex's jacket and flings him against the wall. Alex's head clunks against the hard concrete.

"I'll kill you!" Kevin's wrist is pressed against Alex's throat. Kyla sees Alex gasping for air—sees the color of his face changing. She screams silently and looks around. Why isn't anyone doing anything?

"Stop it!" she yells.

Then one of the guys steps forward, the one who was hanging out by Alex all evening.

"Are you crazy?" Val yanks on Kevin's arm, hard. "Let go of him!"

Kevin is so surprised that he loses his grip on Alex's jacket.

Alex sinks down onto the floor, coughing. He feels a hand on his back. When he looks up he sees Kyla, water spilling from her puppy dog eyes. Everything in his head is spinning. Kevin is standing with a dumbfounded sneer on his bloody face, staring at Val. He can't get a word out.

Val is breathing hard. "You have no idea, Kevin!"

Kevin flings his arms in the air. "What? What are you talking about?"

"What do you think? All your shit talk. Get it through your head. *Alex. Isn't. Gay.*"

Kevin looks to the others for support. "He's *not gay?*"

No one reacts. Kevin breaks into a nervous smile, then walks over and thwacks Val on the back. "Come on, man."

But Val backs away. "You're so clueless!" He pauses. "I'm the one who's—"

"What?"

Val raises his head. His body is so tense, his muscles ripple under the skin.

"I'm the one who's gay."

Kevin's smile freezes.

"Surprise! It's true. I've been gay this whole time. Totally gay, gay as a queen, gayer than gay! Guess you had a problem *smelling* it. So you can knock off all your bullshit with Alex and direct it at me. That is, if you're man enough."

Val turns to Alex and gestures toward the exit with his head. Alex casts a last look at Kyla, who's standing there shaking. She looks at him pleadingly. But he can't feel sorry for her. She makes him sick. He turns and follows Val out the door.

It's not until Kyla gets home to her apartment, once she's locked the door to her own room and flung herself down on her bed, that she cries. She held it in all night—for all those hours in the city before the next train to Los Angeles left at 6:10 a.m. She just wandered around bumming cigarettes off people who didn't look too crazy, and telling all the guys who wanted to talk to her to go to hell. She wandered up and down streets, back and forth, until the station opened, without tears. Not all day, or the whole way home on the train either.

It's early evening. She's lying in bed sobbing. She crawled under the covers in her grimy clothes and curled up into a ball. In the middle of all the crying she starts hearing what it sounds like. An almost cartoonish wail, "Boohoo, boohoohoo!"

There's a knock on her door.

"Kyla, honey?"

"Go away!"

She doesn't want to talk to her mom. There's no comfort, no help for her. What's done is done. The doorknob turns back and forth several times.

"Kyla! Kyla, please open the door!"

Kyla tries to sniffle quietly, but it doesn't work. She knows her mom can hear her, knows it's torture for her to stand out there, but how could she possibly be any help? Frail, feeble Mom who tried to abandon Kyla once before.

"Kyla, you have to open the door! I know it's hard . . . I know life sucks sometimes, but what if we talk about it? I might understand more than you think."

But Kyla doesn't want to talk about what a horrible excuse for a person she is. She muffles her sobs with her pillow. There's silence. The sniffles slowly abate as her body shakes in small, soundless, almost epileptic jerks.

Will her mom think she's asleep and leave her alone?

No. She doesn't give up.

"You got to comfort me, Kyla. Can't I come in and comfort you? Honey? You don't need to tell me what happened. I promise, I won't ask anything. Please, sweetie . . ."

Kyla raises the covers. She moves slowly over to the door and unlocks it. Her mom is inside in a second. She embraces her, holds her hard. Kyla opens her mouth and lets out a long wail.

"Cry," her mom whispers. "I know how it feels, sweetheart. Just cry."

They sit on her bed for a good half an hour, Kyla in her mother's lap like a little baby. Strangely, she knows she doesn't need to be scared anymore. This is her mom showing her that she won't try to kill herself ever again. It's two of them now and forever.

Her mom rocks her back and forth. "We can help each other, honey. Promise me that. You and me, Kyla, we'll stick together."

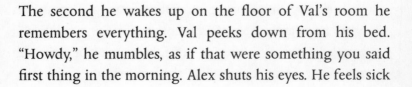

The second he wakes up on the floor of Val's room he remembers everything. Val peeks down from his bed. "Howdy," he mumbles, as if that were something you said first thing in the morning. Alex shuts his eyes. He feels sick and grimy, and the events rehashing themselves in his head make him feel like he's drowning.

Val seems to want to talk, though, and there's no avoiding him. "What a night," he says, almost elated. "Wonder what things will be like now."

"Hmm?"

"Tell the truth. Did you suspect at all?"

Alex thinks about Kyla's hair that day in the forest, how it got big and frizzy from the exercise, and of the face she made when she slipped by the stream and got soaked. And then her face as she sat on the rock: *Imagine not having to deal with anything.*

"Huh?"

"I asked if you suspected anything!"

"I really should have." Alex is thinking about Kyla's e-mails, so often filled with stories of raging parties. "I really should have had some idea of who she was."

"No, not Kyla, dude. Me! That I'm, you know . . ." Val's face changes colors. "Gay." He shakes his head. "It sounds so crazy weird. To say it."

Alex suddenly wonders: Could Val be a real friend?

"No, I never suspected."

Val lies back down again, staring up at the ceiling.

"Not even you. I thought that in some way *you* always knew."

Alex slowly slinks home from the bus stop. Outside his door he stops and waits a few seconds. He didn't call to tell them where he was last night. His parents must be sick with worry. What if they even called the police?

279

But his mom isn't standing there when he walks in, doesn't even come hurrying to the door. It feels strange. He hears low murmurs in Russian from the kitchen.

"Poor girl. Her poor parents. Such a shame . . ." he hears his parents saying.

What happened?

"Dancing," his father sighs. "Really, not everyone can . . . it is lucky you were able to stop in time."

"Was *able* to stop?"

"Yes, that you stopped before it got serious. Would you have been able to handle a professional career?"

It's silent for a few seconds.

"*You* wanted me to stop!" Alex's mom wails, practically screaming.

"Olga—"

"It was just *you, you, you,* always *you.* And for me: *You* must stop dancing and move to America with me, *you* must have a bunch of children that *you* should take care of . . . "

"Olga, dear—"

His mom tries to imitate his dad's voice: "*I* have so much *I* need to do in my life that I can't do here in Russia. There are no opportunities in this country for *me. I* must get an education. *I* must work."

"No, that's—"

"And what about *me*? What about what *I* wanted? *My* dream? You did not care about that!"

"Do you even know what you're saying? Olga, lie to the children if you must, but how can you lie to me as well?"

"Lie?"

His father's voice is calm and gentle. "You know what it was like. You were not . . ." Deep sigh. "You were not good enough. This is how *they* thought. The theater would not keep you. It was very well for us to move to America right then."

Alex reels. *Not good enough?* She always said she was the best.

"And besides, you were pushing yourself too hard, you had impossible standards . . . it was just as well, what happened."

Alex is holding his breath. All those years she talked about what a star she was, all those years he was told that he took after her, that they had the same unique gift, that he was going to follow in her footsteps. It was all . . . a lie?

He stands there for maybe a minute. Not a sound comes from the kitchen. Then someone comes out. Alex jumps. His mom stops and stares at him, her eyes glazed.

"There you are." It's a simple statement of fact. She looks small and sad. "Paulina called. She wanted to talk about the schedule and what it will be for the fall." She puts a trembling hand on his shoulder. "But . . . it's terrible, Sasha. Christina is not coming back to our studio. She must *stop* dancing."

One day a package arrives with the clothes and toiletries she'd left at Alex's house. She searches frantically for a letter, but there is none, not even a hastily scribbled note. She tries to unpack her things but can't bear to look at them, so she flings the box into the hamper and shuts the lid.

But it's hard to put things out of your mind, especially when you spend so much time alone. She doesn't see Therese and Susanna anymore and hasn't managed to make any new best friends. There's always someone to hang out with at school; after all, she's still popular. But on the weekends, she mostly stays home. She stopped going out at night, doesn't dare go to parties. She's so scared of what might happen. She still doesn't trust herself, but at least the slut rumors have subsided.

After a few weeks she tells her mother what happened in Oakland. It just comes out when they're sitting in front of the TV one night, slowly and with all the details. She doesn't censor anything, and her mom listens without saying a word.

When the story's done, she puts her arm around Kyla's shoulders and pulls her in close. Kyla wishes she would say something comforting, but she doesn't. She's simply *there*. And she doesn't judge.

The next day when she gets to school she sees Lucas's car idling. Her heart is suddenly in her mouth. But then she notices someone in the front seat. When she gets closer she sees that it's Therese. She's not surprised; it feels as if she'd known it all along. Is it true love or revenge? Kyla realizes it doesn't matter.

She starts walking toward the school. She knows Therese is watching her. What's weird is that it doesn't feel sad or upsetting. This end just feels like what was supposed to happen all along.

Val and Alex reach the soccer field, and start to gear up—Val with much more gusto and anticipation. Kevin basically disappeared after everything went down at the concert, and things have reached a normal pace. But practice is starting to feel more and more pointless to Alex. It's not exactly boring, it's . . . something else.

It's been a long time since Alex considered his every opinion before he spoke—by a few months after . . . what happened, he could keep up with conversation as if it were natural. He told Val he almost feels like the son of Bob Jones; in the other guys' eyes surely he is. They'd both laughed, but Alex has a feeling lurking inside, gnawing at his gut, telling him something's *off.*

He straightens up and stares out at the grassy green field. At times like this, he thinks about Kyla. He doesn't want to, she just pops into his head. It hurts just as much each time.

Sometimes, late at night, he checks his e-mail—as if he were hoping. So dumb.

When he stopped seeing Christina at dance class, he realized he'd never been in love with her. She had been a dream to him, nothing more. How *could* he love her? He never actually *knew* her, and that was his own fault.

She's been living in rehab for the last few weeks. At least, that's what he's heard. No one from dance is permitted to contact her, and perhaps that's just as well. In the end, what could he offer her? And vice versa?

The next day, halfway to soccer practice, he just stops on the sidewalk. He's completely still for a moment, then he slowly turns around and goes back home.

Without anyone seeing him, he goes up to his room and grabs his dance bag from where he'd stuffed it in the top of his closet. Then he trots off to the bus stop.

When Kyla gets to the stables, Elizabeth is in a stall curry-combing a horse. They're equally surprised to see each other. Kyla had no idea Elizabeth rode *here*. She must come on different days, for the more advanced classes.

"Hi," Kyla says. It would be absurd not to say hello.

"Hi." To her amazement, Elizabeth returns the greeting.

Is that a little smile she glimpses at the corner of Elizabeth's mouth? Anyway, there's no open hostility. Neither of them has said a word to each other since that time in the elevator. It's been at least a couple of months.

"You ride here?" Kyla asks.

Elizabeth nods. "I've started teaching classes, and taking care of Blacky too. So it's me and a bunch of little girls."

As Kyla tries to learn this posting business, she suddenly realizes that she doesn't resent Elizabeth anymore. But when she gets back, Elizabeth is gone.

Just a few days later, they come out into the hallway at the same time.

Both of them are wearing breeches and carrying a helmet under their arms. Kyla can't help but laugh. Elizabeth too; it's so obvious where they're going.

They sit next to each other on the bus and walk from the stop to the riding school together. They don't talk about anything but horses. After the lesson, Elizabeth waits for her and they head home together. Kyla tells Elizabeth about her mom, how she's started skipping riding to do other things. Now she wants to learn everything at once: French and Photoshop and even yoga.

"She's nuts," Kyla sighs, even though she's actually proud.

"So she's doing better now?"

Kyla's surprised. What does Elizabeth know about her mother? More than what she saw in the stairwell that time?

Elizabeth notices her reaction and blushes. "I saw you—and the ambulance—when they took your mom to the hospital."

Kyla squirms. She never thought of who might have been watching that night.

"I guess after that, I realized things haven't been easy for you." She pauses. "I was angry when your dad left and you stopped hanging out with me. I took it personally, but—I should have understood. I should have been a better friend."

Kyla is stunned. Do people actually get second chances?

She swallows the lump forming in her throat. "We were twelve. There's no way you could have known."

They're quiet for a moment, then Elizabeth changes the subject. She leans in conspiratorially. "So I met that new guy you're seeing."

Oh, God. "Lucas?"

"No, that other guy. You know, the guy you were e-mailing."

Alex? Kyla feels dizzy.

Elizabeth grins. "He was super-nice. I'm sure he thought you and I were, like . . . friends."

"What did you guys talk about?" She hears how scared she sounds.

"About you." Elizabeth looks embarrassed. "I get it if you think that's strange, considering you and I weren't exactly . . . you know."

Kyla just nods.

"But he said your mom wasn't doing well . . . just when we were going up in the elevator, I mean. He was a little worried about you, how you were going to manage."

Kyla snaps out of it. "Yeah, my mom's doing better, a lot better." She doesn't want to talk about Alex.

"When I met him, I started thinking about you differently. It made you seem more like your own person, like someone no one thought."

Slowly Kyla feels warm inside.

"So when *that stuff* happened at the party . . ."

That stuff. Kyla wants to pull the cord, press the button, rush up to the bus driver and to make him stop so she can run away. Elizabeth continues, ". . . well, I was so surprised."

"I know," Kyla adds quickly. "It was inexcusable."

"But . . . then you said you were sorry. And Erik . . ."

Kyla feels the color rising into her face again. This is torture.

" . . . despite the fact that he's a total loser, he said that you changed your mind. That you two never did it."

"No, but still."

The seconds tick by. Elizabeth offers a soft smile, something like forgiveness. Kyla opens her mouth to say thank you but can't get a word out. There's so much more she wants to explain. She looks down at her boots, ashamed by her inability. Cautiously she lifts her head again. Then she realizes that she doesn't need to say anything.

Elizabeth understands.

Alex doesn't say anything to his mom, just that they're playing four times a week now. That's how often he puts on his cleats and carries his bag full of dance clothes out of the house. Then, as soon he gets out of sight of the kitchen window, he changes direction and goes down to the bus stop.

Paulina has promised not to tell. The first time, she was speechless. He was there for an hour before she saw him, dancing like he'd just come out of hibernation—dancing until he forgot where he was.

Without a word she came over and threw her arms

around him. That was all. Then she let go of him and started class. Now she lights up whenever Alex steps into the studio.

Val was fine when Alex quit soccer. He joked that they were going to lose a whole lot more games, but he understood Alex's decision. He needed to do what made him *himself*—now that he'd figured it out.

They get together sometimes, go over to each other's houses to play Wii and talk. Or they ride their bikes or try out a recipe—it turns out Val is quite the chef. In the beginning it felt weird, but Alex got used to it over time, started sharing some of his feelings, kidding around.

One night, Alex tells Val the whole Kyla story, from the beginning to the end. When he's done, Val is quiet for a moment. Then he asks, "Are you in love with her?"

"Are you nuts? After what she did?"

"Yeah, but if that stuff with Kevin hadn't happened, would you have been in love with her then?"

"We're about as different as can be."

"You didn't answer my question."

"Yeah, well," Alex stumbles over the words. "She's, well . . . I mean, she's so . . . we don't have anything in common."

"What did you used to write about then?"

"Everything."

Val smiles. "Then you have everything in common."

Val thinks Alex should write to her again, but he can't.

He will never go crawling back, it's as simple as that.

~~~

One day when Alex comes home from school he finds his mother in the kitchen with a letter in her hand. She's holding it up to the light, squinting, and doesn't see him standing there in the doorway.

"What is that?" Alex asks.

"Hmm?" His mother drops the letter on the table, caught in the act.

He picks up the envelope. "This is addressed to me!"

She's embarrassed. "I know it is. I was simply curious . . ."

"Don't read other people's mail."

She doesn't respond. He turns his back to her and opens it. Doesn't whoop with joy, because it says exactly what he was expecting. He got into the City Ballet School. He stuffs the letter back in the envelope.

"You were admitted?"

"To what?"

"Please, Sasha . . ."

He turns around. She looks gentle and loving. "I know that you have been dancing again."

He's completely shocked. All this time he's been sneaking around behind her back. "How?" he asks. "Did Paulina . . . ?"

"No, Paulina has not said a word. But a mother, she knows."

"Why didn't you say something?"

"I thought it was better for you if I stay out of it."

He feels no anger toward her, weirdly enough. He ought to feel dumb for walking around pretending all those months, but he doesn't. He's just grateful that she kept her distance—that she let him have this for himself.

Alex pours some water into the kettle and opens the cupboard to get out some cups. "Do you want some tea, Mom?"

Kyla tries to write to him. Elizabeth nags her into it. She says Kyla can't let a guy like that go, *he's not like all the others*.

All the others. God knows, there have been quite a few.

Every evening she writes a new e-mail, but it's never anything she wants to send. With each attempt it gets harder and harder. It's been such a long time.

She often thinks about all Alex's done for her. In a way it's thanks to him that she and Elizabeth got to be friends again. They see each other pretty often now, just the two of them, mostly at the stables.

Elizabeth's other friends don't ride. Elizabeth, whom Kyla always thought of as perfect, says she feels inferior to them. They're so smart and scholarly, they're musicians and writers—and she's just good at cramming and is not particularly creative at all. But she does love horses.

They go out on the town. Sometimes they meet new guys at some café. But Kyla hasn't had a boyfriend since Lucas. Elizabeth goes on dates with a couple of guys, but nothing serious. She's just having fun and glad she's no longer with Erik the Sleaze.

One day Kyla finds out she didn't get the grades she needed for her AP courses. She expected that—but Lizzie says there's still a slight chance. Kyla talks to the school counselor, who says that she can take extra classes over the summer and tests in the subjects that are required to get in. Then she e-mails her dad. He's willing to pay for the classes. Mostly it's Lizzie who cheers her on.

Kyla is struck by how Liz has taken Alex's place in her life—and in the same instant feels an intense sense of longing.

> dear alex,
>
> if u only knew how many times i've started writing you, how many times i've deleted every-thing. i know it's 2 late for a bunch of i'm sorrys, but i have to try.
>
> it feels like 1000 years ago, that weekend with you, the worst weekend. there's no point in blaming alcohol. no one poured it down my throat against my will. so what should i say? i don't know if you could tell, alex, but when we saw each other, i still hadn't figured out anything about myself or what i wanted in my life and i was still sad and terrified about what my mom had done . . . i was so looking forward to that weekend and

had such high hopes and really—it *was* amazing at first.

but then i got insecure and suddenly i had no idea how to be . . . and then that same day we went to nina's concert your mom had a talk with me. she told me it was my fault you quit dancing and that i'd ruined ur life. i couldn't bear the idea that it might be true—that *i* might have caused u to give up the one thing u really love. so after that i kind of wanted to wreck everything between us.

i don't know if this explanation helps, but at least now i've said it. u don't need 2 answer and i understand if u hate me.

but i want u to know, i'm changing. nothing is the same really. my mom has been in the same job for over 3 months now. i've been going to summer school and i managed to get into the ap courses i wanted! studying is going all right . . . i'm feeling good about it. i'm feeling happy! and you were right—i'm *not* dumb.

well, that's about all. I hope ur happy 2, i hope that so much. and i think about u often.
kyla

ps yesterday i finally did it! I galloped through
a meadow on a horse!

He reads the e-mail several times. His new life at his new school with all his new friends, Friday evenings at cafés in San Francisco, the rigorous dance training—it's helped his memories of Kyla fade, but now, in a flash, he's back with her.

His mother. He should have known she had something to do with Kyla's weirdness. He should be angry, he should want to march up to her and really let her have it. But it's so long ago. What good would it do now?

Besides, his mom is so different these days. Happier. She's started working as a receptionist at the school and enjoys it. She no longer waits for him in the entry hall when he comes home from dance. More and more she leaves him in peace, and her *Sasha*-ing bothers him less and less. It feels risky to stir up the past.

He's doing so well. He goes to concerts and listens to music, which is opening things up inside him. And he doesn't want to go back to a relationship filled with waiting and misunderstandings.

He reads her message again and reflects on how his body sort of tingles, despite the fact that this is the third time he's reading it. He sits perfectly still for a moment, then he quickly deletes the e-mail and empties the trash.

It's her mom who sees his name in the paper.

"*Alex Borodin.* Isn't that *him*?"

Kyla was just on her way out of the kitchen. Her heart skips a beat. It's been three months since she e-mailed Alex. He never responded.

"What?" Kyla squeaks.

Her mother points to the paper.

"Alex Borodin. His name is right here. He's going to be one of the finalists competing to represent the U.S. in some international dance competition."

Kyla reads over her mother's shoulder.

"It's going to be on TV too."

And there's his name with about ten others: Alex Borodin from Oakland.

Kyla heads for the door. She doesn't want to be late.

"It's going to be right here in L.A. Don't you want to try to get tickets?"

"I'm sure they're sold out." Kyla slips on her cotton jacket.

Her mom stares at her for a moment. "Boy, are you chicken."

Kyla bristles—her mom looks almost *mad*. "What do you mean, chicken? He's made it clear that he doesn't want anything to do with me."

"No one said you have to stand up during the show and yell 'Here I am!'"

"But . . ."

Her mom rises from her seat, lays a hand on Kyla's shoulder. "Honey, have you ever seen him dance?"

Alex was the only one chosen from northern California. His mom is beside herself with pride. But he notices that she tries to tone it down for his sake. His father just smiled with bewilderment when he heard that Alex would be competing. As long as Alex gets good grades, his dad is quiet, like always. That never changes.

When the plane landed, Alex thought of Kyla right away—Los Angeles and Kyla were inseparable. He was prepared for the thought, but it still stings.

That sense of being close to her, it was almost unbearable the first few hours. It took a lot of energy to concentrate on the competition.

They spent the night at Vladik and Eva's and then there were rehearsals all day. He forbade his mother from wandering around backstage, so she wandered around Hollywood instead. But of course tonight she's one of the first ones to take a seat in the audience.

Her lips are dark red and her hair is piled so high on her head that it ought to concern the people sitting behind her. This is her big night too. Alex peeks out from behind the curtain with anticipation. The audience slowly fills with people.

He finds himself searching for Kyla's face and gets irritated with himself, lets go of the curtain, and returns backstage with the other competitors.

He's longing to be out on the stage and yet weirdly calm. The calm is what surprises him. All the dancers seem talented. Several of them are two or three years older, but it doesn't matter. He chats with them, fully aware that even if he loses, he'll never stop dancing.

The nerves backstage are palpable. The girls are traipsing around in toe shoes, all of them equally thin and long-legged. For a second he thinks about Christina, who seemed so delicate and unique. Several of the girls here are near duplicates of her, swinging their legs through the air and leaning forward with their necks elongated gracefully. In an instant he's afraid of what might happen to them, or to the guy standing in the corner hyperventilating with all the muscles tensed under his too-pale skin, but now is not the time.

He's going to dance barefoot in a tank top and tights. Many of the others have picked music from well-known ballets, but he did his own choreography to a contemporary song. He's so sure it's right. But when there are only ten minutes left, his thoughts start spinning: What if it was stupid not to do something classical? What's wrong with him that he isn't nervous? Aren't you supposed to be A, nervous; B, really nervous; C, really really crazy nervous . . . He smiles privately, recalling the supportive congrats Toby had e-mailed the day before.

Before the emcee steps onto the stage, he gives the whole group the thumbs-up.

Alex just nods and awaits his turn.

Neither of them has been to a ballet performance before. It's lucky Elizabeth came with her, even if she won't stop commenting on every single thing she sees. But they're welcome distractions: "Wow! What a gorgeous building. That's one *huge* stage. Look at all these people!" and "How nervous do you think they are?"

Kyla brought flowers at Liz's urging. She thought about dropping them off before the performance, but they made it to the Walt Disney Concert Hall in the nick of time. So much for that plan. Lizzie tries to cheer her: Maybe they'll find someone afterward who can make sure he gets them. But Kyla still isn't sure if she wants Alex to know she's there.

They have good seats. The TV cameras make everything momentous, and signal that what's going to happen is of the utmost importance. Kyla feels the tension—everyone looks so eager. She feels like people can tell she doesn't belong here. Everyone else is surely siblings, parents, or classmates of the people who'll be competing—and she, well, what is she to Alex? An old acquaintance? An adoring fan?

She realizes that Alex would hardly recognize her now. It's been nearly a year since they've seen each other. So much has surely happened in his life as well. Her eyes settle on an amazing hairdo a few rows in front of her. Before she knows it, the woman has turned around. Kyla jumps instinctively.

"What is it?" Elizabeth wonders.

"Alex's mom," Kyla whispers.

Mrs. Borodin scans the audience in excitement. And then, boom, their eyes meet. There's no way to avoid it. They stare at each other for several seconds, and neither of them makes any attempt to nod in recognition or smile. Kyla can't read what she sees in Alex's mother's eyes. Is it contempt or just surprise? Then the lights go down and the woman and her hairdo turn back to face the stage.

Kyla's heart is racing.

Elizabeth, who's been following the drama, grabs Kyla's hand and squeezes.

The emcee steps onto the stage and bids everyone welcome. He introduces the jury, which consists of all kinds of famous people Kyla's never heard of: prima ballerinas, national award-winning dancers, ballet school headmasters and choreographers. And when the dancing starts—Kyla is amazed. It's like the girls are from another century the way they float across the stage in their stiff tutus. She's both befuddled by them, and impressed. She and Elizabeth look at each other and smile, but sometimes they raise their eyebrows, full of admiration at what people can do with their bodies.

After six dancers, they present Alex Borodin. Fear floods her body at just the sound of his name. As if she never believed he would really be there. She feels dizzy. What if he still recognizes her and stops dancing in anger, or trips in surprise? "Crap!" she whispers. Elizabeth squeezes her sweaty hand again and she suppresses the will to flee.

The music starts before anyone even catches a glimpse of him: deep bass notes without any obvious rhythm or melody. Then he slowly strides in. She doesn't recognize him at first; he seems like he's grown. He's a man, not a boy, as he makes his way to the middle of the stage. She's struck by how *handsome* he is. It's ludicrous, but she really never noticed until now.

Enthralled, she follows his body on the stage. Each motion is perfect and natural. He leaps, he spins. He is really, *really* good. Is it relief she feels? Did she actually worry he'd embarrass himself up there?

When the music is over, she forgets to think about what you're *supposed* to do. She stands up, cheering and whistling loudly. Alex bows proudly and smiles happily at the audience.

"Wow, he's really hot," Elizabeth giggles, wiping something off Kyla's cheek.

Kyla swipes her own fingers across her face. Only then does she realize she's crying.

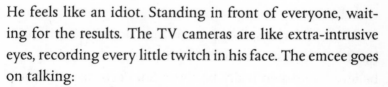

He feels like an idiot. Standing in front of everyone, waiting for the results. The TV cameras are like extra-intrusive eyes, recording every little twitch in his face. The emcee goes on talking:

". . . all this talent gathered onto one stage . . ."

Alex senses the presence of the other competitors around him, their rapid breathing and nervous throat clearing.

". . . our esteemed jury has finally reached a decision . . ."

The audience holds its breath. Alex's mother sits stiff as a rod, her eyes unblinking.

"Let's welcome the chairman of the jury onto the stage . . ."

He didn't do a perfect job. His body was tense in the beginning and he was self-conscious. But then he got a grip on himself. The audience response felt good afterward, but you never know.

". . . and the time has come to let all of our anxious competitors know who . . ."

They start with third prize. Alex realizes he's hoping it will be him, just so the torture will be over.

". . . Natalie Landin!"

One of the ballerinas flashes a smile, mixed with relief and disappointment. She steps away from the others and goes over to accept her flowers.

Time for second prize. He closes his eyes, both wanting it and not wanting it.

"Tonight's second prize winner's name is A . . ." It *is* him! ". . . Adrian von Seth!"

He's almost astonished when the guy next to him walks forward. The next second, the fear finally arrives. What if he doesn't win *anything*?

Only now does he realize how important it is to him to show everyone back home how wrong they were about him. Only this moment does he realize that there's one person he's thinking about—the one he wants to impress most of all. Why? Why does he want *her,* whose e-mail he didn't even answer, to stare dumbfounded at his name in the newspaper and watch him get first prize on TV?

Why, after everything, does he still care?

He looks like he's in his own world. His eyes are trained somewhere far behind everyone's heads. Kyla wonders what he's thinking about. The prize that will take him to Italy for the international competition? The future successes that will give him work all over the world?

His life is so different from hers. She was so beside herself with pride at acing her summer courses and getting into the AP classes. It's enough for her to have one friend she likes and an activity in her free time that isn't completely devoid of meaning.

Meanwhile, Alex is on his way to conquering the world.

"And now it's time to announce tonight's well-deserving first prize winner . . ."

She holds her breath.

"I'm pleased and proud to present the person who will be representing the United States in the international competition for young dancers in Venice . . ."

The emcee pauses. Alex is standing motionless, his face frozen. The whole audience is dead silent.

"Alex Borodin!"

Yes! Yes! Yes!

Kyla completely forgets herself, raises her arms up in the air, and yells at the top of her lungs. Only one other person is as ecstatic. Alex's mother is cheering like a madwoman. Alex himself mostly looks confused. He looks out at the audience, astonished. For a second she thinks he sees her. Her chest pounds when his eyes stop on her, but then his gaze moves on. When the emcee repeats his name, Alex snaps out of his trance and strides over to accept his prize.

He doesn't look overwhelmed now; his smile is just pulling at the corners of his mouth.

He still hasn't recovered. He's sitting in the dressing room, drinking champagne right out of the bottle, as if he were legal. His mom just laughs—he can do whatever he wants right now. The other competitors and jury members have left, there aren't any more congratulators. Just his mom. She cried so much, her makeup ran so dramatically, that her face is a riot of different colors and shapes.

"Oh, Sasha," she whimpers for the seventeenth time tonight.

But a moment later, she's all business. She glances toward the doorway, claps her hands. "We must pack up to leave! Off to the showers now!"

Alex has no desire to rush. "What's the hurry?"

His mom casts a quick glance toward the closed door—again.

"We will eat at beautiful restaurant, of course! I made reservation!"

"Okay, take it easy." Alex chuckles.

"Hurry hurry!"

She tosses a towel at him. He ducks and it lands on the floor. "Let's go!"

They're interrupted by a knock. Alex's mom freezes and stares at the door in dismay. What is she afraid of? That someone will come and take the prize away from him?

"Sasha, I do not think—"

"Come in," Alex interrupts.

The door opens slowly. First he sees the big bouquet and assumes that it's yet another jury member to wish him well in Venice. But then he notices her face above the red blooms. Kyla.

He feels a twinge. Cold and hot at the same time. He's at a complete loss. Was she here all night? Sitting out in the audience watching while he . . .

"Hi," she says. Nothing more. As if it weren't at all strange that she's standing there. As if countless months hadn't gone by since they'd last seen each other. As if she hadn't gotten completely wasted and made out with Kevin right in front of his eyes.

She looks different. She has bangs now. She looks pale and has black eyeliner on, no lipstick. Her chin is hidden by a gauzy yellow scarf. It hurts to look at her, she's so beautiful.

"Um, I thought . . ." She smiles uncertainly. ". . . Congratulations!" She holds out the flowers without moving. He snaps out of it.

"Come in."

She takes a couple of steps into the room. Stands there with the flowers in front of her chest, as if protecting herself. He takes the bouquet. "Thanks."

Her arms drop limply to her sides. Her gaze darts quickly toward the door.

"Um, my friend is waiting outside. Elizabeth?" But he doesn't know who she's talking about. "She was actually the one who thought I . . ."

She looks down, but her eyes glance up behind her bangs. Is she doing it on purpose? Trying to melt him with her crazy charm?

"Well, I was a little scared to . . ." She trails off.

Alex looks at his mother. Thinks of her hurry to leave. She must've noticed Kyla in the audience.

"Can you leave us for a minute?" he asks.

"But we must go!"

His mom's afraid. Of what? That Kyla will ruin him? He smiles to himself.

"Go on," he tells her.

Reluctantly she leaves. Kyla gives him a look of gratitude and searches for a smile. He gives her no response. He can't. He can't deny he's happy to see her, but the old hurt is still there.

"I thought you'd seen me," she says quietly.

"From the stage? Oh, no. The lights. You can't see any-thing."

She looks down at her shoes. "I wanted to say that . . . Well, you were unbelievable out there." More intensely: "I'm sure I don't understand all the reasons they picked you, but you were . . . *different* from the others, you know? Everything you did looked strong and sure and natural. I mean, compared to the other dancers."

She stops. As if she'd realized she was talking too much. Her words warm him.

He'd wanted so badly to impress her and, well, mission accomplished.

"Thanks." It's the only thing he gets out.

She looks at the door again. "Maybe I should go."

Maybe. An unmistakable hedge. But he doesn't know what he wants, what she wants. She waits for his response, then starts moving toward the door. In five seconds she'll be out of his life.

"So now that things are going so amazingly well for me, you don't want to trample on me anymore?"

It comes out quickly. He's almost surprised himself.

Just coming to see him, asking the way to the dressing room, knocking on the door and delivering the flowers, even that was so much more than she'd planned.

Elizabeth said she'd regret it her whole life if she didn't

do it. Kyla had gathered all the courage she had. But now—this bitter accusation.

Alex looks unmoved.

"It just seems like you've changed your attitude," he continues, setting the flowers on the table. "Is it because I performed in this big fancy theater? Because people clapped for me? Because I won first prize?"

It burns.

"What do you think?" she asks.

He stops, his eyes trained on her.

"I know how people are."

"I'm not *people*."

But he doesn't let up.

"If you wonder why I don't exactly trust you . . ." He pauses and swallows. ". . . then maybe you don't remember how it feels to be humiliated and betrayed."

She casts a quick glance toward the half-open door. It's only three steps away. He studies her, for a long time.

She can't hold the tears back. "I was drunk and crazy. I've felt so awful about it. I've tried to apologize. And I've changed a ton of things about myself just so I could stand to be me."

"Oh, really?"

Is that *sarcasm*?

"Do you honestly think so little of me?"

"I don't know what to think." All the anger seems to have run out of him. He's just sitting there and looking inconsolably sad.

"My e-mail—didn't you get it?"

"Yeah."

"Then why didn't you answer? I tried to explain." She stops. "Are you—are you really so cold?"

Silence. He looks pensive.

"It came so long after everything. I had already . . . hardened myself against you." He hesitates. "And then I met someone."

Alex with someone else?

Of course, she thinks, *of course. Just look at him.*

She feels sick, doesn't want to know any more. They look at each other one last time. His brown eyes almost knock her over. She tears herself away.

"Yeah, um . . . sorry," Kyla mumbles. "But that's not what I was here for. I just hoped we could be—I have to go."

He just nods in response as she slips through the door.

He watches her disappear. His mom comes in two seconds later with a phony look of distress pasted on her face.

She lets out a pitying *tsk*-ing sound. "Poor girl. She didn't look happy."

He picks a towel up from the floor and heads for the showers. He shuts the door, takes off his tank top, and looks in the mirror. He sees *her,* her sad eyes under her bangs, her hands, fidgeting nervously, her teeth, biting into the pale pink of her lower lip. He shuts his eyes to erase the vision. But she's still there just as clearly. That bright smile, the eagerness when she's about to say something, the sudden anger.

Kyla, who he lied to.

Kyla, who he loves.

"You don't understand," Kyla whispers again.

But Elizabeth doesn't back down. "If he's such a prick that he can't forgive you when you've really shown him that you're sorry, then he's not worth having. It's as simple as that."

"You're the one who kept going on and on about how I can't let him go!"

"That was before I knew he'd pull this."

Kyla looks over her shoulder at the street behind them. As if somewhere inside she still held out hope.

"To hell with him. Put him out of your mind." Elizabeth tries to pull her along.

"How can I possibly do that?"

"You've just got to start working on it. Come on. Pinkberry. My treat."

Kyla doesn't respond. They walk on in silence for maybe another fifty yards. Then she thinks she hears something and stops.

"What was that?"

Elizabeth sighs. "Um, a car? Some random noise. Come! I want to get you as far away from here as possible."

They keep walking. But then she thinks she hears it

again. Someone is yelling over the traffic noise—yelling her name. She turns around and searches the people on the sidewalk. She doesn't see anyone she knows, doesn't see anyone . . . sees someone.

A dark-haired guy comes running, a guy who looks shockingly like Alex.

"Kyla!" he yells.

She turns to Elizabeth, beaming.

"Alex!"

"He still has a girlfriend," Elizabeth reminds her gently. She gives Kyla a quick hug. "I'm heading home. Call my cell if you need me."

He's breathing heavily when he gets to her. He tries to say something, but can't get a sound out. She waits for him, in silence.

"I forgot . . ." Alex begins.

"What?"

"I forgot to say that . . ."

"Yes?"

His jacket is hanging open over his naked torso. His feet are jammed into his shoes without socks. But what's most naked is his face.

". . . that I was a coward too. I mean, that time by the stream. That I didn't just say it like it was, that I wanted to be with you. And later I should have told you to stop what you were doing. I don't know."

That pained expression. She wants to pounce on him and kiss him, she's so happy that he's here. But then she hears Elizabeth's words echoing in her head: *He still has a girlfriend.*

"I should have just pulled you aside and forced you to say what the problem was. Then that stuff with my mom would have come out," Alex continues. "And it wouldn't have been too late."

"We were both idiots. But mostly me."

They're standing so close together she can feel his breath on her face. He nods and still looks troubled.

"I'm sorry I was so nasty before. But it was kind of a shock when you showed up." He stamps his feet to keep warm. "Actually I was . . ." He glances down. ". . . thrilled."

She strains to smile at him in a friendly way, and not an in-love way. It's just so hard to do.

Neither of them says anything for a minute. What does he want? Just this, just forgiveness? Or something more?

He laughs. "I must be totally nuts."

"Why?"

Oh, God. Those brown eyes again. How can she ever be just friends with him?

She's standing so excruciatingly close to him and smiling. He can't guess what she's feeling and isn't up to contemplating it. It doesn't matter. Tomorrow he's going home and if what he does is wrong, then they never need to see each other again.

He takes a deep breath. Then he puts his hand around

the back of her head. He just has time to see her surprise before he's there.

It's like it's the first kiss there ever was, that's how new it is, how strong: It's like being completely lifted from the earth.

Afterward they look at each other. She's breathing fast. Blinking her eyes, confused.

"What about your girlfriend?"

"I lied."

Her face changes color. "That's not true."

"Don't you know I never stopped thinking about you?" Alex murmurs. "It's always been you. Only you."

She sparkles. He pulls her close again. Brushes his lips across her forehead, back and forth. Her skin is so soft.

"What about you? Did you ever think . . . I mean, about me?"

She looks up at him and nods.

He has to kiss her again.